Owen Marshall has written, or edited, twenty-four books. He has held Fellowships at the universities of Canterbury and Otago, and in Menton, France. In 2000 he received the ONZM for Services to Literature in the New Year Honours, and in the same year his novel *Harlequin Rex* won the Montana New Zealand Book Awards Deutz Medal for Fiction. Marshall is an adjunct professor at the University of Canterbury, which awarded him the honorary degree of Doctor of Letters in 2002.

Owen Marshall
Living as a Moon

VINTAGE

A VINTAGE BOOK published by Random House New Zealand, 18 Poland Road, Glenfield, Auckland, New Zealand

For more information about our titles go to www.randomhouse.co.nz

A catalogue record for this book is available from the National Library of New Zealand

Random House New Zealand is part of the Random House Group

New York London Sydney Auckland Delhi Johannesburg

This collection first published 2009
'Another's Shadow' first published *Takahe*
'Anacapri' first published *Landfall*
'The Don Fernando Motels' first published *Sunday Star-Times*
'Mid-canvas Figures' first published *New Zealand Listener*
'Patrick and the Killer' first published *New Zealand Listener*

ISBN 978 1 86979 251 0

Text design: Laura Forlong
Cover illustration: Getty Images
Cover design: Sarah Laing
Printed in China by Everbest Printing Co Ltd

In memory of my father, who loved books.

CONTENTS

LIVING AS A MOON

I'm not going to pretend that when I was just myself I was always happy. There were plenty of times I was fed up with being a twenty-nine-year-old retail worker with a tendency to put on weight. I worked at Mademoiselle Coquette Fashions as assistant floor manageress, and it wasn't any picnic. You're not allowed to sit down in those jobs: you've got to look your best so as to give the customers confidence, and some of them are right pains in the butt, but you can't say a word back. The other girls there were a great bunch, though, apart from Shonagh, and you got twenty-five per cent discount on all the clothes. Some good labels too. I was actually saving a bit of money when I worked there. Not because I was paid much, but because I was still at home with Mum and Dad, and not minding it. I was able to go out most Friday and Saturday nights to the pubs and clubs: I was seeing a fair bit of

Nigel Nesbitt on most of those nights. Nigel is noise abatement and signage officer at the council, and has a house of his own. I could've done a lot worse than Nigel, like Shonagh's Morgan, who would snort anything and flatted with five other losers. It was a routine sort of life, but a lot of people had worse.

Estelle Page was the reason I became more than just myself. Estelle was originally from Darwin, but came down to Sydney, where she pretty much took the place by storm. Her face was suddenly on all the mags, she was doing gigs at all the best night spots and mopping up guest appearances on the television. She started off as a singer, but there were plenty of better-looking girls with better voices too. What Estelle realised was that she was a natural stand-up comic — sassy, lippy and tons of confidence. The punters loved the sexual banter and quick repartee between the songs better than her singing, and she saw the potential. There were plenty of guys who did stand up comedy, but hardly any women, well not in Sydney that I can think of. A couple of gag writers, a good manager with all the contacts — the girl's a star. You have to say she's got something.

Right away people said she looked like me: well, I looked like her was how they put it. Even without any imitation of clothes, or mannerisms, everybody said I was the spitting image of Estelle Page. Even before she was on television, people who saw her at the clubs noticed the resemblance. One of the reps coming to see Mr Littam was the first, I think. As he was walking past me at the specials rack he suddenly reared back. 'Jesus,' he said, 'I'm seeing double. You're a sitter for that woman comedian I saw last night at Dominoes. It's bloody snap, darling.' I was fitting security tags on the garments, and didn't know what he was on about.

I soon did. As Estelle's star rose, pretty much everyone knew her, and those who saw me recognised the similarity. Sure, she was a bit taller, and had her teeth whitened, or capped, or something, but she could have been a twin. There were the big boobs, big eyes, round face, the smile, short neck, heavy thighs, even the Kelly nose — the whole ensemble I spent time looking at in the mirror, deciding how to accentuate the positives. It was spooky, really, to sit at a table in Dominoes, or in front of the television, and see how much we were alike. And Estelle had trademark habits that were so easy to copy, like the 'duh' pose with head forward and mouth open at the conclusion of a punchline, and sitting with her knees wide apart when wearing a dress.

Sooner or later I was bound to play on it, I suppose. The first time was the Christmas staff party. I wore a slutty, low-cut lace blouse, full skirt and slingbacks, which were the sort of things Estelle liked for her act. Sonia and me made up this bit of patter about Coquette Fashions, the staff and some of the regular customers. The party was at the Littams' place and there must have been more than thirty people with partners and everything included. I did the duh look and the knees apart. People just about wet themselves, and raved about it most of the night. Only Mrs Littam didn't like it, but that was because it wasn't ladylike. She didn't like Estelle Page, she said. Couldn't abide smut coming from a woman, and in public too. I hadn't been offensive, but I looked so much like her, didn't I.

Mr Littam thought it was classic. He asked me to do a turn at the Business Association's fundraiser for the East Balmain Hospice. He offered me $200 of his own money: a sort of indirect donation. You don't know when you start out on something where it'll take you. Hundreds of people do an amateur turn, and that's the end of it. For me it was just the start. I recorded some of Estelle Page's television spots on *Better Believe It*. She became a regular there in no time, and her backchat with host Ricky Ryall became the sort of signature sign-off for the programme. I got her mannerisms by practising them in front of the TV, and did my hair in the same dizzy bouffant style.

People afterwards seemed amazed that I could be so like her, but the thing that was really unusual was that I had no nerves at all. I'd never even been in a school panto before that, never sung in a cruddy band like Shonagh, or been karaoke mad like Ellie and Natalie. Over three hundred people at the Business Association's fundraiser, and I went on the stage and did Estelle Page without hardly raising a sweat. It was that easy. You learnt the stuff and the moves, and you looked out into the lights, and the laughter came back at you like a warm, uplifting wind. I didn't tell people, but I was surprised how easy it was: being someone else was a complete disguise, like wearing a full mask at the ball.

I was a natural, said Wayne Esler, a complete natural. Wayne came to see me being Estelle at the Beach Carnival cabaret a few weeks after the fundraiser. He had his own showbiz agency for impersonators. I had no idea such agents existed, but he was full-time at it, and had an office above a computer shop in Annandale. He had almost anybody that mattered on his books — the prime minister, Elton John, Russell Crowe, Rupert Murdoch, Nicole Kidman, Olivia Newton-John, Robert De Niro, Hugh Jackman, and several Tom Cruises, Clintons of both sexes and Elvis Presleys. 'You're a natural, Estelle,' he told me. He called all his impersonators by their stage names, and the habit spread. 'You're not just a dead ringer, but you've got the accent as well, and more than that, you belong on the stage. Not a nerve in that gorgeous body.'

I've never liked Wayne, but I'm not going to make him out worse than he is. He isn't a financial cheat, and after the first time he tried it on with me, he's stuck to his word about being strictly business. He put his hand on my boobs, to compare them with

Estelle's he said, and I told him I was having none of it. 'Fair enough, darling,' he said, 'you can't blame a man for trying,' and he never came on to me after that. He's got no class, but he's a shrewd bugger about sniffing out jobs and money. Some of the impersonators thought they could do better going it alone, but that didn't work for any I know, and they all came back to Wayne, or dropped out. Robbie Williams hung himself when he got too fat for his original; Clint Eastwood ended up selling Aboriginal tourist curios in Alice. On the other hand there's Goldie Hawn, who married a wine millionaire from the Barossa Valley. It's getting enough regular work that's the thing, and getting people to pay a decent appearance fee. Until you're in the industry you don't realise how many people want everything for nothing. It's for a good cause, they say. You'll really enjoy the crowd there, they say. We're a non-profit organisation, they say — 'Yeah, but we're not,' Wayne would say.

After the Beach Carnival he contacted me officially, and asked me and my parents to come in to see him if we were interested in me being Estelle Page professionally. Dad and I went to his one room and alcove office above the computer shop on a wet Thursday morning. The rain spat on the window behind his desk, and the posters advertising his clients lined the walls above the coffee machine and filing cabinets. Brad Pitt, Tina Turner, John Clarke, Prince Charles, Kevin Rudd, Mel Gibson, Bryan Brown and so on. And sporting heroes that meant nothing to me, although I did recognise Ricky Ponting. The outlines seemed to blur just slightly in the flicker of the fluorescent light. They were both true and counterfeit at the same time: you knew there was something not quite right, but couldn't put your finger on it.

Someone told me Wayne Esler had been a primary school teacher in Queensland, and had some sort of breakdown there.

He doesn't speak much like a teacher. He has a lot of hair on the back of his hands, and favours light-coloured formal shirts. He's more than average height and weight, but has these very small feet. Sometimes when I see him standing, I wonder about the small amount of shoe that shows from his trousers, and half expect him to overbalance. He's got this really nice leather jacket that he wears on special occasions. I checked the label once when it was lying in the back seat of his car as he took Prince Charles and me to a corporate do in Birchgrove. It was made in Milan. I can always tell the wonderful suppleness of Italian leather. Somehow even that doesn't give Wayne any class, though. But then if you're not sleeping with him, or married to him, all you want are the gigs he drums up and the money.

He said to Dad and me the thing was I had a good chance to do well as Estelle. Not only being a natural and that, but the closeness of the physical fit, my voice, and because Estelle had got famous suddenly so there wasn't much competition around. He said we'd be surprised how important it was to get in early; that impersonation can become a brand almost in its own right. All we'd need to do physically was to have special built-up shoes for the height thing. Maybe the teeth. 'How much do you get paid at the clothing shop?' he asked, and when I told him he reckoned he could guarantee fifty per cent more over a year with twenty per cent of the hours. Dad and me were pretty impressed. We decided to give it a go.

'You can always go back to retail and be none the worse if it doesn't pan out, love,' Dad said. That showed how little we knew then.

You've got to hand it to Wayne: he's professional in his way. I didn't do any gigs for more than two months. I worked on being Estelle every day, and Wayne saw to the special shoes and the job on my teeth. He advanced money for clothes even more tarty than Estelle's. That's the thing with successful impersonation, he said. Everything has to be just a bit more pronounced, slightly more obvious. Not a lot, or you fall into parody. There's such a fine line, Wayne told me. He had a gag writer come up with a bunch of jokes that could easily be adapted for almost every occasion and venue, and I learnt Estelle's songs too.

A league club dinner was the first gig I did. It was to farewell some big guy transferring to an English side. Wayne drove Dad and me there because it was the first time. I got $500, and that seemed a lot of money, even though twenty per cent went to Wayne. Wayne didn't come just out of kindness, of course. He wanted to see how I'd go: whether I'd go down with that sort of crowd and if I could hack it. He knew what each of his people could do, and what they couldn't. He said he didn't put his people beyond their comfort zone. 'I knew you were a natural,' he said afterwards. 'There's a few timing things, and you need to pick the right punters from the audience to come on stage, or you're buying trouble, but you nailed it, Estelle, nailed it.' Dad reminded him of my name, but Wayne took no notice. 'We can swing right into lining up appearances, I reckon,' he said.

It's exciting at first, being on stage, being the focus, having the laughter gust towards you and the applause follow you off stage. And if a few guys shout out they want to see your tits, well that's part of being Estelle Page. There's always an element of excitement, but the more you do it the more you wonder what's happening to your own personality, your own life. Because you're not in control, see. My friend Elton John said it's like shadow dancing, and we're the shadows. Elton and Kylie Minogue became my best friends. A lot of the impersonators on Wayne's books I hardly saw. The politicians, sports stars and moguls appeared at very different sorts of functions. I might just see them briefly in the office, or on the stairs. There was one time I did a show with Kevin Rudd at an Australia Day in Dubbo. We travelled together and stayed in the best hotel in the place. He was a nice guy, but very reserved off stage.

Elton pointed out to me that impersonators are either fixed, or double-sided: he meant some were always in the role, and some took a lot of trouble to be unrecognisable when they weren't in character. He was right. The top Elvis Presley wears beach shorts and his head's shaved; Dolly Parton's always in character and loves creating a stir in supermarkets. Elton has a lot of theories about what this says about them, and what the psychological effects are. A good deal of it went over my head, but he got me thinking. He and Kylie and me did quite a bit of stuff together. Elton has an MSc and had been a polytech tutor for years before going full-time. I think he might be gay, or maybe he's just so good as Elton John. It doesn't worry me. Wayne knew that the three of us got on well, and he worked up a bit of a three-bill package that did very nicely. Elton would accompany Kylie and me, and do his own big solo hits as well. I was the comic element, of course, and expected to have the odd wardrobe malfunction. We did two Australian tours, and sell-outs over the ditch in Auckland and Wellington. You get to know people so well when you travel and work together. All those pressures, and the potential for rivalry, but we stuck together. It was great money too, for Wayne and us.

The high point for me was April last year. Estelle Page was at the absolute height of her popularity, and Wayne persuaded the television channel to run a competition for a double as part of her six-part series. The competition segments were in the middle of the shows, peak viewing time, and Estelle herself judged the final. It was a close thing there between me and Estelle from Melbourne, but I won. I think Wayne had financial talks beforehand with Estelle's management, but that's showbiz. A lot of the contestants were amateurs, and didn't really stand a chance with professionals. The Melbourne Estelle was great, but she suffered from nerves in the final. I always have the confidence that I'm an almost perfect physical fit and a natural as well. Hundreds of thousands of people saw it on television, and Wayne said we'd be able to pick and choose our gigs from then on. 'I always said you're a friggin' natural, Estelle, didn't I?' he said.

It should have been a great moment. It was, I suppose, but meeting Estelle Page at last was real unsettling. She didn't want any of us to be introduced to her in the preliminary rounds, but she came on stage when I won to give me the award and pose together. And she and her manager shook my hand in the dressing room afterwards. It was weird to touch her, to be beside her and realise how closely we matched. Her skin wasn't as good as mine: I remember that. The sweat from her final act affected her make-up, and that sort of orange peel roughness on her cheeks was just starting to show through. I'll always know I've got a better complexion than Estelle Page. She just said I must be pleased to have won, and good on me, and as she and the guy went away down the corridor, I heard her say, 'Well, that's the end of the freak show.'

Elton John was the only person I told about that afterwards. We were in the Matrix Bar in Double Bay. Elton reached over and took my hand. 'Don't let it throw you,' he said. 'Let it go.' He's got that mouth like a frog that goes right round his face, and it makes a sympathetic smile, comforting somehow.

'But why would she say that?' I asked him.

'We don't know the pressure these people are under. They have to cut through the swell and we're just dinghies towed along behind.

Estelle's made it from nothing. She came from an inland farm in kangaroo country. She's managed something pretty unusual in entertainment here, but she'll know better people will follow: not impersonators, but women with more talent and just as much guts to take her place.'

I can see it starting to happen. She's slipping just that bit, and better-looking women are coming through with stand-up routines. Estelle's getting more raunchy to keep media attention. Elton John reckons she'll end up in the niche category of men's clubs and stag parties. I'm expected to follow. That's the thing with impersonators: you have no control over who you are. I don't much like Estelle Page, or talking dirty, but that's the future if I keep going, I suppose. Every success has its cost, Elton says, even petty success.

Most people would say I've nothing to moan about. I can see that. Being Estelle Page has made a big difference to my life. It's meant more money for a start. I've got an apartment not far from the zoo with a manageable mortgage, money in the bank, and I've been able to help Mum and Dad buy a new red Corolla. They've never had a new car before. I get a kick out of seeing how proud of it they are, and they appreciate any help I give. I've got fab clothes to wear when I'm not Estelle, some of them made overseas. There's a sort of fame too, that comes from appearing in public and winning that competition on telly. People often want to come and talk to me after appearances, some of them quite well known, and I get some fan mail even. We don't give out my address, but messages and emails come through Wayne's agency. He's quite strong on professional distance. Most people admittedly are wanting to know how to become impersonators themselves. They start by praising you, and then get on to their own abilities and how they're the spitting image of so and so. My old high school asked me to come and present the cultural prizes at the end of year, and Mr Littam from Mademoiselle Coquette rang up to congratulate me after the television appearance. Nothing from Mrs Littam.

Being Estelle though meant I lost my retail friends, and Nigel Nesbitt. Showbiz is a different world. Nigel was supportive at first, but soon stopped coming to the gigs. He hated the way I was on show for the guys, and their interest afterwards, and he was at a complete loss with Elton John, Kylie and my other new friends. I think he got a hard time at the council offices about us too. I don't miss him, I'd have to say. There are plenty of guys keen to take me out if I want fun. Johnny Depp and I have had several weekends at Surfers, and he's as sexually energetic as I can cope with. It seems a sort of competition for some guys, doesn't it. I think I've got more from people like Elton, Kylie and Rove McManus, who I wished lived closer than Goulburn.

The thing is, being Estelle gives me a different sort of life, different people and expectations. I'd never have met a friend like Elton John working in Mademoiselle Coquette. You make a choice and you live with the consequences, because yes, there is a cost. It's not just the travelling and the repetition and guys shouting for a look at your tits, and wondering how long the work will last.

More it's about the value of what you do, and who you are. Last Thursday I went to an overnighter in Newcastle: a private birthday party for a big noter in horse racing whose name you'd recognise. It was one of those gigs that didn't go so good. You get them from time to time in this work. I was feeling a bit flat, the sound system was shonky and a couple of girls started stripping off during my act and got most of the attention. Everyone in showbiz has times like that, but they're a bit of slap all the same.

Last night Elton and I were talking about it at Dominoes. John Clarke and Scarlett Johansson had just left, and the two of us were there by the window, overlooking the marina that was like a black and white photograph. I told Elton about Newcastle not going so well. I tried to explain to him why I wasn't getting the same pleasure out of being Estelle Page as before, but it wasn't clear in my own mind. Elton John has been in the business longer, has a university degree and likes to examine behaviour. 'It's living your life as a moon,' he said. 'That's what it's all about really. We give up our identity and become just a reflection of another personality, like the moon having no fire of its own and being just a pale reflection of the sun when it's not there.'

I think he's right. That's what's been bothering me. All the advantages of being Estelle Page, the good money, the laughter and applause, people knowing you, come because you pretend to be someone else. You're not at all significant for being yourself. 'You don't get anything for nothing,' Elton John said. 'Me, for instance. I like the guy, but I'm not good enough to be him overseas: not musician enough. So I'm Aussie Elton, that's my slot. It's just a business, Estelle, and you've got to keep yourself apart. You've got to have people who know who you really are.' He's right, isn't he. I've made up my mind to ride the Estelle thing out for as long as I can, while still keeping myself going. I bet you can do it with the right friends, like Elton, Kylie and Rove.

MANHUNT

Serial rape, murder, smash and grab with senseless violence — these are things that force politicians and celebrity weddings from the front pages. The people responsible are household names for a time, and then mostly forgotten, unless in some way you have a personal link, as I had, fleetingly, with Tony Ballard. Ballard was a contractor with a small property close to Feilding, and he killed a bank official and a neighbour with a Hollis 12 gauge, let the bodies lie and went on the run. I knew nothing about it at first, because I was on exercise at the annual camp that territorials had to do as part of national service. Ours was an infantry battalion, and we'd been in the field for three days practising contact and ambush drills, with some regulars as the enemy. I'd been back in barracks only long enough to get cleaned up when the adjutant sent for me.

'How are you feeling?' he asked. I told him I was okay. 'Yeah, well something's come up we'd like you to handle. Heard anything about this Tony Ballard guy in the news?' I said I hadn't seen a paper, or a television, since getting back, and he told me about the shootings and Ballard taking off into the Kaimanawas not all that far from Waiouru. The police wanted help in the search, and the CO offered a platoon. 'Better than doing the same old, same old, anyway,' said the adjutant, 'and it'll be good for your map-reading skills if nothing else. You operate under the police guy of course. He knows all about this sort of thing. Senior Sergeant Hoskin — a bloody good man. Your platoon will need only their small packs, and the police will feed you. I don't see it as more than a couple of days at most. We'll truck you up there and set everything up. No weapons, of course. Best go and warn the lads, and then come back for a briefing. I wouldn't mind getting out of the bloody office and up there myself for a nosey in the fresh air.'

The adjutant was an enthusiastic type who had stayed in the army even after his term of national service was done. He loved the formal mess nights when the port was passed to the left, and getting done up in his dress uniform for special public parades. In real life he was a chiropractor in Palmerston North.

Less than three hours later the twenty-seven of us were on the way to a creekbed in the Kaimanawa foothills that was as far as vehicles could go. The police had set up there, not far from Ballard's abandoned ute. There was no use setting the platoon to anything until I knew the situation: maybe the guy had already been caught, or turned himself in. Sergeant Vince Hoskin was looking at a topo map he had spread on a small wooden table in the shade of a police van. He must have been not long back from a recce, because the sweat shone on his balding head and darkened most of his shirt. He was a big man I judged to be in his mid-forties, and he wore fragile reading glasses as he leant over the map. They had thin wire frames and caught the sun as he turned to meet me. He put his head down in an oddly equine way to look at me over the rims. 'Ah, yes,' he said. 'Cometh the army.'

Hoskin was disappointed, I think, that I was a junior officer still in my twenties. 'Wow, a full lieuy,' he said. 'The army certainly believes in sending top brass, and I'm only a sergeant.' There were other touches of sarcasm as he briefed me, but I let it all pass. They hadn't found any sign of Ballard, and he wanted a search the next day, right up into the bush and tops.

A platoon and a police team couldn't hope to cover even a part of the high country, but Hoskin was working on Ballard's need for water. It was a hot, dry summer and not many streams flowing in that part of the Kaimanawas, he said. As I talked with him I realised he was a shrewd guy with a lot of experience, just as the adjutant had said. What did it matter in the circumstances if he was friendly or not.

I asked him what it had all been about, Tony Ballard shooting the man from the bank and the neighbour. Hoskin told me that he'd got into debt and the bank was going to sell him up, and Ballard couldn't bear the thought of losing his small holding. He'd had some hare-brained scheme to do with alpacas, or llamas, and he'd spent thousands on the wrong breeding stock, and the whole thing was a flop. 'A dreamer and a loner,' said the policeman, 'and he drank himself silly before the bank guy came out. The neighbour was actually one of his few mates, and came to the house when he heard shouting, to smooth things over, and ended up copping it as well. You never want to see someone who's been killed at close range with a shotgun, believe you me. Ballard just left them there by the doorstep and took off. He's got hardly anything with him and can't last long up here without food. The poor bugger will be in a right state emotionally too.'

'No sign of him so far?' I said.

'We've had a look in the obvious places today. We'll have to go further up, I'd say. Partly he'll be walking just for the sake of it. But no use doing anything else today.'

Adrian McLintock was my platoon sergeant, and we got the guys settled in. There was plenty of light in the evening and we had the tents up, sleeping gear out of the trucks, and a latrine dug before twilight. The police had food brought through from Turangi and we ate with them, sitting in the creekbed close to the vehicles as the sun went down. My guys seemed happy enough: the search for Ballard was better than square bashing, or weapons drill, and most of them preferred to be in the field. Almost all of the police team were older than us, but, apart from Hoskin, they were friendly. One of them had been at the same school as Adrian, and sat by him and me, talking of their common experience. It became cooler, and I lay back and watched the light gradually leave the clear sky, which lost its shell-like sheen and began to show the soft depth of dusk. Adrian and his friend were reminiscing of old teachers with nicknames like Snapper and Toots, and there were voices and low, relaxed laughter from guys further away. A small community was being established, while somewhere in tougher country Ballard was hiding out. I remembered being rather surprised when Vince Hoskin called him a poor bugger, but he was, I suppose, even though he'd killed two other poor buggers.

I had no dreams of murders and manhunts that night, and the only interruption was sleepwalking Pita Wiremu, who blundered into one of the vehicles and cut his lip. He'd been on his honeymoon in Taupo with the sexiest woman in the world. They were about to go to bed. Pita said he was pissed off he hadn't had just a few more minutes of his dream before hitting his face on a tailgate and waking up on the creek shingle.

A Sioux chopper went over the next morning early when we were preparing to move out. Hoskin was talking on the police radio about the area he wanted covered, but when I joined him he said that the flight was pretty much a waste of time. There was too much cover and the noise carried a long way. 'But you know HQ,' he said. 'Must put on a show, oh yes.'

'Maybe he's not even up there,' I said. 'Maybe he's snuck back down and thumbed a lift back to civilisation, back to some mates who'll hide him away.'

'He hasn't got any mates,' said the sergeant. 'Not even a mother to love him, and his wife walked out on him yonks ago. No, I pick he'll be up there all right, stewing in it as he sobers up. You know he's still got the shotgun?'

'I guessed as much.'

'You told your men?'

'Not yet,' I said.

'Okay,' said Hoskin. 'Let's have a look at the map here, and then we'll gather everyone together and set things up for the day.'

Hoskin gave us a good briefing, full of experience and common sense, free of puff and exaggerated drama. Afterwards, though, I saw him giving more detailed instructions to Adrian, and individually to my section corporals. I didn't want to get all uptight about chain of command, but it wasn't on, and would only get worse if I didn't say something at the outset. When he was putting his pack on, I went up and said I wasn't happy about it. 'Jesus,' he said, 'don't go all regimental on me.'

'I'm not,' I said. 'We're here to do it the way you want. There's no problem with that. It's just that individual direction should come through me and Adrian. You know how it works. You lose cohesion otherwise.'

Hoskin gave me a level look and a half smile of weary tolerance. 'Okay, bright eyes,' he said, 'point taken, but if it comes to the crunch out there today I'll tell any bastard what to do on the spot and expect it done pronto.'

'Fine by me,' I said. Hoskin re-tied one of his shin-length boots: expensive trampers, almost beautiful, and a contrast with my black, army issue, and the rest of his police field kit. He looked me over.

'Binoculars?' he said.

'No.'

'Jesus, you're no good to me up there without binoculars. Come down to the van. I think there's a pair still in there.'

It was a still, clear day and the heat built up quickly while we moved as a party into the hills. It was good to reach the bush, and we rested there for a bit. Hoskin pointed out on the maps what areas he wanted gone through, and the trig point where we were to regroup. The link between the army radio sets and the police ones wasn't that flash, but we hoped everyone would be able to keep in touch. The police line went off quietly: I spaced out my sections over the gullies Hoskin had allocated, and we began working uphill, paying special attention to any likely water points. It was cooler in the bush, with soft green light, spirally ferns, tree trunks to hold up the canopy, and mulch beneath our boots. No one expressed it, but most searchers I think must have felt it was a hit or miss affair. Thousands of hectares of steep bush, open tops, scrub and scree, and one man in it, not wanting to be found.

I made a bit of a fool of myself in guiding my guys to the trig point at midday. Map reading was never my strong point. So much depends on the ability to grasp scale — the spatial relationship between what's on the map and what you see, or expect to see, on the ground. It comes with experience, but early on you can be standing on a feature and looking round for it because you expect it to be so much bigger, or smaller. We ended up twenty minutes' walk from the designated place, and I found it only by using the binoculars to see the police sitting in the open on a knob high above the watershed. We arrived to find the cops already eating and resting up. 'Better late than never, bright eyes,' said Sergeant Hoskin. 'We'll give your boys a bit of a blow before moving on.'

The flies came as I sat with Dave Saunderson, one of my section corporals, and opened my lunch pack. Dave was a powerful guy, but got migraines sometimes. The warning was when his eyesight started to blur. He took a couple of aspirin, and thought he'd be okay if it didn't get any worse. I told him if he thought he was going to start vomiting then he was better off going back to vehicles, but I knew he wouldn't want to do that. I'm always surprised by those flies that come around high in the hills. What the hell do they feed on when there's no one around, as is the case almost all the time? They like to get at your sweat. They're bigger than blowflies and have bodies of a wonderfully blue, or green, iridescence. If they weren't flies people would think them beautiful.

The boys got a bit of a blow, but I didn't. Hoskin wanted to get up the mountainside high enough to work out the best places to check in the afternoon, and he wanted me with him. We set off up the ridgeline, with the cop setting a cracking pace. He was bloody fit for a guy of his age and size, and chose ground well, but he'd picked the wrong activity if he wanted to show me up again. Tramping's always come easy to me, with pack or without. I enjoy it, and your fitness is at a peak in camp. Hoskin may have had the flash boots and be shit-hot with maps, but he'd taken on the wrong guy if thought he could drop me on the climb. I kept just behind him: when he put a bit of a spurt on, so did I; if he slackened then I eased off. He talked a bit at first, perhaps to check my breathing when I replied, but then he just put his head down and got stuck in. Faster and faster, but when we got to scree slope, where it's better to cross on the trot when the shingle and rocks start to move, I left him lagging behind.

'Okay,' he called at the other side, 'let's take a gander from here.'

'A better spot up a bit by the bluff,' I said, without stopping. I was sitting there when he caught up, chest heaving. I could taste my own salt sweat, but Hoskin was dripping. Nothing was said about our little contest. It was tacit, but registered all the same. 'We can see a hell of a lot of country from here,' I said. We were above most of the trees, could look down on jumbled hills and bush, see the cones of Ruapehu and Ngauruhoe to the west.

We sat with our maps and checked them against the country. Hoskin showed me the areas he wanted the platoon to cover, but didn't make any comments about my deficiencies of the morning. Rather he seemed more inclined to talk. 'What do you do normally?' he asked, and when he found out I was with the Grasslands Division of DSIR, he was quite interested. As we went back down to the others at an unforced pace, we talked about introduced plants in the South Island high country, and then the whole question of genetic modification. Hoskin was well informed. He was doing a law degree he said, and wasn't sure when he completed that whether he'd stay with the police or not. 'Maybe I'm too long in the tooth,' he said, 'and after a while you find most of your friends are doing similar work, have the same interests.'

'I suppose there's a lot in common between the law and police work.'

'I have a good deal to do with court lawyers,' said Hoskin. 'Some are good value, but Jesus, there's some average bastards that need a kick in the bum. Think they're God's gift. We have to put up with a heap of investigative work wasted because of incompetent prosecution.'

When we rejoined the others, Hoskin gave a briefing and we moved off again, groups working away from each other as they headed for the most likely search areas he'd identified. The heat was sapping, but at least movement stopped the flies gathering, and the bushed areas were welcome when we came to them. Well spread out as we were, and moving quietly, there was a certain feeling of unreality. I found it hard to take seriously the chance of finding Tony Ballard in all that wild country: difficult to imagine some wild-eyed guy with a shotgun behind a tree. And what would he do, or I do, if we came across each other, despite the sergeant's order not to engage? No, it was like yet another exercise that you knew would end without significance.

But that time was different, wasn't it, and so clear in my mind while dozens of routine manoeuvres have merged, become indistinct, the specific purposes forgotten. Late in the afternoon, with the sun still blazing, Albie Gale from two section caught up with me, and said they'd seen something: some bald-headed guy in dark trousers. I was going to check it out before telling Hoskin, but then thought better of it and got him on the set. 'Do nothing till I get there,' he said. 'Nobody's to do a bloody thing till I get there. Tell your guys to lie low, understand.'

'Is Ballard a baldy?' I asked.

'You just keep your lads quiet and out of sight,' said Hoskin, 'I'm on my way.' So I guessed the answer. I left Adrian to gather the rest of the platoon and move them back down to the vehicles, and followed Albie to link up with two section. Hoskin was a good deal further away, and I suppose it was tension, rather than a wish to arrive before him, that made us cover ground so rapidly.

Dave Saunderson had pulled his section back from the gully in which they'd sighted Ballard. He and I went back to the ridgeline, and I kept my camouflage floppy hat low on my forehead as I used the police binoculars. Dave said he'd glimpsed the guy in a scrubby bit by an overhang, but I couldn't see anyone. Both of us were keen to get closer, but I knew the right thing to do was to wait for Hoskin, and besides, if it was Ballard then most likely he still had the shotgun.

Sergeant Hoskin seemed a long time coming, and when he and one other cop arrived, he had a rifle that I hadn't seen anywhere earlier in the day. Hoskin wasn't in any hurry. He had a careful look with the glasses. 'Okay,' he said, 'you two stay here, and we'll go and have a gander.' He meant Dave and me to stay behind.

'I'd like to come too,' I said. 'It was army guys spotted him.' I expected Hoskin to be opposed to that, but he didn't seem much bothered.

'Okay, bright eyes,' he said after a brief pause, 'but you stop when I say so, do what I tell you, right?'

The three of us moved down the ridge, taking advantage of any scrub cover. I was tail-end Charlie, and not wanting to draw attention to myself. The bush was a bit thicker in the gully, and the creek, barely running, was pooled among the rocks. We worked our way up quietly until a bare knob with a view of the rock overhang and the scattered scrub there. Ballard was sitting well back in the shade, but was clearly visible. He had his hands on his knees and his face down.

I suppose I thought the three of us would sneak up on him, that there'd be a rush and we'd overpower him, or Hoskin would shout out that he'd have to come walking to meet us without the shotgun. It wasn't like that. Hoskin took a light plastic, sleeveless vest from his small pack and put it on. It was bright yellow and had POLICE in blue on both back and front. He left the rifle with the other cop, and walked up to the bare knob in full view. It wasn't all that foolhardy because a shotgun's range isn't great, but I wondered why he showed himself so openly. He gave a musterer's whistle in fact, to get Ballard's attention, and when he had it, just stood there for a time. We were too far to see the expression on Ballard's face without the binoculars, but after looking steadily at Hoskin without movement, he got up and moved further round the rock and out of sight.

The sergeant wasn't in a hurry to close the few hundred metres. 'Let's give the poor bastard a chance,' he said, and when I heard the shotgun blast I knew what he meant. Hoskin and his offsider didn't quicken their pace: just went on calmly and with caution. It was possible, I guess, that Ballard was foxing.

There wasn't much to see in the overhang where Tony Ballard had spent two nights: a blue tartan Swannie crumpled in the stones and dirt, a tin of beans that looked as if it had been hacked open with a sheath knife, a supermarket bag with odds and ends. Hoskin had been wrong about him having no food at all. The guy himself was in the open further round, lying on the scree amid the sparse yet tenacious scrub. The shotgun had slithered down the slope a bit with the recoil, and Ballard looked small and bloody, with what remained of his head cast back unnaturally. He looked very alone, which might be an odd thing to say about a corpse.

Hoskin put the Swannie over him, but touched nothing else. 'You could do a good thing for us,' he told me. 'You're fit as a buck rat, and I'm about buggered. Could you get a radio set brought up here, and then see where's the nearest place we can get a chopper in? We can't be lugging him all the way down.'

'Sure,' I said. I was keen to get away. Unlike Hoskin, I wasn't familiar with death, and he'd been right when he said you never want to see someone who's been killed at close range with a shotgun.

Hoskin came to me as I was about to go. 'You okay?' he asked. And then, "Think what he had in front of him, the poor bastard.'

'I suppose so.'

'And behind him too, come to that. What you've got to do, I reckon, is show some discretion. You never get used to this sort of thing, but you start to get a sense of the choices.' Hoskin took off his beret and his yellow vest. His shirt was mottled with sweat, and his face glistening with it. His features seemed to sag as the tension left him. He opened his shirt and flapped the edges to cool his hairy chest. 'Ah well,' he said drily, 'I guess we've kept all the good people safe from another desperate criminal. All over, and nobody hurt.'

BUNSEN VERSUS THE REPUBLIC

As a defence lawyer it's my job to do the best for a client irrespective of my own views, or the personality of the accused. Professionalism becomes a form of emotional insulation, as it must for a surgeon, say, who does his utmost to save the life of a murderer shot by the police. Yet there are people who are difficult to treat objectively, and Liddell Bunsen was one of those.

I saw him first at the main helipad after he had been brought from the Wellington police station to the remand centre. He was tall, blond, gangly, almost boyish, with the inoffensive stoop that some tall, thin guys have, almost as apology for the superior height nature has given them. His pale ears poked through his straight hair like pig snouts through straw. He didn't look an incorrigible person, didn't seem that bad.

Bunsen was charged under the Death, Damage or Detriment to Living Organisms Act of 2062. It was an act the judiciary were applying with increasing severity because of rising public indignation. For a while botanical killings had been treated rather differently from those involving animals, but there was more and more opposition to any distinction. I was prepared to do my best for Bunsen, but privately I thought that if he was sentenced to anything less than five years supervised virtual reality then I would have done a pretty good job. He was a serial killer, a recidivist offender, and there were several witnesses to more than one of his rampages.

We met in a third-storey interview room that looked out over the uncut grass, then the small harbour, towards Eastbourne. Lawyers and their clients are legally entitled to privacy, but I suspected the authorities often didn't bother to turn off the sophisticated recording devices that cover the entire remand centre. 'Don't say anything in these interviews that might advantage the police,' I told Bunsen at the outset. 'This place is full of bugs.'

He threw back his head in an exaggerated way and shouted to the ceiling, 'Hey, snoopy bastards. Haven't you heard of citizen's rights? Fascism is alive and proliferating in the twenty-first century.'

'Just something to bear in mind. No need to antagonise them.'

'What else is there for the pricks to find out?' Bunsen said. 'There's just me eating vegetables for Christ's sake.'

Two or three hundred years ago, cannibals may have said something much the same, and fifty years ago people were still slaughtering lambs and hormone-treated chickens to eat, and gaffing magnificent tuna from the ocean. You could slit the throat of a pig on your own land, haul the carcass up to dress, and neighbours didn't do a thing. Incredible. My own father was accustomed to seeing mussels and lobsters being tossed alive into boiling water in top-class restaurants, and no one batted an eyelid. Cruelty is defined by social fashion as much as anything else, he said.

At the beginning of the new millennium there were still whole shops devoted to sushi: people who considered themselves quite civilised openly ate the uncooked flesh of fish. Even recently, caterers would twist the heart out of a living lettuce and stand talking of Hollywood, or rugby, while the white blood dripped from their fingers. Despite the abundance of food that plants provided naturally — fruits, nuts, nectar, gourds, berries and grains — it wasn't enough to dissuade people from killing plants in a sort of orgiastic greed. For years there was a concerted propaganda attack on Professor Muzzovich's evidence through tissue contraction research, that plants were susceptible to pain. Change, particularly against established tastes, is bitterly and instinctively opposed by most of society, and yet when we look back after the accomplishment, it seems so manifestly right. Until thirty years ago whole forests had been planted for the sole purpose of slaughter for building materials, and now they've been heritage embargoed, and people picnic and tramp in their oxygen-regenerated shade. Chemically constituted material these days can provide all the foods and material we need.

What's the use of talking about sanctity of life to someone like Bunsen, though? He's one of those young intellectuals who make a cult of the idealised past. I looked at his slouched figure on the vinyl chair, his long legs tucked untidily underneath. I don't think he realised what serious trouble he was in; what a stiff sentence he was facing. To tell the truth, as I went through the trial procedures with him, I couldn't work up a great deal of sympathy.

'It's important in the courtroom to project a sense of remorse,' I told him. 'Some sensitivity towards the victims.'

'We refuse to recognise any victims,' he said. 'I'm standing up for a way of life that has existed for thousands of years.' He had faded blue, prairie eyes in an unlined face. I was aware of a chilling, china doll viciousness in the guy.

Bunsen and a few other throwbacks had no respect for life, and even the law hadn't been deterrent enough to stop him from raiding the wild leek and asparagus beds, the firm, bright beetroot in abandoned market gardens, the mushrooms growing around the protein feedlots for dairy cows and sheep, or in the grassed macadamia farms.

Commentators consider it a form of lust, and likely to remain a problem in the depraved minority who lack self-control and respect for others. After all, rape still occasionally occurs despite hundreds of years of condemnation and the most severe of penalties.

'Didn't you feel any pity at all for the plants you systematically maimed, or killed — all the living stuff you ate?' I asked him.

'Hey, look, they're not like us,' said Bunsen. I think he really believed it, just as the slave owners had two hundred years before.

'The police claim that you had onions knotted together and suspended from racks in your garage, that your house stank of cooked cabbage to such an extent that hardened officers went outside and vomited. One report claimed you admitted to breaking off living stalks of celery, plunging them while still weeping into salt, and then eating them. It said that you had baby carrots in the cellar that you'd scrubbed raw, and the widow lady next door saw you tearing handfuls of parsley and mint like an animal and taking it indoors at mealtimes.'

'It's natural, okay?' said Bunsen. 'It's the way things were meant to be: the way life evolved. Eat or be eaten. Kill or be killed, okay?' Bunsen became animated, evangelical rather than distressed or defensive. I wondered briefly whether I should plead of unsound mind, but aberrant beliefs probably aren't enough to substantiate that course. 'I bet even now there's people somewhere in the Amazon, or Papua New Guinea, who are eating birds of paradise, scooping out shellfish and uprooting and cooking plants,' he said vehemently. 'Natural, unspoiled communities in tune with nature.'

I could have slapped him, but professional discipline held me back. In tune with nature, eh. That's a great line to use for a race that has succeeded by killing, laying waste, exterminating and genetically modifying. I just said, 'But we're not in the Amazon, or Papua New Guinea, Mr Bunsen, and you'll be tried under international environmental law.'

He didn't say much more; gave one quick look at the ceiling with sneering exasperation, then seemed to draw back into himself in a fatalistic sort of way. His fair lashes drooped over his prairie eyes, and his long, pale fingers lay spread on the table. Perhaps he realised that I wasn't some simpleton to be taken in by self-serving rhetoric. It came to me, regarding his lanky awkwardness, his straight, fair hair, that despite his perversity he didn't look a hardened criminal, and that was surely the way to pitch his case — present him as misguided, pitiable, rather than psychopathic. A man captivated by false theory, rather than an unscrupulous killer. A young guy who could have been a top basketball player perhaps, but who'd lost his way and followed the most base of his appetites. If I could hide my natural repugnance sufficiently, maybe I could pull it off, and he'd receive a sentence of only two or three years. After all, I was paid to find mitigation for Bunsen, not judge him.

THROW DOWN YOUR GUNS

They lay on their backs in the dark, looking up to a ceiling they knew was there. They talked about their son's seventh birthday, about how they would put aside their own issues for a time and make sure he had good memories of the day to go forward with. 'Let's give him a birthday and a half,' she said, 'before we have to dump other stuff on him.'

'Absolutely,' he said. 'Maybe I could take the whole bunch of them to a movie and give you time to get all the party bits and pieces ready,' he said.

'Yes, maybe.'

The counsellor had surprised them by saying that the grief and guilt of breaking up a family can lead to a good deal of false sentimentality. She said that kids were a lot tougher than most people realised, and that having the continued, reliable affection of both parents was the main thing. Some kids didn't have any parents at all, for Christ's sake: some were beaten to within an inch of their lives. Some children grew up despising their parents for the loveless partnership they'd persisted in. And what about those kids chained in wash-houses, fed cat food and forced to sleep with Uncle Neddy?

So the birthday party for Dylan became the watershed. Both Gavin and Freya recognised the subterfuge, but were emotionally drained enough to welcome it. The party was an event in itself of family significance, but also a tacit marker for their separation.

In the dark Freya recalled the holiday they had in Fiji not long before Dylan turned five. They went then partly because it was a last chance to have an extended holiday in school term time, and so avoid a lot of families. The size of the people surprised her, and the passivity of many of them. The sun and moon were much bigger there too, and the sea full of light and colour. Like swimming in an aquarium, Gavin said. Fiji was a beautiful setting for the first serious difference between them. Before that she had always loved the smell of the ocean, but after Fiji, to experience it was to feel her heart constrict. Gavin's firm had offered him the top position in its Sydney branch. He'd been saving the news to tell her on their holiday, and he did so with little Dylan at the margin of the colourful ocean, with theatrical palms behind them, with a vast and naked sun swelling in the sky.

She told him she didn't want to go. There was her family she was close to: her mother was marvellous with Dylan and that gave her opportunities she wouldn't give up. There was her own part-time work for Mickleburg Hooper that she much enjoyed. There were her friends, and there were her fears of being a nobody in a new place.

'It's the best opportunity I've had,' he said. 'You turn down something like this and that's it. You've put your hand up as a stick in the mud. Jesus, and I thought you'd be so pleased, after talking about how shit-hot Phil was at his job and that he and Anna were likely to get a posting to Europe.'

'The timing's off,' she said. 'All that we've spent on the place to get it nice. And just when Dylan's got a group of kindy friends to begin school with. It's just the timing, isn't it, otherwise it would be great.'

Their talk continued in the hot sun. You couldn't call it an argument: no shouting or abuse, rather a sort of reasoned disappointment and mutual, unexpressed, but powerful feelings that each should be willing to sacrifice something for the other. Freya noticed nearby the faintest line of detritus at the high-tide mark. No plastic containers, wrappers or jandals, just small, pale pyramid shells, foam flecks like horses' sweat, and filigrees of fine seaweed already pressed quite flat. 'It doesn't mean I don't think you've done bloody well to be offered the job. You have,' she said. 'You should be proud of that.'

'Right,' he said. 'Well, not quite the celebration I expected, eh.' He put his hands behind his head, lay back on the towel and covered his face with a floppy, yellow hat he'd bought especially for the holiday.

'Well I'm sorry, but that's how I feel,' Freya said. That was the beginning, really, of the end.

They cleared the kitchen table on an evening of summer twilight, and encouraged Dylan to make his own invitation card. The lettering in his own oversize hand and the drawing of him riding what looked most like a bulldog. They'd suggested using a photograph of Dylan as a wizard in the school play, but he wanted himself riding the bulldog. 'That's fine,' Freya said. 'Whatever you like.'

'Absolutely,' said his father.

They were grouped at the table, and the garden outside was gradually erased by the night, but there was a dry, autumn wind and the leaves bustled before it on the paved barbecue area with a sound like a water fountain. 'You can help get it through the computer,' he said, 'and then we'll use the colour printer.' Dylan smiled. For an almost seven-year-old he was pretty savvy about computers.

'I want to put the names and stamps on the envelopes too,' the boy said.

'Well, okay,' said Gavin. 'Putting the names on is fine, but most of them won't need stamps. You can take them to school and give them to your friends there.'

'Maybe some of his class might feel left out that way, though,' said Freya. They explained it to Dylan and decided to mail all the invitations.

'I reckon it's more exciting to get them that way anyway,' the father said.

As he and his son worked on the invitations it occurred to Gavin that he'd have to talk with his wife about who took what of the array of computer gear. When Dylan carried the prototype invitation back to the lounge to show Freya, and Gavin had turned everything off, he stood for a moment in the darkened office, with just a slab of indirect light through the doorway. He could hear the fountain of leaves outside in the night, and the voices of his wife and son in another room. There was a rich glimmer on the brass umbrella stand that had belonged to his mother's grandfather, and that he used as a wastepaper basket. His mother said her grandfather had owned coal barges in the Midlands and had been a rich man.

A few nights later they talked about the prizes and presents — not those for Dylan, but those for the other kids. That was the way these days, said Freya. Everyone got a loot bag to take home. They spent quite a lot of time talking about the possible contents and pricing them. The birthday party raised no issues causing pain, or bewilderment, or accusation. Freya said you didn't want all lollies after a big birthday tea. Better to have items the kids could play with. 'What about that two-dollar place?' said Gavin.

'That's a great idea,' said Freya. So they took Dylan there one Saturday morning, and guided his choice of a number of little junk purchases that he was delighted with. They placed a limit of six dollars each for the loot bags, and the boy enjoyed making them up at home. The chocolate frogs remained his favourite, despite his parents' views.

Freya watched as Dylan and Gavin taped up the bags, and the small presents that would be discovered in the treasure hunt, or won during pass the parcel. How open and easy was her husband's smile when directed to his son. She had brothers, though, who could be good role models and companions, and male colleagues. And anyway, she'd told Gavin she was happy for him to have as much part in their son's life as possible. There was nothing of harm in her husband. It was just they didn't find each other essential any more. Paths divide in life, the counsellor had said.

Freya thought a lot about the party, and talked with her friends. Even kids of seven can get scratchy late in the day after a lot of excitement. Better to start at one, have the food at three, and all the guests away home by four. And there were a couple of younger children, siblings of Dylan's neighbourhood friends, who would be heartbroken if they were left out.

She and Gavin talked about the birthday also. It was an event full of small decisions on which they could entirely agree and support each other. They realised that their determination to make it a wonderful party was partly guilt, but neither of them mentioned that.

On the day itself the weather was fine, and they were able to have the treasure hunt and some games in the section. No permanent damage was done: just a protea broken down, a red plastic ball lost over the fence in the Harris's garden, and Zeb Riley struck in the face with the half-size cricket bat. He cried a lot and his mother came and took him away just in case his nose was broken. Despite his injury, Zeb had the presence of mind to ask for his loot bag before he left.

Gavin was in charge outside, while Freya and neighbour Susan Munro prepared the party food. Sue had two children at the birthday and was happy to help. Of all the women Gavin knew, she was the hottest, and had something of a reputation. She liked a joke with innuendo, kissed easily, but he'd never tried it on with her. Maybe it would have been easier for Freya and Gavin if that had been the problem: one of them falling for someone else. Something clearly identified and therefore surely subject to remedy, or clear cause for parting. Personal growth is sometimes at the expense of existing relationships, the counsellor said.

The kids loved the food. There were fifteen of them in all, counting the two younger ones and leaving out Zeb. Gavin had picked up pizza and chicken pieces, but Freya made all the cakes, sandwiches and fudge. There were old-fashioned jellies: a sort of motionless cordial. The chocolate birthday cake was in the shape of a Mississippi paddle steamer. 'I don't honestly know how you do it,' said Susan. 'How you manage everything so perfectly.'

'Absolutely,' said Gavin.

Dylan coped well with the excitement until almost the end, when he had a meltdown about sharing some of his presents. The super transformer actually, that Patrick Leask said he just wanted a look at. Gavin had to carry his son from the room for a time out in the bedroom. Dylan had one of his self-induced coughing fits and brought up his share of the paddle steamer over the pale rug, but he was reasonably okay again by the time parents began turning up at four o'clock to take their children home.

Despite Dylan being sick, the party was a success. It's a relief, though, for parents when a child's birthday is over. Gavin was surprised how little usable food was left. There was a lot of it on the table and some elsewhere, but most of it had been gnawed a little, or disfigured in some way. The paddle steamer was unrecognisable and bereft of the pebbles and sliced jubes that had adorned it. Over the next two days Gavin and Freya found bits of food secreted about the rooms, and two treasure hunt prizes that the kids had missed.

Dylan took most of his presents to bed, heaping them up at his feet. 'We'll go in when he's nodded off and move them,' said Freya.

'Absolutely,' said Gavin, and later he went into his son's room, removed the heavier things and stood for a time watching Dylan as he slept. The night light showed his smooth forehead and open mouth, the easy and silent breathing. The smell of sick lingered in the room, but Gavin didn't care about that. He sometimes thought there was only so much happiness in the world, and therefore satisfaction for any individual must be at someone else's expense.

He wondered how different it would be coming to visit his son in the house they had all lived in together: a place utterly familiar and bearing the evidence of his rather mediocre DIY skills. He imagined that his conversations with his wife would be much the same — they had learnt to avoid painful topics — but he had a great fear that Dylan might be lost to him in some way.

As Freya and Gavin worked together to tidy up after the party, they talked about their own birthdays when children: how their families had dealt with such things. Gavin's recollections were the more pleasant, for Freya's father had been a discontented man who had wanted an academic career, and ended up a success in business. Money disguises failure, but never compensates for it, she said. It was a conversation in which both of them fully engaged. They were able to talk quite freely about the past.

When all was tidy, when the signs of another passing year in Dylan's life had been smoothed away, they took glasses of chardonnay outside to the patio, and sat there in the glow of solar lamps Freya had placed on the garden edge. The night was quiet: easy laughter could be heard from the house two over where students flatted.

'We shouldn't blame ourselves,' Freya said.

'No.'

'And if we're both in the same city he shouldn't miss out on much at all. Some kids' parents are working just about all the time anyway.'

'Can we manage things without the bloody lawyers?' asked Gavin. 'At least at the beginning, I mean, until we see how it goes. The whole world doesn't have to know, does it.'

'I'm okay with that,' she said.

She was sitting forward in the wooden chair, her arms resting on her knees and her hands clasped. He could see the shimmer of tears on her cheek, but knew there was no response that offered solution. The distanced laughter of the students drifted in the dark air. 'Actually I'm pooped,' she said.

'Yeah, it's been all go.'

'You think he had a great time, though?'

'He's a lucky kid,' said Gavin.

'It's important we see a lot of each other while he gets used to us being in separate places,' she said. 'Nothing abrupt at all, don't you think?'

'Absolutely,' said Gavin.

SEGUE DREAMS

'I REMEMBER NOTHING THAT HAPPENED WORTH RELATING THIS DAY. HOW MANY SUCH DAYS DOES MORTAL MAN PASS?'

Diary of James Boswell, Thursday, 21 July 1763

'Would you like to make love?' Graeme asks his wife.

'No,' she says, and goes into the bathroom for her shower. Where the bedroom curtains don't quite meet he can see a strip of sky, and it's all cloud. He enquires loudly if his wife expects a busy day, but there's no reply: not because she is out of sorts at all, but because the plumbing is particularly sonorous when the shower mixer indicator is at that one point of the 360 which delivers water at the desired temperature.

An inconsequential dream is fading; something about mountaineering and the crevasse death of a fat boy who bullied him in Standard One, and whom he hasn't given a conscious thought in forty years. He remembers now how the mud used to cake on the bully's big knees in the winter playground, and how his pink gums showed when he sneered. When Graeme pulls the curtains he sees from his neighbour's dogwood tree that the wind is southerly and therefore cold.

'So, you've got a busy day?' he asks his wife at breakfast.

'Absolutely flat out,' she says. 'And then there's the meeting tonight to organise the thingy.' His wife is a school dental nurse, and the thingy is a conference on fluoridation. 'How about you?' she says. He could tell her that the futility of his existence gapes before him, that he was bullied in Standard One by a fat boy, that the lustre of the world is now quite worn away.

'The Mycenaean kingdoms at eleven, Ionian cities at three,' he says. They are lectures he has given many times, and he feels a twinge of guilt that yet again he hasn't got around to updating them. The Ionian lecture, in particular: there is new material on the influence of the Persian satraps which needs to be included.

'Would you mind going round to that Powys street address sometime today? I won't have a chance,' his wife says.

'What address?' he asks.

'Where they advertised the used bricks. I told you we should consider them for the barbecue surround.'

'Ah.'

'Don't make a decision on the spot. Just see what condition they're in, and if there's still mortar sticking to them.'

There is time after his wife has left for work and before he must leave for the university, for him to get some of the satrap material into the computer, but he doesn't do it. Without a conscious decision he makes a cup of coffee instead, and reads the newspaper. There is a story about a Nigerian faith healer who made a woman parade around him naked while he sprinkled her with camel urine and recited incantations to increase her chances of receiving immigration papers for England. Female nakedness is always newsworthy: nothing else in the story is of the slightest concern. Prurience has taken a trivial incident from African obscurity and placed it on the breakfast table of the world.

Cicero, a terrier with hair like the bristles of a worn toothbrush, whines behind the door. He is let in and impatiently waits to be fed from the Doggie Woggie Giant Roll with heart and kidneys. Graeme talks to him, draws fingers through his sparse coat, but Cicero has become self-absorbed and depressed with age. No longer does he display disinterested affection, bring in the paper or hold up his paw in a greeting. Only his appetite and body odour are undiminished. Domesticity and abject loyalty have palled for Cicero, and his joints grown stiff. 'Good fellow, aren't you, yes,' says Graeme, 'and you like that Woggie Woggie don't you just, old fellow. Yes, you do.' Cicero says nothing.

Graeme has a glimpse of the red-jacketed postie passing, and stops talking to his dog to concentrate on a new distraction. Letters and emails are moments of possibility in his day. The air is cold on his bald head as he walks to the gate, and the daisies on the lawn, rather than having a wildflower allure, remind him of yet another duty. Yet, there is a good handful of mail, and he resists the inclination to check it out until he's back in the house, seated by the window and upwind from Cicero.

All, however, is winnowed away without leaving solid grain or gain. The rates demand, the 134th issue of the *Ancient History Review*, a credit card statement, a slip announcing the milk round has changed hands, with apostrophes twice missing from abbreviated it's, a note from a former colleague, now in the States, saying she has married an evangelical preacher from Alabama, seven multi-coloured advertising circulars, and a donation envelope from the support group for those with clinical flatulence. What more did he expect? But he did, of course — he yearned for a gift unsolicited and undeserved, a lightning strike that would galvanise his world. 'Cicero, old boy,' Graeme says, 'I cannot believe the earth is not flat.' Cicero doesn't bother to reply.

His eleven o'clock lecture is in Room C25. It's a long time since Graeme has visited Mycenae, Tiryns and Pylos, and years of reading and conferences have dulled that bright immediacy. He makes an effort with the PowerPoint display of the burial treasures, but the majority of students are impassive. Yet the lecture is well attended and a good many students stay after its conclusion. The reason for both occurrences is soon disclosed: the third assignment is almost due and half the class want extensions. The applications are more statements of entitlement than requests for clemency. He listens to their trite justifications and allows all their requests from weariness rather than goodwill.

In the staff club he lunches with Brendon Connor of Linguistics and a visiting Fellow from East Anglia who is an expert on the economic consequences of war. They talk of rugby, the naked African woman and the loss of savouries since the new caterers took over. 'I used to have curry wontons two or three times a week,' laments Brendon.

'Not even a sausage roll now. Jesus. It's not right. Who makes these decisions on our behalf is what I want to know,' says the East Anglian Fellow. Graeme thinks he may say something about the demise of pinwheel pastries with bacon and corn, but instead gazes at the full cloud cover clamped over all the campus. Everything seems on a small scale, and shrinking further.

In his room, J47 on level four of the Humanities Block, he works on a departmental submission to the university library, which has decided to reduce its subscriptions to academic journals on classical antiquity, then has a session as supervisor with Carl Lemms, who is preparing a PhD thesis on the rise of equestrian political influence in Rome during the second century BC.

Lemms is a toiler who twenty years ago would not have been given the opportunity for a doctorate: a glum, uninspired and prodigiously determined young man, with hair like dry pine needles, and sprouting ears that threaten to ramify. Graeme knows the future for Lemms and others of his increasing tribe — a rotation of lesser, untenured academic appointments and the final bitterness of expectation unfulfilled. In the present, however, Lemms scratches in his dry hair and looks about Graeme's room with a stolid avarice. His glumness is a contagion, and Graeme feels its emanation.

The afternoon lecture is poorly attended, perhaps because no assignment is due, and there is a flickering fluorescent light close to the lectern, which is unpleasant. Also Graeme has no PowerPoint display to bolster his unrevised Ionian notes, and a commonplace boredom drifts in the still room. He is aware of the lack of animation in his voice, but cannot manage even spurious enthusiasm. No one waits to ask anything of him concerning Cyrus the Emperor, or the city of Miletus, and a tall, young guy leaving with others slaps his open hand to his temple in what Graeme takes to be mockery of the time spent in the lecture.

As he drives home Graeme remembers the advertisement for used bricks, and finds it in his case. Powys Street is in the older part of the city, and Number 189 is a weatherboard house, but despite that there is indeed a large dump of bricks on the tufted front lawn. No one answers his knock at the front door and then the back, so he goes to the brick heap and makes an appraisal. Most of them seem to be damaged in some way, and most have an icing of mortar. Graeme scrapes one brick against another to check the grip of the mortar, and judges it difficult to remove. He then stands for a moment, a brick in each hand, in the grass of a stranger's unkempt section and wonders what he's doing there. No one comes, no neighbours are to be seen.

Where have they come from, these used bricks piled outside a wooden house? What disintegration of dreams do they represent? Who owns them, yet doesn't bother to be there for a customer? Why on earth would he and his wife wish to corral their barbecue trolley with old bricks? When does the world end?

He's about to leave when a small and battered car pulls into the unsealed drive. A woman gets out, waves and then ducks back into the car to retrieve a bag of groceries. A tall, rather gaunt woman wearing tracksuit trousers with a yellow stripe, and what looks like a man's corduroy jacket. 'The ad for the bricks,' says Graeme, in explanation, and gestures towards them.

'Come inside, come inside,' she says boisterously, and leads the way through the front door with hardly a pause.

Down the burrow of a narrow hall they go, and into an old-fashioned kitchen with a table in the middle. The woman dumps the groceries on it, and whirls disconcertingly towards him with a hand outstretched. 'Sally,' she says. 'Some call me Sally Army,' she adds with a barking laugh.

'Graeme,' he says, and is surprised by the strength of Sally's grip. 'I was just having a look at the bricks, but I don't think they're quite what I'm after.' He feels he's inside the house, has been greeted with familiarity, on false pretences. 'Sorry.'

'They belong to the former tenants. The landlord said if they hadn't collected them by last week, I could sell them off. They're a bit of an eyesore, aren't they.'

Sally Army looks like a man. She has a lined face of character, without make-up and with bristling eyebrows. Her hair is long, grey, parted tautly in the middle and held at the back by a blue band. 'Forget the bricks then, and give me an honest opinion,' she says.

'Pardon.'

'I've just been down to the gallery to see the curator about my exhibition there. Forty-two pieces and only three with a red sticker. She said my work doesn't appeal to the man in the street, and she said it unkindly. You're a man in the street, well on the doorstep anyway, and you can tell me what you think.' Sally tilts her chin and gives a laugh free of bitterness.

'At the gallery?'

'No, here, here! There's plenty of my work in the studio here. You give me your man in the street views and I'll give you a cup of coffee, or maybe the old bricks you want.'

'I'm no expert on art,' he says.

'That's the point — Graeme isn't it? That's the point, Graeme. The man in the street, the curator said.'

'I do have an interest in ancient pottery and sculpture as part of my studies,' says Graeme. He's trying to suppress a slight affront at being assumed a representative of the proletariat.

'So much the better: history provides perspective. Excellent. I'll just put these peas and fish fingers in the freezer before we go through.'

She does so, then opens the back door and leads Graeme to what he'd assumed to be a garage, but which has become her studio. The afternoon sun has escaped the cloud and slants through the small window, but Sally snaps on the lights as well. Graeme's first impression is of a bizarre produce show, or harvest festival. Dry pumpkin and marrow like ornamented shells on a trestle table, a scatter of incising tools, coloured leather and foil leaf, beads, lacquers, paints, brushes and bubble wrap. 'Don't say a word,' she says. 'Don't say a word till you've had a look round.'

Sally may not want Graeme to say a word, but she can't repress her own enthusiasm. 'Gourds,' she says. 'I tell people that my art is always gourd.' She laughs in his ear, bending to see what he's taken up from the table to examine. 'The calabash gourd was the first plant species ever domesticated. Long before pottery, gourds were used as containers and for display. Creek Indians in the US used gourds for centuries as purple martin birdhouses as well as storing corn. They knew purple martins fed on insects that damaged their crops.' Her hand is halfway towards the gourd he has picked up, as a mother's instinctive movement when another picks up her child. 'Bicolour pear,' she says. How light and balanced it feels in the hand, how glowing the red and yellow geometric patterns Sally Army has given it.

'They're lovely,' says Graeme. He feels slightly uneasy in the glare of Sally's almost obsessive enthusiasm. For a stranger to reveal so much emotion is almost an exposure.

Sally is delighted to have someone she can instruct, assuming everyone was bound to love a gourd. 'People think of pumpkins and Halloween jack-o'-lanterns,' she says, 'but there's a whole culture tied up with gourds. Musical instruments even — marimbas, maracas and gourd banjos. In some places they were a currency.'

'The decoration is so intricate, so colourful.'

'The galleries tell me they won't sell at the price, though, that I shouldn't spend so much time on each one. People don't understand about the curing, polishing, the special paints and gold foil and everything. There's cheap ones brought in from overseas. Stuff done for the tourist trade with machine scrolling.'

'Where do you get yours?' Graeme asks.

'I grow them on my son's farm at Ashburn. He and his wife

think I'm potty, but they humour me.'

'They're not actually pumpkins, are they?'

'No, but all the same family. Pumpkins are the world's largest fruit. Did you know that?'

'Really.'

'In 2002 in New Hampshire there was one officially weighed in at 1337 pounds.'

Graeme shakes his head, not in disbelief at giant pumpkins, but to convince himself that he's here, in a backyard garage with a tall, mannish and ageing woman who spends her life creating wonder on vegetable shells. 'I'd better be on my way,' he says.

'But as the man in the street, what's your opinion?' asks Sally.

'I think they're beautiful.'

'I knew it. I knew the man in the street would appreciate them. If only men in the street went into galleries. Which one would you like to buy?'

Sally asks with innocent confidence, and Graeme hasn't the heart to refuse, perhaps not the inclination either, although he hasn't had time to consider. He hasn't a lot of money with him, he explains, but he likes the small one with the colourful, geometric pattern and slender neck. 'Long handle dipper,' says Sally. 'I'll tell you what I'll do. We'll pick up the supermarket receipt in the kitchen and that'll be the price for you. You'll find it's even got a faint fragrance of its own. It's in the drying of it, and the soil type, just like wine.'

She would gladly relate the full history of each piece, but Graeme says he really must get going. His wife has a meeting after tea. Sally wraps the gourd in bubble paper, leads him back to the kitchen table and takes the receipt from among the remaining groceries in the bag. It's $61.32, and Sally rounds it down. She comes out to see him leave, shading her eyes in the low sun with a large hand. 'If you want the bricks as well, just get in touch,' she says. 'And tell all the other men in the street where to find true art. My stuff will be worth a fortune in time.' She waves to him as he leaves.

At tea he tells his wife the bricks are no good, but that he bought a gourd at the place in Powys Street. 'A what?' she says. 'You bought a what?'

'An ornamental gourd. A work of art.' Rather than describe it, he fetches it from the hall table and puts it beside her fettuccine. She picks it up with her free hand, and gives it the sudden fierce and brief attention that is typical of her.

'I like it,' she says. 'It's wonderfully light and smooth. The patterns are in keeping with the thing's shape and the colours are optimistic. How much was it?'

'Thirty dollars,' he says.

'Good one. I like it a lot.'

She has no curiosity concerning Sally Army, because she is preoccupied with the meeting that night to organise the conference on fluoridation. She asks his advice as to the best composition for a planning committee, and they discuss the value of co-ordinators for the various jobs. Graeme gives his opinion that effective planning is like scaffolding, essential for success, but forgotten afterwards. He warns her not to expect any gratitude. 'Would you like to come tonight?' she asks him, but he doesn't fall for that.

When his wife leaves for the meeting, Graeme takes the gourd into his study and places it by a lump of kauri gum he discovered in the Hokianga bush. The pressing cloud finally breathes a drifting drizzle into the twilight, and the neighbour's spaniel yaps at phantoms. Cicero sits silently with his back to his master. Graeme tells himself he will soon work on his academic paper concerning the fluctuation of precious metal content in coinage as a general economic indicator in late Republican times. Already the day's activities have been leached of feeling and are pale, receding ciphers. He is mildly alarmed to feel no vital involvement with anything that's happened. The gourd still pleases him, but its provenance is already insecure. Is there a Sally Army of such resolute and admirable artistic commitment to the place of gourds in the world, or has he made a mundane purchase at the Trade Aid store, and all the rest surreal?

Cicero goes to his bowl and regards it without making any noise, or even looking at his master. Their moods may well be similar, but that's no consolation to either of them. Graeme cuts the last of the Doggie Woggie Giant Roll for Cicero, and sits at the table to read the fine print on the dog food wrapper. 'You're a spoilt boy, aren't you,' says Graeme. 'You're a lucky rascal, that's what you are.'

Cicero doesn't bother to reply.

SLEEPING IN THE AFTERNOON

When I was at varsity I used to sleep sometimes in the afternoon: especially late in the year, around exam time when I should have been swotting. The heat would do it, and the futile, rote revision. Sleep was a temporary escape, like alcohol, or gambling. My room in the flat faced north and the sun blazed in while I sat in shorts, and tried to tabulate amino acid indicators, or the evolutionary pattern of change in the shell markings of brachiopods. I would wake in the early evening, over heated, full of despair and self-loathing. During sleep at other times I often had dreams, but I don't remember one dream during those lost afternoons. They were pits of oblivion. The shrunken remains of a burst balloon hung from the light cord. It was there when I came to the flat, and also when I left after two years.

After varsity I never slept in the afternoons, except maybe after sickness, or a long-haul flight. I was busy with things that mattered to me: wife, family, career. I have no patience with people who are both idle and unsuccessful. The thing is to gain some control over life, limited and transient as that may be. So it was most unusual last Thursday when I went quietly up the stairs to the master bedroom, took off my tan shoes and lay down on the cream duvet of the large bed.

Emma was downstairs with our new neighbour and her four-year-old son. Normally I would have been at the office, but I was working on a corporate mission statement that I hoped to email in. I had spent some neighbourly time with Summer Neil and her son, Jack. I wondered if Summer had decided on a traditional name for her son because of the liberty her own parents had taken. She was attractive in that slightly washed out way of some thin, blonde women. I found her pleasant to talk to, but later, when I was outside with little Jack looking for the cat that had more sense than to be found, her disembodied voice had a slightly querulous tone. When Jack and I went in again, Emma and Summer were in one of those apparently trivial, relaxed conversations that women use to decide if there's any basis for friendship. My wife never finds the need to change her initial assessment of character in any significant way. By the time Summer and Jack returned to their house across the hedge, Emma would know what intimacy, if any, the relationship would have. My own first impressions are less secure and less accurate.

I'm not sure why I made the unaccustomed decision to lie down: maybe because the bedroom faced north and was warm on a cold day, maybe stooping to little neighbour Jack, in the way I had to my own children twenty-five years before, had tweaked some unaccustomed muscle; maybe it was just that I knew no contribution of mine was needed in the conversation downstairs. I lay still and relaxed in mortuary position and regarded a smoke alarm on the ceiling. For a brief time I ran through the main points of the corporate mission statement, but then just enjoyed the warmth of the sun on my face and hands. No demons came.

Jack's cry came through the thickened atmosphere of half sleep, and then the clearer cries of his mother and Emma. I went downstairs to find them in the bathroom. Jack had gone outside again by himself in search of the tabby, and tripped on the raised concrete drain, cutting his eyebrow, which bled freely. His howls were not so much because of the pain, but the horror of the blood running into his eye. When that was stopped, and his eye bathed, he became manfully stoic. He stood in the bathroom, pale-faced, solemn, and with a large wad of bandage taped above his eye.

'I think it needs a stitch or two,' said Emma.

'Why don't I run him in to Dr Posswillow?' I said. A man is expected to show initiative in such times of crisis. 'You ring him and say we're on our way.'

So within an hour of sitting quietly in front of my computer, I was driving into town to seek medical help for a four-year-old boy and his mother. Two people I had never met before, who until a day or so ago had lived in a different city in a different province. 'How is he now?' I asked.

'I think he'll be fine. Good to check, though, about a stitch in case of scarring. It's so good of you to help, and I only came over to introduce myself.'

'You're welcome to use my cellphone to get in touch with your husband.'

'That's kind,' Summer said. 'If you don't mind I'll do it after we've seen the doctor, so he knows how it's panned out.'

My wife had told me several days before that she'd heard that

Summer's husband was a solicitor, but I was about to ask as a conversation filler when a police car drew alongside and motioned me over. It was that long straight by the industrial estate, and I pulled into the forecourt of a small business that made irrigation equipment. The officer had noticed Summer's son on her knee rather than in a car seat. Yes, we told him, we were well aware of the law, but had been overwhelmed by circumstances. 'Okay then,' he said, 'but straight home after the doctor, right?' The extravagant patch above Jack's eye was indisputable evidence of our story. 'Perhaps your husband could come in with your own car and the seat for the child.'

Usually a policemen is just a policeman, but this guy was young, and even I could see that he was handsome — the sharp features and thick, black hair of an Italian gangster. 'Wow,' said Summer as we drove on, but more as a release of anxiety, I think.

'Is that the doctor?' asked Jack.

'No, sweetheart,' said his mother, 'but we'll be there in a minute.'

And we were. Sitting in the worn, communal reception room with a pile of women's magazines, a red plastic tub of small toys and a rack of free pamphlets on tinea, flatulence, lactation problems and Alzheimer's disease. We were to be fitted in before the two bowed and silent old women already there, the receptionist said. 'I must thank Emma for ringing ahead,' said Summer. 'And I'm taking your time up when I'm sure you're busy.' I didn't tell her that I'd been lying on the bed when Jack took his fall. I noticed her hands trembling a little, and the tendons clearly visible beneath the pale skin.

'We're happy to help,' I said.

Summer and Jack were only a few minutes in Dr Posswillow's surgery. No serious damage and two small stitches. Dr Posswillow came out with them briefly, and told me that he'd been called to our golf club earlier that day. Brian Annders had collapsed and died on the ninth tee that overlooks the brook. 'Out like a light,' said Dr Posswillow. 'Massive cardiac failure from all descriptions. Massive.' I was sorry to hear it. Brian was a pleasant guy: a builder who had made an excellent job of tiling our garage to match the house roof. His brother represented New Zealand in skeet shooting.

'I'm sorry about your friend,' said Summer.

'He was a good guy. Did some renovation work for us.'

'You just never know, do you,' said Summer. She had no handbag with her and was embarrassed about her temporary inability to pay. I told her that it was okay, she could fix me up later, and I rang Emma to tell her about Brian Annders' death, say we were on our way and that Jack was fine. He was grinning, in fact, because Dr Posswillow had given him a lolly. The death of a builder was nothing to him.

By some coincidence we were passing the irrigation machinery factory again when the car began playing up. The gangster policeman was nowhere in sight when needed, but I managed to stutter on to a garage in Hulme Street. I was annoyed. You don't spend $43,000 on a car to have trouble with it. It would be the electrics. Modern cars are reliable, but they've got so many bells and whistles now, that when something does go wrong it's the electrics.

The mechanic was a thin oldster with a good deal of hair in his ears. Obviously he lacked the wow factor of the cop. He lifted the bonnet with the authority of a fat lady opening a box of chocolates.

'Alternator,' he said, after some poking about and an attempted start-up.

'I thought it would be electrical,' I said.

'Alternator,' the oldster repeated, as if to deny it at all connected with the electrics, or to indicate my guess not specific enough to score agreement.

'Emma,' I told her on the phone, 'wouldn't you know it. There's something wrong with the car's electrics. We're here in the industrial estate, at a garage, but the guy reckons he can do the job in half an hour, so we'll hang on. Anyway, Jack's fine, and we shouldn't be long.'

'Ask Summer if there's anything at the house that I need to go over for.'

'Emma wants to know if there's anything she can do,' I told Summer. 'You've nothing turned on, cooking, anything like that?'

'No, but thanks,' she said.

'No, everything's okay she says,' I told my wife.

At the side of the garage was a bench seat with a view of the workshop and the equipment hire business next door. Jack played among some worn tyres along the wall, and his mother and I sat and waited. 'If you want to ring your husband now,' I said.

'It's okay, thanks,' she said. She had a habit of scratching her elbows through the fabric. She was naturally blonde, I decided, because I could see the downy hair on the back of her neck. I asked if she'd rather wait inside because of the cold, but she said she was fine, that Jack needed something to keep him occupied.

'It's Murphy's law,' I said. 'The one time it's something of an emergency and the electrics give out.'

'But better now than when we were on the way to the doctor.'

'That's true.'

'I could ring my husband, but we'd be back before he could get here from work,' she said. We watched a couple in the hire yard struggling to lift a rotary hoe into their off-roader. The woman seemed to have the heavier end. 'Actually, I need to get home before he does,' said Summer. 'Things haven't been so good for us lately. That's one of the reasons we came here from Hamilton. New place, new start, new resolves. You know how it goes.' For the first time that I was aware of she held my gaze, and smiled: a tight smile that caused fine wrinkles at her eyes. 'Jack, be careful, sweetheart. Don't climb up on those tyres,' she said.

Her face was pink and white because of the cold, and the tendons moved beneath the skin of her right hand as she scratched her left arm. Better not to say anything in reply, in case she didn't want to pursue her marriage as a topic. She did, though. 'Paul had so much pressure at work,' she said. 'People think lawyers have it easy — money by the minute and long lunch hours in suits with corporate clients.'

'Envy, I suppose, and suppressed anger when they have to seek professional services themselves, and then get the bill at a bad time.'

'Paul had a falling out with his partners, and it all got pretty nasty. It comes home, doesn't it, one way or another. I don't mean anything physical, nothing like that. Just impatience and loss of involvement. Nothing you do is good enough for an unhappy person.'

We were two people who had no connections that weren't entirely circumstantial. Summer had come to introduce herself to her neighbours and ended up sitting between a garage and a hire firm while her son with fresh stitches in his eyebrow, played among second-hand tyres. And she was telling me of the difficulties in her marriage and her hopes that the shift to a new place would solve them. She had no one else to talk to I suppose.

'A new start can be a good thing,' I said. 'How does your husband like the firm he's with now?'

'Yeah, he does, but he's lost a lot a confidence. He used to be quite gung-ho, and now he has this oppressive fear of failure.'

'It could be just a bad patch,' I said.

'I told you not to do that, Jack,' and she half rose from the seat and then sat again when her son obeyed. 'You don't think of someone changing that much when you marry them, do you?' she said. 'You imagine one personality for all the time. That sounds stupid I suppose.'

'Not at all.'

'We've both been so unhappy.'

'Maybe the shift here will make the difference,' I said.

'If it wasn't for Jack I don't think we'd make a go of it at all. But then you have to go through stuff, I guess.'

I thought she might cry, but was relieved when she got up and went over to play with her son. It was getting colder in the late afternoon, and in the hire yard a tall, slow man was putting tarpaulins over some of the equipment. I wished I could say something to Summer that was as candid as her own admission, but far more encouraging, something about love, resilience and sacrifice, but I was too much on the outside of her life. We retreated to talk of the cold, Jack's dexterity on the tyres and his lack of concern with Dr Posswillow's stitches.

The mechanic was as good as his word. He had the car right within half an hour. Jack sat on his mother's knee on the way home, but the Italian heart-throb didn't appear. Emma insisted that Summer come in to warm up and have a drink, and she'd dug out some of our children's old toys and had them on the carpet for Jack. I recognised them all with a twinge of family nostalgia. The wooden duck with oval wheels to make it waddle, and the robust jungle jigsaw that was more suited to Jack's age.

Summer appreciated the kindness, seemed almost reluctant to

leave, although she said she needed to get back to her own place. 'God, what a strange day,' she said. 'I come over to introduce myself and end up imposing on you both for the whole afternoon. And relying on you to find a doctor, and not having my purse to pay him. I don't know what you must think.'

'We're glad to help,' said Emma. 'I'm just so pleased that Jack's okay. That's all that matters.'

'You've been so kind.' Summer took Jack's hand and we followed them to the door. The little boy's patch had become an accustomed part of his face. She thanked Emma and then me. 'Thanks, Robin, for the help and the understanding,' she said.

'Good luck,' I said.

We watched them going home to their own lives. 'Good luck?' said my wife.

'She said a few things about why they shifted. Just semaphore really. There's stuff going on in the marriage.'

'Yes, there is something, isn't there.'

'Anyway, after all that excitement I could do with a rest.'

'You know you never sleep in the afternoon,' Emma said.

OE CALLS HOME

Who's that? — Oh, you, Spam. Yeah, things are okay, but look I need to talk to Mum. — Italy. I'm calling from a place in Italy called Ventimiglia. — Yeah, of course it's filled with hot Italian women. What do you bloody expect, Mexicans? — Yeah, yeah, of course I am: more bangs than hot dinners. I'm beating them off with a stick here. But I haven't got time for you to be rabbiting on, this call's costing heaps. Put Mum on. — Okay, you too, you big dork. See you, bro. — Hi Mum. I'm fine. How are you? — Yes I did. I got all of those, I just haven't had time to reply because I'm on the move so much that I never seem to get to a post office and that. I've actually got cards in my pack written out to you and some of the rellies. — I'll do that. Okay. Look, the thing is that I'm over my limit on the credit card, and I wonder if you and Dad could kick in a few bucks just to tide me over.

— Well, I know you did, but everything costs a packet over here. You wouldn't believe it. — I know I did, I know, but there weren't as many picking days as they'd hoped because of the rain, a rat ate some of my Euros, and I had to pay for a mirror that got broken somehow in the room I shared with this Dutch guy. — I've no idea. I think the Dutch guy was an epileptic, or a stoner, or something. — Stoner? Well, it doesn't matter what it is, Mum, the thing is I had to cough up for the mirror, and someone had been sick on some linen, or something, I don't know. You don't argue with these people. Konrad is a white giant, and besides I don't speak Dutch, or Italian. — You wouldn't, Mum, believe me you wouldn't. — No, it just doesn't work that way here, Mum. Anyway, as I say, one way or another I just need a few hundred to tide me over until I get a job. This Russian girl I met at the backpackers' says they're crying out for English speakers to work on the cruise boats around the Greek islands. — Well, I was heading for London, but the exchange rate of our dollar to the pound sucks. — Yeah, but when I do have some, the exchange will crucify me. You see it's all this pressure that I'm under at the moment. I wasn't going to bother you, but actually I haven't been feeling so good. I was crook in Switzerland most of the time. — Well, the symptoms were just general, Mum, you know, I kept feeling bad in the mornings, might be the altitude, and now the heat here on the coast fries your brains. A few times I've had to go without food. — Yes I did, and thanks very much. It was a lifesaver, but unfortunately I got this court fine in Paris which took most of it. — Oh, they reckoned some guys were drunk in a cruddy fountain, and I happened to be resting nearby and got grabbed as well. — I don't want to go into it all, everyone's on the take here. Money's everything, and I hate that attitude. It's sickening, and if you can't speak their language the French go ape. — I'm not saying that I need to come back. It's just if I could feel there was a little emergency money, you know, probably I wouldn't need it, but it's the peace of mind. — I know I did, and I'm sorry it worked out that way. — Well, it's what I thought at the time, but things change quickly here, Mum, it's a different world. — No, I'm not travelling with Kevin now. He got all sour when there was a miscalculation at Istanbul and we had to pawn his watch. — Well, his mother *would* see it that way, though, wouldn't she. — Anyway, the Croatian girl was just someone I thought we should help out. You and Dad brought us up to offer a helping hand, I thought. Getting back to the money thing, what do you reckon? — Yeah, well I'm pretty peeved that Granddad mentioned that to you and Dad at all. I mean I asked him to treat that request just as a private arrangement between him and me. Anyway, I'm letting you know the situation 'cause you're my family, and what action you take is up to you. — Sure, sure put Dad on. That's great. I haven't actually got a lot of time before I try to get something from a chemist here for my skin, and the call will cost me an arm and a leg, but I thought it important to check in with you all. — You too. Hi, Dad. — Not too bad all things considered. I tried calling from France a week or so back, but there's always some foul-up on the exchange in these places. It's mad, but people just don't seem to understand English over here. — Sure, sure, I will, you bet. — I don't want to go on about money you know, it's just — I did, yes, — What's that? — No, nothing like that, not that sort of thing, I keep to myself, it's just being under pressure, run down, and crook in the guts sometimes. I try to be responsible and that. Actually I didn't like to mention it to Mum, but one of the things is I'd like to bring back something decent for her, you know? There's some beaut jewellery here. — Well, I did yes, I was about to use what you sent for that, but I was robbed in Naples. — I thought I told you that? Yeah, yeah, I'm sure I did. At least I wasn't injured much. — No, the bruising's pretty much gone. Anyway, I'm mainly ringing just to check in and say I miss you all. You know my card number. — Sure, I understand that. No sweat, but just think about it — Eh? — Well, I thought I had, Dad. I'm sure. — Is it that much? I haven't kept an exact tally. — No, no that'll be all right, and I appreciate it. — Yeah, I can see that. Anyway, better go. Calls cost a bundle here, Jesus. — Yes, you too, you too. — That's okay, see you. Bye.

VAPOUR TRAILS

'Bums, aren't they,' said Matthew. 'In the States they're derelicts, winos, bag crap, hobos, vagrants, tramps. Jesus Christ.'

'Not that so often, I reckon,' said Felicity.

'What?' Matthew stood at the office window and looked down on the small group forming in the alley off the busy street. 'They'll all be on P, or some bloody thing. Fucked up by being groped by an uncle, or some such, so they'll tell the courts. Useless buggers.'

Matthew, who imported office equipment like the rest of us, stood as a big guy by the window in the cheap, black shoes of a lower echelon city suit. The vagrants didn't have to put in the hours he did, had no responsibility, were never going to provide a client base. Their essential, dilatory uselessness and weakness pissed him off.

Usually they were later coming back to the alley, but the day was cold and the wind came up the street from the harbour with a drizzle before it like a swarm of sandflies. The alley offered protection, and ended in a plot of bushes and zigzag steps to a car park accessed from another street. There were cartons and light, Warehouse garden sheeting made into shelters in the bushes, a suitcase in which a Labrador slept. Close to the steps was a deep, rear doorway in a commercial building where the vagrants gathered to drink and shout at one another. 'Useless, noisy fuckers.' Matthew never got used to them.

'Language,' said Felicity.

'You're not doing a hell of a lot yourself,' said Ramon.

Here we call them street people, or the homeless, don't we. It's more PC, and collective terms somehow seem less invidious, more suggestive of society's neglect rather than personal failure. We knew of the alley dwellers because of the noise they made and the openness of their lives to others' gaze: they knew nothing of our closed community on level four. We were aware of them, while knowing next to nothing of the people who shared the building with us — like those who sold insurance from level two, the dental practice and insurance brokerage that shared our floor, Acme Investments, Catalogue Empowerment, Scientific Aromatherapy, level three, and the legal firm of Ramage, Browne, Poole on level six. The Icarus Private Academy of the Performing Arts, always deathly quiet above us. Each day an army of people came through the same street-level main door, nodded perhaps, and went to their own stations. For the life of me I wouldn't have been able to pick out Messrs Ramage, Browne, Poole or Icarus, in a police line-up.

I knew Sex Slut from the alley: not her face so much because of the bird's-eye view, although I had passed her in the street, but the fall of her lank, brown hair, or the green beanie in winter, and the shouts and shrieks of her name. And she would shriek foully back, or laugh, which was a shriek too. Alcoholics and druggies need to be loud from the fug of their addiction, or maybe it's some unconscious defiance of everything around them. The street people were loudest at the end of the day, when they gathered in the doorway and bushes by the steps after their meanderings. Maybe noise was the only way they could impinge on the world. If I was working till half six, I would have a window open to the limited extent the mechanism allowed — was it feared we would cast ourselves to death? — and listen to the ravings below.

Sex Slut had a shrill voice that carried well, but I learnt to identify others as well: Puli the Pacific boy, Jimmy in the grey overcoat who owned the dog, I think, the thin man with a bald top and yet long hair down his back that he sometimes wore in a pony-tail. When they shouted his name it sounded like Saucer, but must have been something else. Mostly they were guys. Mostly they seemed to hate each other: fierce abuse, dramatic collapse into sobs, savage group persecution of each member in turn, especially Sex Slut, who would retreat down the alley to scream back at them, sometimes wander quite away, but usually rejoin the others in time. Abuse could turn to laughter within one phase of the distant traffic lights, and sometimes they went into a huddle like a basketball ball team to share some dirty secret, or some substance to put coloured stars into their firmament. Late at night they must have slept there in the deep doorway and the bushes fashioned into bivvies with scraps.

Our own community was so much more civilised and fortunate, yet so similar in disillusion. Matthew, Ramon, Felicity, Becky and me in the main office, and Mr Cusip in the glassed-off alcove by the photocopier, the fax machine, the hiccuping water dispenser, the yellowed Zip and the notice board that bore no tidings. After Mr Cusip, Matthew was senior by virtue of long service and institutional knowledge, but he was denied any formal title to recognise that status, and received bugger all more money. Matthew was a model study in thwarted ambition. He would often come and put one half of his substantial arse on my desk, and talk in an undertone of how his loyalty and talent were insufficiently recognised. He wasn't a great one for cultural sensitivity. 'If I chose to toss it in here,' he'd say, 'old Cusip would be in the shit, for sure. Whole show down the gurgler in no bloody time at all.'

'Think of the disruption to the office equipment supply industry throughout the country,' I'd say, or some such. Actually, although I didn't like Matthew, it was true that he kept the place going. Cusip was like a rabbit in burrow, fearful of the ferret. In all the time I worked there he never addressed us as a group, but sidled up to us individually if there were instructions to be given.

'I see you as someone with a career path in this office,' he said to me once, and touched his nose like a character from Dickens. How Ramon and I laughed at that on the roof: how we teased out the magnificence of a career path among the five of us in that office.

Ramon showed me how to get onto the roof. He and I kept it as a secret. You went to the top floor and at the end of a corridor next to the fire hose was a ceiling flap and a counter-weighted folding ladder that you pulled down. Lunchtimes sometimes we went there, using the ladder only when all was quiet. The roof was flat concrete with drain grilles and ducts and pipes poking up. We'd sit in the sun, forget about the office for a while, forget about the inventories of business equipment and exchange rates and the rudeness of people you have to deal with. Even there occasionally, even in the middle of day, we would hear people shouting in the alley, and could look down on their foreshortened figures.

Ramon's name was ludicrously inappropriate. He was a tall, red-headed Californian named after some forgotten matinée idol.

Almost everything about our jobs was a source of humour for him, but then he was younger than me, and knew it was a passing phase of his life. He was waiting for his overseas accounting qualifications to be verified, after which he'd float upwards into a rarefied professional world in which office equipment was just something you sat on, or manipulated, without thought. He hadn't told that to the others, and when he was rebuked by Matthew, or patronised by Felicity who'd been to a private school, he'd take it with mock contrition, and a glance towards me. I would have enjoyed a greater share in his derision had I been as assured of a future. Maybe in ten or fifteen years, following the career path proffered by Mr Cusip, I would inherit Matthew's seniority in the office, still peddling mundane merchandise, still at the same desk hearing the shouted profanity from the alley below, still wearing cheap shoes, while Ramon flew to business deals in Singapore, or wound up national corporations as official receiver.

'You should sign up for one of those evening courses at university,' said Ramon on the roof. His lunch was a supermarket brie cheese that he ate like a bun.

'I'm okay,' I said.

'You'll get screwed down there. You'll end up like Cusip, or Matthew.' Felicity and Becky didn't count. Felicity made the most of herself, went to the right parties and would marry security with a big dick. Becky would stop working when her husband agreed to have a kid.

'It's a job,' I said.

'You need to move on, man. It's no way to spend your life down there. Those people, they're just rotting.' Down there meant the office on level four, not the alley. In the alley people were already rotting surely, but then you don't look below you, do you, you look at those doing better than yourself. Dissatisfaction and envy are ambition's goads. Yet I couldn't persuade myself that Puli, Jimmy, Saucer, the limping guy with the grey hoodie, the Sex Slut and others would be breaking their necks to move to level four, except for warmth.

'I've got plans, don't you worry,' I said. I had no plans: dreams, yes, but there was no bridge between dreams and the office on level four. I needed a plan. Sometimes at my desk with invoices, or being belittled on the phone by the manager of some tin-pot store in the provinces, I felt a sort of panic rising because my life was unchanging, yet passing in futility day by day. It would move through me like a liquid shiver and leave just dull despondency.

'The thing is, you got to make things happen sometimes. Strike out on your own in some way. Badminton's no bloody living,' said Ramon. 'No good just waiting for Godot.' He was testing the last of the cheese round in his fingers, and the sunlight brought out the ginger in his hair, although he didn't have a single freckle. There was cloud drift over the hills, and the traffic noise rose like the sound of a great river in a canyon. Gusts of car fumes and the persistent fragrance of the ethnic food malls overlay the smell of the tar sealant on the roof. Sensory perception was most acute, yet the sum total of it had no connection with my life.

'Don't you worry about me,' I said. I could do that for myself.

'You need to get your arse into gear,' he said.

Ramon was a friend outside work as well. On a Friday or Saturday night we often drank at his place until midnight or so, and then went into the city. It made a cheaper night of it. But weekday nights he did advanced courses in business management and book-keeping, or accounting — I'm never sure if there's difference. And he didn't play any sport at all. He said it was non-productive, a debit not a credit, unless you were able to do it professionally. Apart from women's beach volleyball he never even watched it on television. I played a lot of badminton myself. I was a top club player and that was as far as it went. It helped me forget what I did weekdays on level four: the physical focus of it and the team mates who cared nothing about the supply chain for office equipment. Sometimes when I was on song there were moments of euphoria, moments when the shuttle seemed to hang above like a light bulb, and the high leap to connect with it was effortless. Exquisite relief to put all into an overhead smash, and with the next shot delicately finesse the shuttle a whisker from the net. While Ramon beavered at evening classes during the week, I played badminton, or watched asthmatic, psychopathic serial killers hunted down on television. At weekends we went together into the city in search of one-night stands, though hangovers were the more regular outcome. What could I offer a woman that wasn't over with the orgasm? It was life in a holding pattern, but whereas Ramon created prospects for better things, I had no real hope of deliverance.

It's odd, isn't it, that often nothing changes for a long time, and then several things happen at once, almost as if pressure has been building without awareness of it. It was a clear, blue Thursday, almost time to finish on level four, and Becky and I were at the big window above the alley. Two guys in black jeans were going through to the car park and started kicking the Labrador that was in their way at the bottom of the steps. 'Look at the bastards,' said Becky. Some of the street people came out of the doorway, including Puli, Jimmy, Sex Slut, the bald head with a name like Saucer, and an older, heavy woman with fingerless gloves, who was only there occasionally. They shrieked and capered like a baboon band, and the two guys shouted in reply and pushed their heads forward to show they weren't backing down. Matthew, Ramon and Felicity came over to the window to watch. Mr Cusip stayed in his office. It was like being high up in a theatre, seeing something nasty from life being played out below, but safe from the threat of it.

'Listen to the silly fuckers,' said Matthew. He seemed indignant that the alley people were capable of outrage.

'We should ring someone,' said Becky, but we stayed there at the window as safe spectators.

It's the only group fight I've ever seen, and not at all like those sequences in the movies. It was all pushing, falling, heaving, breaking apart and closing again: all clumsiness and malicious opportunity. I can't remember one clean hit, and the noises were more disturbing than the actions. Raw, unrestrained sounds that were unsuitable for people. The two guys fought their way up the steps, disengaged and stood at the top swearing for a while before leaving. Your eyes follow movement, and it was only when the men were gone that I noticed Saucer lying on the ground by the steps and deep doorway. From such a height he looked small, almost restful. The other alley people came and gathered about him. Sex Slut and Jimmy knelt down. 'I'm ringing the cops,' said Becky.

'Better had,' said Matthew.

We were too far away for any blood, or bruises, any twitching, or eyes rolled back, but the shouting went on. They stood and knelt around Saucer as they would around a brazier on a cold night, and argued. I even thought I heard a laugh. After a time Puli left the group and walked up the steps, and soon afterwards the woman with the fingerless gloves went too, looking back at first, but then determinedly, ignoring the cries behind. They had reasons to avoid attention, I suppose. Some ordinary people joined the group before the police arrived. One man put his coat under Saucer's head, and another seemed to be arguing that he should be picked up. When the police and then ambulance officers arrived, I could still recognise Jimmy and Sex Slut among the little crowd, although they'd stopped shouting. When Saucer was taken away on a stretcher, Matthew said the show was over, and so it was. It was only then that it occurred to me that none of us had thought to go down from level four during all of it. The alley people weren't of our world, and it was a long way down.

Ramon and I went up to the roof at lunchtime next day. Busy Friday and with the weekend to look forward to. A clear sky again, but not all that warm. We sat with our backs to one of the air-conditioning outlets and ate bought sandwiches from clear plastic containers. 'The vagrant died,' said Ramon.

'How do you know?'

'When you were out doing a round the cops came asking what we'd seen. He was dead on arrival, they said.' They're expensive, those bought sandwiches, but fresh you have to say. Even though Saucer had died, we could still hear shouting from the alley, even at lunchtime and after what had happened. Sex Slut was screaming about something, and then laughing about something. How could they laugh like that from such lives. 'They still don't know who he is,' said Ramon.

Ramon also told me that his academic accreditation had come through and he'd been offered a job in a firm of accountants two blocks away. More than three times the money he and I were getting. 'Jesus, that's great. Good on you,' I said, and I tried hard to be pleased as he deserved, but was cast down by the reflection on my own shitty situation. He left me there on the roof and went down to see Mr Cusip and hand in his resignation. 'Make sure you stick it to Matthew,' I said.

The cops didn't know who Saucer was. They meant he wasn't anybody. I told myself I was in a totally different situation, and would soon have a plan. Jesus no, you're not the same, I said to myself. I leant back on the air-conditioning shaft, listened to the jostling voices from the alley below, and watched the vapour trails of the planes above: strings of silver Christmas tinsel dissolving slowly in the blue.

FREEZING

A late autumn day with the colours of the dying leaves defiant against grey sky, and a drift of air that was almost a breeze and would have passed unnoticed but for its chill. I was walking down the hill from the university, and making ground gradually on two women in front. They both wore dark, winter skirts and high leather boots. I knew one of them, Alexa Pope, who worked in the registry. As they stepped across a gutter to cross the road, the other woman slipped and fell with surprising force. She lay still for a moment because of the impact, her skirt rucked up to show the scope of inner thigh, a smooth expanse in the soft autumn light.

Viv said I laughed at her fall, but surely I didn't, and if so it was the laugh of someone caught off guard by the suddenness of trivial misfortune, and the guilt of finding eroticism in it. Alexa and I helped her to a low, garden wall and she sat there for a few minutes.

She was angry, I think to be introduced in such circumstances. 'No, I'm perfectly okay, thanks,' she said.

There was no blood, no apparent damage to herself, or her clothing. She said then that she fell on her hip, and, months later, when we were friends, that she landed on her bum.

There is in the psyche of every man an unconscious, archetypal image of how a woman should be, and when he meets someone who fits that template, a feeling arises of ineffable fascination, and sadness too. The woman may not be beautiful, may not be gifted, but there is a throb of recognition, the sense of something intrinsic that is glimpsed in the moment.

Viv had long black hair, pale skin with several dark moles on her neck. She was natural and graceful in movement, and her face possessed inquisitiveness without malice. So womanly, so sisterly almost, that I wanted to go to her with something that would make her smile, and then come back having done no damage whatsoever. She was tall and rangy, and always looked better in winter clothes than those of summer. In light, sleeveless things she seemed slightly dispossessed, but winter clothing fleshed her out, contained her height, her straight, dark hair and pale skin. Even after we were married I never told her of the powerful jolt I felt at the sight of her thigh after she had fallen on the street, the accidental exposure of herself to a stranger, though often as we lay together I would run my hand to the top of her legs.

Meetings and partings mark the chronology of our experience, with memory having its own criteria. I remember almost all the occasions on which I last saw people important to me, but not always how they came into my life. Yet how clear the recollection of the two women walking, the changing leaves, the close, grey sky, the sharp sound of their boots, and then Viv's sudden fall.

I saw her three days later: she was coming from the university medical centre towards the tower block. She had a bruise on her hip, she said. 'It's just as well that any treatment's free for me,' she said. Viv was a nurse, but wore no uniform. Instead, close-fitting jeans and a black jacket with long pockets, which hid her hands and wrists.

'Why not come and have a coffee in the staff club?' I said.

So something important in the lives of both of us began, though her recollection, as I said, was somewhat different, and our opinions of the outcome may not have been the same. Whatever the subject of our talk at that first coffee, it was an easy conversation, perhaps because we had come together by accident rather than one of us having made a move towards the other. There were no conditions and no expectations, and we made no arrangement to meet again, and so parted with the same ease we'd begun. I didn't see her again for several weeks, but remembered her boots, her relaxed and inquisitive face, her habit of bulging her cheek with her tongue if she was amused.

The third meeting had nothing to do with our lives at the university, and so the more unexpected. My father was involved in organising hot air balloon rides as a fundraiser for children with disabilities, and I went to Ashworth Park with him to help the balloon owner set up. I'd never realised what a lengthy and complex business that is: the aligning and laying out of the fabric, the positioning of the basket, the initial propping of the mouth until the controlled blasts from the burner slowly inflated the fabric, and it began to swell on the ground like a fat man. The burner was fierce and loud: great care had to be taken to ensure its flare didn't damage any tackle. The balloon man was at first quite tense, and spoke sharply to us as casual assistants, but once the thing had lifted off, mushroomed into the still air, he laughed a lot, and enjoyed the wonder expressed by the people who began to gather.

I watched the first groups go up. The balloon was on a long tether that was never let go, and so the short trip was all about elevation, and enough for those in the carrier to see the city spread out beneath them, take photographs if they wished, and then come back to the same spot.

Viv came with a tousle-haired guy with a pleasant voice.

The three of us talked briefly, and he told me his work concerned the classification of historic buildings. I was surprised how much I envied him as they stood close together and smiling in their ascent, until they were too high for me to see their expressions. Before they came back to earth I moved away, but I'd made a decision that I should be the one who stood beside her as she smiled, or cried, or rose, or fell.

I rang her at the university clinic, and asked her to come with me to see *Gloomy Sunday*, which became our film, in the way that couples have our tune, our meal, our wine, even our quarrel — all seared into their lives by association with falling in love. Only much later did she tell me that Jay, the man in the park, had wanted to marry her.

All that is seventeen years past, and I saw Jay's photograph in the paper two days ago, taken at the opening of a refurbished movie theatre in Wanganui. Viv wouldn't have been beside him if they'd married: she's been dead for thirteen months. Cancer of the spleen — lymphoma, which is an ugly word. A rapid form of the disease, but by no means painless.

It's customary to say that victims of disease are bravely resigned in their suffering. Viv wasn't. As a nurse she had a special bitterness concerning the path she was compelled to take. She became a changed woman, an angry, sometimes vituperative person. The specialists told me that was to be expected, but I hadn't. Her death was pain enough, but to have her personality corrupted by disease and the despairing knowledge of its outcome was quite terrible. Death, it seemed, had taken her, but set up a puppet to mock us and prolong some lesson we failed to understand. That's the last I'll say of it. The last I'd think of it too, if that control was possible. How she was before, and how I remember her now, that's the true image of Viv. Meetings and farewells, meetings and farewells: with Viv it's the meeting I keep my focus on, and our time with Rachel.

Rachel was born on a summer's night when there was a thick flight of the grass grub beetles — small, copper scarabs that blundered in the warm, night air, and lit and crawled on the living and inanimate alike. I'd left the maternity ward with the realisation that something wonderful had happened, and gone out into the hospital grounds. There were beds of severely disciplined roses, the blooms of which had just a tinge of colour in the moonlight. There were short, tapering cypress trees, and borders of long-stemmed lavender. The air was heavy with natural, harmonious scents, and also the drone of beetles, whose bodies struck like pellets. I was reminded of those other pasture predators, porina, whose transformation was not to beetles, but to soft, heavy moths that in rural swarms could so pulp on a car's windscreen that driving became impossible.

What a lovely name is Rachel: how marvellous its biblical origin. Viv and I were completely in agreement in the choice, but then we were rarely in dispute over anything that concerned our daughter. The bulk of people are merely reflectors for attitudes and events around them, but some few have an inner luminosity that sets them apart. Viv had that, and so does Rachel.

The night Rachel was born was one in which my ritualistic father would certainly have proclaimed omens. Even the beetles in their mating dance, the audible flight and pellet impact on solid things, seemed a salutation from worshipful old Egypt. No one else was in the garden, and from the seat there I could look back to the bright, tiered widows of the hospital and forward to the faintly lit roses, lawns and lavender. Winged insects make a sound like string instruments at a distance.

'Go on home now and ring your folks,' Viv had said as I left her cubicle within the ward. 'But don't smoke any cigars inside the house, and put the bassinet in the sun tomorrow morning to air.' I looked back and saw her watching, trying to catch my eye to reinforce our happiness. There was a nurse within earshot: a tall, Fijian girl who quickly glanced towards me, then away. I sensed she felt pleasure from our closeness, and slight envy too. I'd made no reply, gone out like a prince through the long corridors with the lifts at the end, and into the night garden.

After Viv died, Rachel and I were cut adrift from other people, and even, strangely, from each other. Love was not in question, but the oppression of it squeezed out ease of communication. Rachel said nothing to me of her aspirations, her fears, her painful and fluctuating relationships with the flouncing girls and slouching boys who were growing up around her, yet we enjoyed each other's company and carried on a tacit pretence that neither of us was threatened. On my side, at least, I offered a love too heartfelt to articulate, and too natural to require exposition.

It had always been that way. Viv said there was often something idealistic in the relationship between father and daughter, but I had no sense of being part of a generalisation. Love, however, doesn't carry any guarantee of responsible action.

Rachel would come sometimes into my study in the evenings, when I was plodding through essay marking, or lecture preparation.

She would sit sideways in the one armchair and draw her legs beneath her. She might lie her head on the backrest and play with her hair — thin fingers as pale as the hair they moved through. In summer she might watch the japonica bushes blurring into the dusk; in winter she might wait for the neighbour's security light to come on and show a cat she'd know by name, or listen to the television aerial vibrating in a southerly. 'Oh, Dad, stop talking such rubbish,' she might say, or laugh softly at that same rubbish to which she only half listened, while her fingers wove in her hair. Flippancy is a defence against the open engagement that can come unstuck.

How precious trivial memories are, and what intense pain they carry. I find my mouth half-open, as if there were words, or some cry, that would give relief. We hardly ever talked about Viv. There were consequences, of course, of her death, and our responses. Rachel's school contacted me a few months after her mother died. 'Dr Leigh?' enquired the voice.

'Yes.'

It was the deputy principal: she wanted me to come in for a discussion. 'It's a certain situation,' she said, 'nothing to cause alarm, but best talked about together rather than on the phone. Just an area of concern at this stage. Have you perhaps time some afternoon next week? Any afternoon except Thursday and Friday when we're having the winter inter-school tournament.'

'Monday,' I said. 'I can come Monday.' I'm accustomed to interviewing people, and being interviewed, but having some disclosure about your child is quite different, no matter how humdrum the circumstances.

I asked Rachel what I could expect. 'Same old crap,' she said. 'Withdrawal, isolation, social distance. You know the stuff that goes with being a loser and a loner. You don't follow the leader, you're a weirdo.' She was having me on, but she was right just the same. Bravado, too, can be a stance.

The DP and I sat close together in her office as she told me that Rachel was bright, but uninvolved with her peers, or her work, drifting through school. The room was small and all the horizontal spaces above floor level heaped with papers and books. The place smelled faintly of washing powder and dedication. Supermarket cartons used for storage accounted for the former, and Mrs Bridges the latter. She was a small, taut woman brimming with concern for her charges, and possibly fearful of some cataclysmic breakdown of authority. 'There's so little of her, isn't there,' she said. 'Physically, I mean. Such a slim girl. She eats well at home?'

'She's always been thin, but I don't think there's a problem there,' I said. 'I hope not. She doesn't refuse food, just eats small amounts.'

'Her teachers say she'll go through complete periods without volunteering a word, without any interaction with fellow students. We have difficulty getting her to turn her iPod off. Not that she's rude, but she seems to be in another space. She used to be so outgoing, so involved.'

That was true. Rachel was so often in another space, as I was myself, and we could semaphore a sort of whimsical goodwill without either of us comprehending the world the other lived in. As Mrs Bridges and I discussed Rachel's withdrawal, I had a strong sense of Viv's presence transposed on my own, the weight of her concern and her anger that she wasn't there for her daughter as she was entitled to be. Her intercession would have been so much more telling and insightful than my own.

When the interview was over, and the DP held the door open obligingly for me, she looked up, shook her small face briefly as if to clear her vision, and asked me if I would consider coming into the school on the next careers night to talk about the value of history. 'It's the sort of subject for which students don't see that many applications in later life,' she said.

Classes were changing as I walked back through the grounds. How I wished to see Rachel among the mooching, or jostling, streams of kids. How I wished to comfort our skinny girl adrift alone in adolescence, but she didn't come my way. I was failing her, and Viv too. The school kids, both boys and girls, didn't seem to feel the cold. Many wore no uniform blazers, or jerseys, just blouses, or shirts, often hanging loose at the waist, while I wore a jacket and knitted red scarf. I must do more for Rachel, I told myself at the gates where several boys were playing soccer with a soft drink can. 'Pass the fucker, pass it,' said one.

'Useless, man,' said another.

•

I'd get professional help maybe, or we'd go together to some support group for the bereaved — but I knew neither of us would buy it. Therapies that worked by reduction of Viv's memory weren't for us. Withdrawal is a natural reaction to pain, Mrs Bridges had said. I recognised it in myself as well as Rachel. Selfishness is a reaction to pain too. 'We're going to talk about the school thing on Saturday,' I told Rachel that evening.

'Whatever.' A tone dismissive, but not sullen.

On Saturday my laptop was playing up, freezing often and bringing up one error message after another. I complained aloud and bitterly at yet more malfunction, and Rachel replied with high, derisive laughter from her room. 'What's the matter with it?' she said, having come to the door of the study.

'Everything. Bloody thing freezes up. I'm going to take it into town now. Why don't you come?'

'It's freezing out there too.'

'We can go to a mall and have hot chocolate.'

'Big spender,' she said.

'Come on then.'

'Okay, then,' she said.

It was cold, bloody cold. August is often a bad month. There's a sort of seasonal drag which means that even as the days lengthen the weather worsens. On the walk from the house to the car, the cold air rose like ice water up my shins. 'Fuck, it's cold,' Rachel said. Obscenity comes as a surprise from such a slight body and in such a light voice, but I knew not to offer any rebuke if we were to be friends for the day. She had jeans and a padded jacket, but was so thin that surely body heat was impossible to conserve. I had an impulse to hug her, but was afraid to appear maudlin, and my mood was already unsteady.

'What's the matter with it?' the young guy in the repair shop asked. He had a quiff of hair like snow tussock, and elongated nostril apertures showing darkness within as if they bored deep into mahogany.

'That's what I'd like you to find out,' I said.

'It freezes up all the time,' said Rachel.

'Right. Freezing.' He said the second word as he was writing it down on a label that also needed my phone number.

The label reminded me of the polished copper that stood resplendent in our sunroom with a rubber tree inside. The gleams of dark leaves and of the metal sides richly complemented each other. The copper had belonged to Viv's farming grandparents, and with difficulty was broken from its heavy, workaday casing. I had taken it to a metal stripper, and there too filled in a label for identification. After some months and a number of evasive replies to my telephone enquiries, I went back to the business and assumed an authoritative, dogmatic manner. The proprietor eventually admitted that he'd been slack with the labels, and after acid dipping all the coppers in a single session, was unable to identify one from another. He took me out into his yard, and there in the mechanical jungle of a lean-to were a dozen or so coppers. I chose the very best one, bore it home and allowed Viv to continue with the assumption that it represented some special part of the archaeology of her family.

'Don't lose the label,' I told the tussock guy. 'Things get muddled so easily.'

'Right,' he said disdainfully.

'Oh, Dad,' said Rachel.

'When will it be ready?' I asked.

'We give you a ring,' he said. 'That's why I've taken the phone number.'

We had our hot chocolates in a mall. The small tables from the café spread into the thoroughfare, so that people were often ducking past on a shortcut, threatening cups with a swinging handbag, or ankles with a leashed terrier. 'We should have a holiday this year,' I said. I'd been thinking about it since the visit to the school.

'Where'd we go?'

'We can talk about it.'

'I remember when we went to stinky Rotorua.'

'Yes.'

'And we went another time way up north: to the cape and back, and stayed in a motel by mudflats with mangroves,' she said.

'The Hokianga. The place we stayed was Rawene. Your mother got that nasty splinter in her hand from the wooden walkway through the mangroves. Remember that?'

'I'd like to go overseas. Some big place like Sydney with all those shops and people so that you don't have to think for yourself what to do.'

'Well maybe we should do that. Your mum would have liked that.' I was surprised how naturally I was able to mention Viv again.

We normally avoided talk of her, uncertain of each other's ability to cope. I wasn't sure of the duties of a father, apart from love.

'And we need to talk about school — about you not doing so well.'

'Not here. I don't want to talk about stuff in the middle of the mall,' Rachel said.

'Fair enough.'

''Cause it's all about Mum really, in the end it is, or anyway that's what everyone thinks.'

'Is it?' I said. The last time we talked much about Viv was Rachel's fifteenth birthday, when she'd said her mother would've let her friends stay over. She found it difficult to see why having just me made any difference. Was I going to rape all seven of them? she asked.

The mall wasn't the setting for a conversation of any importance: Rachel was right about that. It was a place full of strangers and empty chatter. A place of false conviviality, hard surfaces and futile bustle. 'I don't want to go home yet,' Rachel said. 'Let's go up to the lookout and shout out. Your voice carries so far in winter. When you've finished a shout you can still hear it going away, yet it's not an echo.'

'You know how cold it'll be up there, though.'

'I don't care.'

'Windy too.'

'Come on,' she said. 'Please.'

So we walked to the car and drove around the bays towards

the airport. Rachel in the front seat beside me, was a reminder of our loss, of Viv in that seat and Rachel behind, and the three-way conversation over years, with Viv's face tilted often so that she could see her daughter. When three's a family it's never a crowd.

'I'm worried about the school thing,' I said. 'I don't want you unhappy there the way Mrs Bridges says.'

'I'll be okay, you'll see. It's just I've been quieter and people aren't used to that. I'm okay, really.'

'Do you dream about your mother?' I asked, without knowing quite why I said it.

'Yes, sometimes. They're almost always about rows we had.'

'You didn't argue much though.'

'No, but that's mostly what the dreams are about,' said Rachel, 'but I don't really want to talk about it. Most dreams are stupid.'

'Funny, but I don't dream about her. Lots of memories, though, lots of stuff that's very clear. Lots of really happy stuff actually.'

'Like what?' asked Rachel, without pausing in the scrutiny of her nails.

'Like coming down a sloping street and seeing her for the first time walking ahead under birch trees. Like the time the three of us went to Greytown and then had lunch at a winery with outside tables and a boules area. And you cried because a goose snatched cake from your hand.'

'I was just a kid,' said Rachel.

So she was: just a kid, and Viv and I just her mum and dad and all three of us just a family out for the day. What could be more ordinary then, and more memorable, more painfully special, now. Viv reading from the wine label for me, the debris of the meal on the wooden table, the movement of other people about us who were excluded from our complacent existence as a family. Just the high tumble of a cloud in the blue overhead, the paddocks with grass not grapes, the touch of open air on our faces. Just Viv and me and Rachel, and the white goose breaking in on our togetherness to steal food and make one of us cry. It could be one of those dreams I don't have, instead it's a scene that floats always behind the present view — with that of Viv falling on the street, ascending into the sky with Jay, catching her hand on the rough timber of the Rawene mangrove boardwalk, smiling from the maternity bed as I go out into an Egyptian summer night of whirling beetles, and all the other tableaux from a time when happiness was to be expected from life.

I parked in the rough, off-road loop, and we walked up the winding track through gorse and broom. We stopped talking because we had to walk single file and the wind buffeted words away. Up there, at the crest, is the memorial to the First World War and Gallipoli. I watched Rachel walking up the slope ahead of me, her body so slender that she was able to wrap her coat one and a half times around it, and her thin, denim-clad legs like scissor blades. I felt my face tighten in the cold rush of air, and saw the white scud of wave tops in the strait. A strong wind breaks the complacent unity of a view; makes the elements of it contestable; levers uncomfortably at junctions and unfastened ends.

Rachel climbed onto a ledge of the monument, faced into the wind. The force of it seemed an exhilaration. She spread her arms to feel the lift, as a gull does. 'We're above just about everything, aren't we,' she said, without looking back at me. She took my hand to climb down, and we put the wind to our backs and went down to the car. 'Jesus, it's got so cold, hasn't it,' she said.

'Freezing.'

'Let's not talk about any school crap today,' she said. 'I'll deal with that, okay?'

'Are you sure? You'll say if you need help?'

'Yeah.'

'We'll talk tomorrow then,' I said. 'It's important we talk more. You can see that.'

'Maybe talk about a holiday.' She was shrewd to see some personal advantage amid all this concern.

'Maybe.'

So, no resolution, no epiphany that would ensure understanding between us, just father and daughter getting through the winter as best we can, and lucky enough to have each other. Meetings and partings, dreams and memories, love and loss: hold on tight, that's all you can do in life. Viv would have understood that.

HEAD BUTTING

My job at Foleys market. Vegetables mostly. The trucks come up the side alley and unload. Wally and me take the bloody heavy wooden trays in through the metal sliding door. Sometimes its Shaun. They lock it nights with a fucken lock big as a handbag. You wouldnt believe veges would be so heavy. Drumhead cabbages and leeks. Pumpkins of course, but they look heavy bastards. The buck tooth driver gives me stick. 'Hey, cretin, dont you drop nothing.' Some day Ill have a licence of my own. Keep the truck cleaner too. I could head butt him I reckon. 'Jesus,' he says to Wally. 'Thick as pig shit.'

'Aw, leave him alone,' says Wally.

So after that we take the stuff into the vegetable shed with a plastic screen thing to the shop. Wally does the vegetable aisles and tells me what needs topping up. 'No, not topping up,' Wally says, 'Remember the new stuff goes underneath, or behind old stuff. Kinda like underpants,' he says. 'You dont want old stuff left there forever.'

They mark our clothes at the Home. Everything has TV on it. Toby Vinney. Not that funny I reckon. Things not marked get pinched. Saa wears some of my stretchy things anyway. Hes too big for my coats and trousers. He has the other bed in my room. A big bastard, but okay mostly. Even his dick is brown. Eva asked me when he first came. She wouldve found out when they started rooting anyway. They go out and do it in the van, in the shed. I dont say. I dont mind him. In the first week he took me on at head butting. 'Jesus,Toby, youre a fearless prick though, eh,' he says. 'Youll kill yourself, or someone, you mad fucker.' Ive always been best at head butting. No one takes me on twice. Saa could beat the shit out of me with his fists if it came to it, but he wont take me on at butting. We dont mind each other. Hes okay. He doesnt hurt Eva the way some do.

They keep the temperature down in the vegetable shed. At closing time I bring green leaf stuff back from the aisles and cage it in big tubs of ice water. That way it looks just as good next day. You can eat stuff when they cant sell it. You go off most of it after a bit though. Mrs Graingers dead keen of course. 'You ask, Toby,' she says. 'The more you bring home the better. They throw away bucket loads I bet.' They dont. Theres a pig man comes once a week. Its a crap truck, but theres this hoist on the back for the drums. He lets me work it if hes not hurrying.

'A couple of years and youll have the hang of it, Toby boy,' he says.

Anyway, Mr Simmonds says to take a good deal back on Fridays. 'Its a contribution to that Home of yours,' he says. 'I dont care what you say, but those churches do a good job for people like you.

Take those soft, spotted pears and the outer lettuce leaves pile,' he says. I do.

'It all helps, Toby, see,' says Mrs Grainger.

The Homes okay when Mrs Grainger or William Kaaras there. But Coombes is a bastard. When he has a night stint he gets into the two Mongol girls who take chocolate for it. I can hear it in the next room. Saa just laughs. 'You just keep your bloody mouth shut, Toby,' Coombes says, 'or maybe Ill shut it for you.' I could maybe head butt the bastard, but hes a nasty bastard, eh. I dont want to be sent back to any foster. 'You keep your stuttering to yourself, cretin,' he says. I should head butt the bastard.

William Kaara got me the vegetable job at Foleys. He took me down in the van to see Mr Simmonds. 'I know he cant work out front,' he says, 'looking like that and everything, but he sticks at things. He likes routine and the only stuff hell try and nick are ciggies.' Mr Simmonds hes a bald and skinny bastard. I could head butt him I reckon no sweat. He turned out okay though.

'You look after him,' he says to Wally on the first day. 'Well give the poor bugger a go, but make sure he works. Were not a charity organisation.'

'Well its not rocket bloody science is it,' says Wally.

Wallys not a bad bastard. Shauns more of a selfish bastard. Hes always talking about rooting the checkout girls. Stands at the plastic screen to the aisles and watches them with his hand in his pocket. 'Could do some butting there, eh Toby,' he says. Hes a lazy bastard. Likes to get out of the vegetable shed and into the aisles pretending to stock stuff up. 'So cold in here even the carrots can't keep a fucken hard on,' he says. He knows I could head butt him.

I started serious head butting in my first foster in Wanganui. One bastard son and three of us fostered. The son gave us hell.

Chimp he called me. Hed walk past with his legs bowed out and knuckles in armpits. He used to kick the shit out of us when his father wasnt kicking the shit out of us. I cant remember the names or faces of the other two foster kids. They were usually hiding. I says to the bastard one night, 'How about a bull fight. You know, on hands and knees and then bloody charge.' I broke the bastards nose. His father kicked the shit out of me, eh. I got taken away to other fosters. Youve got to have something youre fucken good at though. I found it with that bastard. I go in hard, over and over. I dont care if I die doing it. No bastard takes me on in head butting now much. Not if they know me. Im pretty much left alone in the Home now. At night sometimes I kneel up and rock so that my head just touches the wall. I can keep it up for hours. I like it. Fuck knows why. 'Youre a sad little prick,' says Saa. Hes okay.

The new guy in the butchery at Foleys didnt know me. He came through the supermarket to see me. Pulled the plastic strip curtain back at the entrance to the vegetable shed. 'This the cretin then?' he says.

'Go back where you belong,' says Wally, but the big bastard laughed.

'I hear the fucker cant even read,' he says. I can too. Paul hes called. He kept giving me a hard time. All the time calling me cretin and that I never had a root in my life. I never have.

'I could head butt the bastard,' I says to Wally and Shaun.

'Take no bloody notice, Toby,' says Wally. 'Keep away from him,' but Shaun reckoned I should head butt the bastard.

'You show him, Toby boy,' he says. 'Cant have the meat boys crowing over us, eh.'

Shaun set it up for knock-off time. We went through to the back of the butchery when most people had gone home. Theres this special door at the back of the butchery with a rail they hook the whole bodies onto and push them inside. Its cold at the back butchery room like the vegetable shed. There mustve been seven or eight dudes. Two chicks still in their smocks. They kept back, laughed a lot and put their hands to their mouths. Big bastard Paul reckoned to box. 'No way,' says Wally. 'We agreed head butting. Toe to toe butting until one pulls out.'

'Christ, what sort of a bloody stoush is head butting,' says Paul. 'Suits a cretin I suppose.'

The first butt he knocked me back a bit. Hes a big bastard, Paul. The second was just as bad. Shit, I felt the old pain by my ear. He flinched the third time. I just went in hard to buggery. You got to be best at something or cop out and die. And him being taller opened his face up a bit to butting. You keep your face down in head butting. He lost his rag after five butts. Started punching. The others pulled him off. His eyebrow was cut and Id fair mashed his snoz. 'Fucken useless cretin,' he says.

'Youll leave him alone now,' says Wally. The chicks were gone. Shaun, he laughed like hell.

Wally ran me back to the Home. 'Look at your head again, Toby,' says Mrs Grainger. She does a wobbly over head butting. 'I dont know.'

'Its not all his own silly fault,' says Wally. 'I did tell him.'

'I cant even put a dressing on it because of the hair,' she says. 'Probably needs stitches. Do you want to stay with us, Toby? You know what Ive told you about head butting,' she says. I dont want to go. Even with that bastard Coombes sometimes on, I dont want to be biffed out of the Home. I could head butt the bastard I reckon. 'I dont know,' she says. 'Well have to see about this. Cant go on,' she says. 'I dont know what we do about you.'

I went to my room with Saa. 'Youre a hard little bastard, eh,' says Saa. 'Good on you anyway I say. Take no fucken shit from the world, Toby, thats the only way.'

Mrs Grainger says Ive been to seven fosters as well as Homes. Cant remember shit about most of them. Says I have brothers and sisters and some siblings. Whatever. I wouldnt know. The Potaka family in Otahuhu were okay though. I remember the Potakas, but they said if I didnt go to school they didnt want me. I didnt go to school. Most teachers were dumb bastards. I didnt know what they were on about. Head buttings too good for them. Schools for fucken wankers, eh. Mrs Grainger says my mums dead. I dunno. Mrs Grainger says my old man jumped to Aussie years ago. See if I care. I could head butt the bastard, just like big Paul the bastard. Saa says Im a mad little fucker. Hes okay for a bastard.

Youve got to be the best at something, or you might as well fucken die.

ANOTHER'S SHADOW

Perugia, hill fortress of the Etruscans. Antony's brother was besieged there by Octavian in 41 BC, and after the capitulation Octavian executed the senate of the city. In the bowels of a building close to the square, is a well two and a half thousand years old, ringed with small, dark bricks and emerald mosses.

The city's university is famous, and I did a four-month course of study there soon after graduation. I spent a good deal of time at the archaeological museum on the Corso Cavour with Dr Germano Lattanzi, and wrote a paper on funeral rituals which was later referred to by several others working in the field. Such work I find fascinating, not at all morbid. We understand people through the manner of their death as well as their life.

I've been invited back several times recently, but it's not the same at all. It's a different city because after twenty-five years

I'm not the same person. Proust said you can never truly go back, because you are looking for a time past, not just a place.

I was lonely in my first weeks in the old city. I didn't speak Italian apart from tourist phrases, and there were few overseas post-graduate students sharing my studies. I was daunted by the exuberant confidence of the Italians and my subdued insignificance.

Somewhat surprisingly however, I acquired a lover. Crocetta Tenaglia was a thirty-nine-year old woman soon to be married to a much older relative. She was one of three tutors with responsibility for foreign students. Her English was good and her temperament completely at odds with the conventional expectation of Latin volatility. Nor was she a beauty. She was small and thin, had a large nose. Kindness, though, is very attractive when you're alone in a strange country, and so is intelligence. So is availability. All that said, I believe I did fall in love, and she was part of it.

Crocetta helped me to choose classes, find a three-roomed, low-ceilinged apartment close to the Etruscan Gate, and not only arranged my introduction to Dr Lattanzi, but accompanied me and made that introduction personally. 'Admit at once that you don't speak Italian, and that your Latin is very bad. He is a sympathetic man and will feel sorrow for you,' she advised. And so he was; so he did. Crocetta wasn't a classics scholar, but spoke four languages, and had written quite a lot on the novelists Umberto Eco and Italo Calvino. 'Realism is only one portal to the depth of life,' she said.

During my first weeks, amid the bureaucratic difficulty that seemed to follow everything I attempted, I went several times to her office, and her helpful, open manner was always the same. 'Something can be done about it,' she would say. 'Let me be strategic with it.' And she would give me a time to come back, and when I did, she had been strategic with my trivial problem and found a solution. My lack of Italian made me often feel foolish and ineffectual, but with Crocetta my confidence would return.

She took me and two other English-speaking students to a restaurant off Via 14 Settembre, on the old fortress walls, from which the green, closely cultivated valley fell away, and gradually disappeared as darkness fell. She ordered no pasta, but pork, fresh beans and some other green vegetables. We had no dessert, but a plate of hand-made chocolates for which Perugia is famous. We drank wine from the shores of Lake Trasimeno, where Crocetta said she would live when she married. She was proud of the long academic tradition of the city and its history.

The other students were an engaged couple from the University of Alabama. Their accents and company were pleasant, but they were interested mainly in each other, and when we had finished the meal, they walked into the inviting night hand in hand. 'It is a happy time for them here,' said Crocetta, 'but they are not serious in their studies. They have no fervour for any particular subjects, and just want to be together in Italy. So it should be.'

We stood for a moment watching the Americans padding away in their jeans and heavy sneakers — big people with the gait of amiable bears. The light from the restaurant was hachured on the street surface because of the cobbles, and there was a faint smell of vegetables — not those we'd eaten, but fresh produce from the market, which was set up most mornings close to the Via Viola. The sun was long gone, but all was still warm. 'I should see your rooms,' said Crocetta matter–of-factly, and so we went back through the main square, still busy with happy people, to the alley close to the Etruscan Gate, to my small apartment.

The only wine I had was very cheap, but she made no comparison between it and what we'd drunk earlier. My second-floor apartment had no balcony, and we sat close to the one window, on kitchen chairs. Crocetta made no pretence of interest in my housekeeping. We talked for a while of my courses and work at the archaeological museum. 'This is an important part of the beginning of your career,' she said. 'From now on you live the life of an adult scholar.'

She was right. The time of living in university hostels and flats, always in a company of fellow students, always in reach of family, was over. The time of irresponsibility, and people's toleration of that, was over too. I told Crocetta of my ambitions for an academic position, and she was both realistic and encouraging in response. In a lighted window opposite to my own, an elderly man was having his hair cut by a much younger guy. Both of them were intent on the task, and the old man held his head almost nobly to receive the attention. It was a tableau like an illuminated postage stamp in the surrounding darkness. The two Italian men were distinct in my view, and yet I would never know anything of their lives.

'This time for you sets a path for the future,' Crocetta said. 'If you do well then opportunities continue to come, each building to the next. Study now is an investment in your future.' I told her that one reason I'd come to Italy was to leave the group I'd been with at home and take work more seriously. I told her I was determined to make a go of it despite my inability to speak much Italian and my weakness in Latin. 'No, the obstacle for you here is loneliness,' she said. 'I see it in foreign students all the time.' She talked of the isolation you feel in a strange country, and how debilitating that is. She herself had spent time at the Sorbonne, and knew that bewilderment, even though she spoke French.

'You have made no girlfriend here, have you?' Crocetta asked me at last.

'No.'

'If you wish we could spend time together. That way you can relax and do well in your studies. In three months you will go home, and in five months I will be the faithful wife. For a time it is quite reasonable for us to have private things between us. We are free to make choices. Maybe only once, maybe I don't want to after it, or you don't want to then. We don't know.' The tone of her voice was just the same as that she used to talk of the university, and she showed no awkwardness as she offered to go to bed with me.

That I was an unimportant and transient foreigner, and she not at all beautiful and almost forty, made it of sensible and mutual benefit. She took her clothes off by the bed quite rapidly, but still folded each garment and put the soft heap on the floor. Her body was almost asexual: breasts like small suction cups on her ribs, which showed front and side. Her thighs were thin and didn't come together at the pelvis, so that light could be seen between them. Her long nose pressed into my cheek when I kissed her. I enjoyed the sex, partly because she did, but physically there didn't seem enough of her and I was aware of my height and weight as I bore her down.

She often spoke rapidly in Italian, or French, as we made love, but would never translate for me, and she would always close her eyes until the climax was past. It was her habit to caress my head and smooth my hair as we lay side by side. 'I wish you to let your hair grow,' she once asked. We spent several hours together that first night, but she said she couldn't come again because it would be noticed. 'What we do isn't happening. You understand?' she said. 'We are free to make choices, yes, but we must be private people. If you want to, I can find a place that is safe.'

Crocetta had the key to a small document filing room in the university library, and we met there by arrangement two or three times a week for the next month or so. I would wait by the shelves of catalogued scientific magazines until I saw her go in and leave the door ajar. Sometimes she couldn't keep our assignations, the door remained shut and I would leave without any gain in scientific knowledge, or physical satisfaction.

The small room was lined with box files, and had an untreated wooden table at its centre. A high window showed only sky. Worlds can be separated by the wooden inch of a locked door. While people studied and browsed in the wider library, Crocetta and I would lie entwined on the mushroom carpet, or, that imperative spent, sit talking at the table. It was a lesson to me that a woman so lacking in physical abundance had such a sexual nature. So much of her body was like that of a stripling, even her short, dark hair. We never talked about our lovemaking despite the power of it. Its necessity was tacit between us. 'We are free to choose,' she said several times to me. 'No one suffers.'

She liked me to talk about the landscapes of New Zealand, its Maori people, and in return to tell me of places and happenings in her own country and in France, where she had worked. After her marriage she was to live in the village of Tuoro close to Lake Trasimeno. It was the site of a great victory over the Romans by Hannibal, and interested me because of that, but she and I would never go there together. She said it was very peaceful, unlike her birthplace of Assisi, which was overrun with tourists. I asked her if she would miss the university, but she said that her intended husband was moderately wealthy, and she would be able to concentrate on her academic writing. 'I would like to come back as an appointment in Italian literature and teach here sometimes, instead of the administrative position I have now,' she said.

Apart from my occasional formal visits to the university office, in which she worked with other staff, and the restaurant off Via 14 Settembre, we met only twice outside the file room. Both times late at night, a rendezvous at her request at the Palazzo dei Priori, and then a long walk arm in arm in the small, cobbled alleys beyond

Via Pinturicchio. Each time the same enduring warmth in the night air, the same easy conversation and easy silences between us, the same sense of a layered past shimmering behind the darkened present. In recollection the two sorties became one, with emotion and frisson redoubled.

Crocetta's friendship made all the difference. I didn't know why she had chosen me from among all the forlorn young guys who were strangers in her city, and over men of her own nationality. She gave me the sexual release necessary to be able to do well at other things. Free of loneliness and crushing frustration, I found my studies a pleasure, and the old city welcoming. All you really need, wherever you are, is one other person close to you.

On a Tuesday afternoon towards the end of my third month in the city, Crocetta told me she didn't wish to make love any more. I had come into the filing room and was already taking off my shoes. She told me quietly, but without explanation apart from the comment that her marriage was coming closer. There was nothing for me to be angry about, and I had no great opinion of myself as a lover. I hoped, of course, that she would change her mind, but she never did. 'Don't think it is because of anything you have done,' she said. 'I like you much.'

We continued to meet as before, but I kept my shoes on after that, and the carpet burns on my knees and elbows gradually disappeared. Secrecy was maintained, though for the rest of my visits nothing occurred that was at all of interest to gossips. Crocetta began bringing in espresso coffee, and often ate her late lunch as we talked: something she'd never done before. I missed the bravado of sex, but our conversations remained high points for me. She was intelligent and knowledgeable but, more important, she was the only person with whom I could talk intimately, the only person in a foreign country I was truly familiar with. She encouraged the studious regime I'd developed. One thing I noticed was that we laughed together a lot more after we stopped making love. I've thought since that maybe the intensity of sex is at the expense of humour.

When my time in Perugia was almost over I told Crocetta I wanted to buy her a gift. She refused, but said that she wished for a farewell meal. It would be seen as quite appropriate, she said, that we would go to a restaurant on the day before I left with my studies completed. We went to the same restaurant close to the ancient wall. Two public appearances, two late nights wandering the hilltop streets, and nothing visible of our many meetings in the narrow library room.

We sat at a table without a view, without the two post-grad students from Alabama, but we had much the same meal: pork and vegetables, the light, red wine from Lake Trasimeno, close to where Crocetta would be living. Cheeses, not chocolates, however. We tried not to be sad, for we'd known all along of the exact time and agreed finality of our parting. Our friendship had never been stronger, but it was easier that it wasn't as lovers we said goodbye. Crocetta told me that Dr Lattanzi's report to the university had commended me for diligence and enthusiasm, and been lenient on my deficiencies in Latin. 'You made it all so special here,' I said. 'I don't know why you bothered with me. Jesus, I don't even speak your language.'

'You were special,' she said after a pause.

'Why?'

'I am honest to tell you because you look like my husband. That's why I needed to be with you at first.'

'You said the guy's old.' I was sure she was meaning some joke.

'No, you remind me of my first husband. We lived in one of the apartments that you and I walked past on those nights together.'

'You never said anything about being married. What happened to him?' I imagined some tragic death, and Crocetta struggling to come to terms with it. Some ecstatic bond destroyed by envious fate.

'He left me for my cousin, who is fat. I had been very happy, but obviously it was different for him. I miss him very much.'

I've met few people capable of such level honesty. So my physical similarity to the husband who deserted her, was what first drew her to me. She said, however, that after those first weeks as lovers, she came to see me as myself. 'I made the right decision then,' she said. Said it with a smile, and with trust in her voice. Her hand moved towards mine on the restaurant table, but stopped before touching. I think I made the right decision then also. I wasn't angry. The whole time in Perugia was subject to different laws. My enduring memory of Crocetta is not of a small, angular body naked alongside my own, or a large-featured face, but of her sympathetic intelligence: her understanding of need, and that history diminishes the present by comparison, yet at the same time makes its brief opportunity the more precious.

THE DETENTION

Friday's detention was held in Room 17, as were all detentions. Room 17 was close to the staffroom, it faced north for the sun and because it was in the old school block the master's desk was on a podium below the board, which made supervision easier.

On most afternoons the master taking detention could stand at one of the windows and watch sports practices on the top field, but Friday was the one day of the week with no practices laid down for any code. Tweetie Pye could see just a dozen or so junior boarders playing the kicking game with the rugby ball they called 'gainers'. Tweetie noticed that Laurie Cramm was the best of them; the boy had a more than passable right-foot spiral punt and also positioned himself well when the opposition was kicking.

Reluctantly Tweetie Pye left the warm, slanted sun and walked behind the five boys copying from their detention sheets, and up to his desk. The detention book showed that seven boys should have been present, and he had already noted the absence of Cody and Nichols. Dermot and Smyth were doing their time for bunking maths, Arvadson had persistently forgotten his PE gear, Crossley had accidently, but stupidly, broken seven test tubes, and Weymouth had been caught writing 'wanker' on the door to the sixth form dean's office.

On another afternoon Tweetie would have done some marking, or preparation, during his detention duty, but Friday afternoon had a sense of relaxation, of the weekend stretching before him. All of Sunday he would have to spend constructing exam papers for his sixth form physics and his seventh form maths, but the Saturday he had set aside to go into the bush at Te Tarehi. There he would not hear another voice for six or eight hours at a stretch. Tweetie would climb up just beyond the treeline and sit amid the rock outcrops and tussock to take photographs of the gorge below.

He left the desk again and walked past the boys to ensure that they were still writing, and writing what was required of them. Crossley had drawn some diamond shapes on his left wrist with blue and red biros. 'If I see any more of those you get a another detention,' Tweetie said.

'Yes, Mr Pye.'

'Get rid of them straight after detention. I'll check when you come to the dining hall.'

'Right,' said Crossley. He was a boy distinguished neither for brains nor physical skills, and so looked for little ways to draw attention to himself. He put his head down and smirked at Weymouth as Tweetie went on to the windows.

The teacher had the pleasure of the late afternoon sun on his face as he watched the juniors kicking and catching. The school was almost empty; most staff and all the dayboys gone, many of the boarders on town leave until 6 p.m. There was a BMW he didn't recognise though, ignoring the 'No Vehicles Past This Point' sign and sliding up to the elaborate stone entrance to the original block. A man in blue trousers and boatshoes got out and went into the building. Tweetie couldn't think of anything that a visitor would be searching for at 4.30 except the detention room, yet the knock at the door was so long in coming that he'd almost decided otherwise.

'Miles Weymouth,' said the man when Tweetie went to the door. They shook hands. Weymouth had a quick smile and a confident posture. 'The thing is,' he said. 'my boy's here and I need to pick him up. The whole family's going yachting with friends and we need to be at the marina pronto.'

'Detention doesn't finish until half five,' said Tweetie.

'That's why I've come in myself to straighten it out. No one's a bigger supporter of rules than myself, and of course Sebastian will do his detention next week. It's just that this weekend we have this opportunity to all be together for a cruise.'

'Sebastian's already missed his detention once and had it altered twice more to suit his sports practices. He's stringing us along, I think.' They both looked through the doorway into the room. Sebastian Weymouth had his head down; the other boys were frankly curious in their gaze.

'The thing is, I'm running behind time already. This place is like a rabbit warren. I'm happy to ring the school office, the rector, somebody, on Monday and go through it all then. Okay?'

Tweetie knew what the easy thing was, the obliging, no-fuss thing that suited the moment, no matter what the end result. Sure, sure he could say, flexibility is everything and no one need ever reach the bottom line. But maybe in the end the trivial begets the great. 'I can't give that permission. I'm sorry,' he said.

'Then I want to see someone who can,' said Miles Weymouth.

Tweetie went back into the room for the detention book. 'Arvadson,' he said, 'you're the senior boy here. I leave you in charge.' Arvadson puffed his chest extravagantly to deflect responsibility. The teacher and father went down the high corridor lined with photographs of past teams and distinguished old boys trapped behind the glass. Several knighthoods, judgeships, membership of parliament — all assumed unequivocally within the gift of the school. Out into the warm sun the two men walked and across the corner of the top field towards the school office. 'I'm not sure if the rector, or his deputy, will still be in their office, but often they are.' After he'd finished the sentence Tweetie realised that there was something grammatically questionable about it, and so went on rather fatuously to admire the weather. Well, he wasn't an English teacher anyway.

Weymouth just looked at his watch and kept himself very erect. By the time they passed the fives courts and the memorial arch, Tweetie had persuaded himself that if the rector, or his deputy wasn't there, then he'd let the kid go. Surely it wasn't for him to stir up a ruckus.

They went up the wide stone steps and through the foyer with the vinyl chairs for visitors. The senior master's door was closed, the deputy rector's door was closed, the rector's door was open and the rector was using the word processor. His glasses were on and his school tie was off and neatly folded towards the front of his long desk. His remaining hair began well back so that there was a considerable expanse of skin above his eyes: thick skin which had three or four deep creases like incisions rather than wrinkles.

Tweetie asked Weymouth if he'd mind waiting for just a minute or two while the rector was put in the picture, and the man sighed tightly and looked about the deserted foyer as if hoping that there might be someone impartial present who could be witness to the inconvenience and inefficiency to which he was subjected. 'Thank you,' said Tweetie. 'Just a couple of minutes. It will save explanation in the long run,' and he tapped on the office door and entered at the same time, knowing that the rector was already waiting.

With a closed door between Weymouth and themselves, Tweetie was able very quickly to cover the ground. Young Weymouth was well known to them both. Tweetie then invited the father in, gave him a chair and sat down himself at the rector's invitation. Miles Weymouth had met the rector several times and judged at first that a line of easy comradeship would have results. 'I told Mr Pye,' he said, after running over the family's weekend plans again, 'that no one supports a tight ship more than myself. That's why the boy's here, but there are other times I'm sure that he could be kept in?'

'He's built up detentions for the next three Fridays. As a concession his form teacher let him choose those times so that he wouldn't miss any sports practices. He's been abusing our goodwill, Mr Weymouth.' The rector turned the pages of the detention book as he spoke, and then a little time after. 'Altogether too many misdemeanours, in fact,' he said. 'You had a letter of concern from the sixth form dean?'

'The usual boys' things. After all, the boarders have to make a life for themselves somehow, don't they.'

'I'm sorry that you've had to come this far, that Sebastian didn't let you know, as he should have, that even though he applied for weekend leave, he couldn't go until after detention.'

'It's absolutely ridiculous. Whatever happens at school should be dealt with in school time. Do you realise that you're not just punishing him, but the whole family?' Weymouth had abandoned the approach of easy comradeship.

'That's partly the point,' said the rector. 'For him to realise that actions have consequences, and that often those consequences affect other people.'

'It's absurd.'

'Sebastian didn't want to do his detention on any other day,' said Tweetie. 'We made two changes for him and now this. Probably he hoped you'd come along, just as you have.'

'I don't mind if you just smack his behind then. Cane him with my blessing. I got it often enough here and it did me no harm.'

'The school doesn't cane any more, as you know. We hope to get the boys to accept greater responsibility for their actions without violence.' The rector's tone gave no indication of the degree of success he saw in that, but his hair seemed even more in recession and his forehead more deeply scored.

'I'm not prepared to put up with this nonsense. Not in this day and age. If I ran my business the way you run this mausoleum then I'd soon be down the road.'

'A different type of clientele, I think,' said the rector.

'Thousands of dollars I'm paying,' said Weymouth. 'Good money and my lad doesn't even like the place. If I go right down to that room and take my boy home are you going to physically stop me? Are you going to forbid me to take my own son from the premises?'

'No,' said the rector. 'I'm not. But if you take him home today, then, Mr Weymouth, don't bother to bring him back on Monday.'

'You mean you'd throw him out for that!'

'When he enrolled here, both of you pledged to uphold the school rules.'

'I'm going right back now and I'll collect my son as I'm entitled to.'

'Very well. That's up to you, but as I say, just don't bring him back on Monday.'

Weymouth, still incongruous in his new matching yachting clothes, left the room without saying anything else. The door remained open and Tweetie Pye and the rector saw him walk quickly through the foyer. 'Do you think he will?' asked Tweetie.

'I don't know.'

'Will the board back us if he does?'

'I don't know, but it's a judgement thing. I don't think you can run a school like the Weymouth furniture factories. Unfortunately, you can't even run it as a democracy. When all's said and done, we're held accountable for what happens here, and I believe that it's only fair that with responsibility goes sufficient authority to affect the outcomes.' The rector knew it wasn't Tweetie who had to be convinced.

'I'll let you know before I wind up tonight if Weymouth completes his detention.'

'Thanks. Yes, that would be helpful.'

Tweetie left then, and as he glanced back from the foyer he saw the rector rub his face, reposition his plain, round glasses and concentrate on the computer screen again.

When Tweetie neared the original block he could see that the BMW was gone. As he walked up the corridor to Room 17, the talking there stopped, and when he went to the raised desk to replace the detention book, he could see that all five boys, Weymouth included, were writing quietly. Tweetie Pye stood at the window again and watched the boys on the field. Things were as they should be.

NO STATIONS OF REMORSE

Margaret experienced relief when her husband died, and so did he in anticipation of it. The last few months of his life had marked an unbearable diminishment in his physical appearance and capability. And for much of that time he endured the knowledge of his dissolution. 'I don't want to be remembered like this,' he told her in the hospice room, where everything was pale, washed out of colours: even his face, and his voice, which had the rustle of a reed bed. Yet that memory of course would be with her until she herself died, along with recollections just as sharp, but far happier and more sustaining. The end of his life was not the finish of hers, but was a marker of unequivocal significance. More was lost, more behind her, than could possibly lie ahead.

Her son, Andrew, had been an indifferent visitor in the last year, but came often to see her in the weeks immediately following the cremation. Avarice was the reason. Margaret loved her son and daughter, but saw quite clearly that Andrew's main concern was to profit by his father's death. He had suggestions for changes to the family trust that would be advantageous to him, but she decided nothing would be altered in the meantime. With prompt zeal he came and took away his father's few tools. Also he wanted her to sell the Beamer and get a smaller car — a Honda Jazz, or a Hyundai Getz, he suggested. Andrew was like that: he knew the model names of cars. She resisted that also, and said she planned a longish trip after the ordeal of the final care. Nothing would be decided until she returned, she told her son.

Greta was truly supportive. She had loved her father, but was aware of the desperation at the end. She brought her two small sons often to the house as a welcome distraction from grief. Their selfish energy and joy, the fresh smell of growth and health, their emblematic proof of family continuity, were more healing than the awkward phrases of adult consolation. Margaret often stood in the semi-darkness of their room, and marvelled at the relaxation of their sleep, the silent ease with which they took breath.

'A trip would do you good,' Greta told her mother. 'You go if you feel like it, just up and bloody go. It's what Dad would have wanted.'

'It's Melanie's fortieth wedding anniversary. And I thought I could have stop-offs on the way up. Maybe the Puriri Street house, seeing I'm going all that distance.'

'Would you like me to come?'

'No, I'll be fine.'

'I could. I could take a few days off and the boys would be okay with Matt.'

'No, but thanks, said Margaret. 'I'll know people at Melanie's do, and there's friends I can drop in on in Christchurch if I feel like it.' There were people, but she had no intention of calling on anyone before Melanie. Just to be by herself; just to have no responsibility for someone else, no obligation to pretend that the process of dying was the same as passing time in other ways. 'If you could keep an eye on the house and so on though, that would be great. I'll text and ring.'

'You always forget to turn it on,' said Greta.

'I'm getting better. I'll be fine. I'll be back and coming round to see you before you know it.'

'Are you sure you're up to it, Mum?' Greta said. 'I can't bear to think of you sad in some crummy concrete block motel.'

'I'll be absolutely fine, and whenever I want to, I can turn around and come home.'

Even preparation was a relief. Just her own needs to consider, and to have them as priority without guilt. Just her own timetable, or lack of it, the indulgence of heaping things in the back seat, rather than containing them in careful suitcases in the boot. She would have to learn to be a widow, to live alone in the house she had happily shared. She understood that, but knew too that there was no hurry. Time enough to live there alone as a widow. The experience was not a pressing one, even though she accepted it as inevitable.

Andrew and Greta knew she intended to visit their old house in Christchurch on the way to Nelson, and Lake Alexandrina where her family once had a bach. She had other places in mind too, for reasons that mattered only to her. Peter had talked increasingly of Ladbrook during his last months, the regression perhaps one way of ignoring what lay ahead. His family had farmed there, close to Roxburgh, and Margaret had visited the place several times before it was sold.

'Cheryl and I used to stand at the road gate summer and winter waiting for the school bus,' Peter had told her after a bad night in the hospice. 'It seemed miles down the track from the house when I was at primary school, but I suppose it was only a few hundred metres. Mr Higginson was the driver for years, and if we were late he'd give a blast on the horn, and the other kids would jeer. Not that we were late often, Mum saw to that. In the winter the grass was white with frost and as brittle as iron filings: in the summer burnt yellow brown. We used to throw stones at the metal flag on the post box, and argue about kids and teachers at school. Because Cheryl was older she couldn't be bothered with my friends. Higginson had two fingers missing on his left hand, and people said he had a secret gold-panning possie in the hills, and had squirrelled it all away.'

Margaret and her husband had been looking out onto the hospice garden from his room. There was a boy of nine or ten idling there, bored no doubt from confinement in a room much the same as Peter's. Maybe the sight of the boy plucking catkins from the small silver birch tree had reminded him of his own childhood. 'Dad was always into some job or other by the time we were at the gate. He'd wave from the tractor, or the sheds, or as he headed off with the dogs. He was hopeless at school himself everybody said, but was keen for us.

And the outcome had been a good one, Peter successful at varsity and becoming a senior partner in his accountancy firm. But at the end it was farm, family and weather he'd talked about, not the figures, not the finance, of his profession.

'Your parents were proud of you,' Margaret had told him.

'I wish I'd done a lot more for them,' he'd said.

'You were a good son to them.'

'Why didn't I do more?'

She hadn't answered. It was grief he was expressing, not guilt.

So Ladbrook was Margaret's first destination, and she left Invercargill in a soft, Irish drizzle and drove through green Southland towards the tougher country where Peter had been raised.

Maybe she should go overseas again. She knew several women who had taken a world trip after the death of their husbands. Denise had married a retired Oklahoma pharmacist she met on a twenty-three-day Mediterranean cruise. She said he gave her the best sex she'd experienced since her twenties. She said her all-round health improved considerably because of it, even the arthritis, although there was a slight weight gain. Margaret was thinking of Denise as she had a flat white in Gore, sitting alone close to a window that showed the main street. Women weren't particularly clothes conscious in Gore, she decided. She liked Denise, the candour of her, the liveliness, but she wasn't looking for a husband, or sex. And travelling alone in a foreign country, especially to those places visited before with someone you loved, must surely have an aspect of regret.

'We had some damn good trips together, Maggie, didn't we? What's the top place you'd most like to return to?' He was in the clear time between the drowsiness of morphine and the preoccupation with pain. Margaret had talked of Croatia and Turkey, and he'd lain there, his eyes intent as he drew up images in his mind to match her reminiscence. His smile was wide, but in those last weeks a parody: the teeth seeming to have grown too large for his mouth, the skin and flesh retreating from the bone and cartilage of his face. 'Yes, Ephesus was great, wasn't it. To think it had been an ancient port and now miles from the sea. Marvellous place.'

'So hot, though, wasn't it?'

'You were always rinsing our stuff out and hanging it overnight in the hotel bathrooms.'

'And you were always working out the exchange rate.'

And as they talked he fell asleep, leaving her looking down on his open mouth, the equine teeth quite strange to her.

In her own country there was emotional challenge enough. Margaret had some difficulty finding the turn-off to Ladbrook after Roxburgh, and even when on the unsealed road, finding the farm wasn't easy. She identified it finally from the green summerhill stone of the farmhouse, built by Peter's parents, and the great, ramifying macrocarpa at the gate where Peter and his sister had waited for the school bus. There was little flat land, and the hills with occasional schist outcrops rose up more steeply than she remembered. There had been a group of assorted fruit trees close to the house, but no sign of them remained. Even country women had given up on bottling, she supposed. There was still the cluster of willows at the turn of the creek marking the one pond on the farm big enough to attract ducks. She and Peter had walked to it during a farm visit before their marriage. Lovemaking was difficult when staying with his parents, and Peter had urged her into the privacy of the maimai, and they had sex leaning against the unsteady side of the hide. Fenceposts, wire and light branches of broom and lupin woven in. Margaret's strongest memory was the feeling of the resilient wire behind her thighs, the fragrance of foliage and the muscular smoothness of Peter's neck. Youth.

She didn't want to go up to the house, to meet people with whom she had no connection, to witness all the changes that had been made since the place was Peter's world. She stood distanced at the road gate, the pulsing sun above her, and thought of her husband as a boy and a young man. This was a place in which he had never been seriously sick, or weakened: a place of natural possession. Where she stood, he had waited as a school boy with his sister, a home-made lunch in his bag. He had ploughed the few flat paddocks for his father. He had mustered the hills, and carted hay to the barn still standing by the windbreak pines. He had shot mallards on the pond, and made love to her there against the wire and brush of the maimai. It was healing to stand in the hot sun and feel Peter's presence. The place was very real, ordinary in the best sense, and the images it conjured for her stood against the memories of the pale hospice room and slowing time. As she drove back to the main road, Margaret sensed she wouldn't go again to Ladbrook. There was no sadness in that.

Alexandra had been her destination for the night, but she reached it by mid-afternoon and wasn't tired. She drove on through the gorge to Cromwell and Lake Dunstan, and booked into a motel not far from the shopping centre and district high school. The woman in the small reception office was thin and wore blue shorts. Margaret judged her age to be mid-forties, but the sun of Central had been destructive for her skin. Lines fanned from her eyes when she smiled, and some parts of her tan had deepened to the colour of the age spots Margaret was aware of on her own hands.

The woman was called Promise. The novelty of it would mean that she, and that Cromwell motel, would remain in Margaret's memory always, although significant in no other way at all. Promise displayed that apparently sincere interest in others that some retain despite dealing with a constant stream of people in their working lives. Some of Margaret's nursing colleagues possessed the same virtue, while she often tired of the press, the expectations, of those around her. 'So where have you come from today then?' Promise asked as Margaret filled out the accommodation form, and she went on to enquire about the weather experienced on the journey and the final destination.

'I'm heading for Nelson,' Margaret told her.

'You live there?' asked Promise.

'No. An old friend of mine is celebrating her fortieth wedding anniversary.'

'It's a credit to her,' said Promise emphatically as she took a pottle of green top milk from the fridge and set off across the forecourt to usher Margaret to Unit 8. 'There's so many marriages hit trouble these days, aren't there. Mind you, I have to say I'm separated myself, but we stuck it out until the kids were safely gone.'

'So often the way.' Margaret chose not to detail her own situation, despite travelling alone.

'Come over if there's anything you want to know,' said Promise. 'Ring the bell if I'm not around.' Her shorts were a narrow cut, but still loose on her thin, brown legs. She moved briskly as if to deny anxiety the time to settle. There were things Margaret wanted to know, but they would be beyond Promise, despite her invitation.

The shopping centre had the uniform architecture of recent creation — stained wood and feature stone walls, full-length windows. Margaret could remember the old Cromwell before the lake was formed, but you had to fight against the impulse to make comparisons, didn't you. It was a sign of age to set Punch past to every Judy of the present. She would curb that tendency in herself.

She ate pan-fried fish and a salad, neither as appetising as those she could make, but that was another comparison she rebuked in herself. She didn't want to become one of those dried-up old women for whom criticism was the only way to gain attention. Like Mrs Ellington one down from them, who gave abrupt and gratuitous gardening advice whenever in other people's sections. She once told Margaret her roses needed dead-heading. Peter called her a bossy old bitch, but not to her face. 'Don't shut up shop,

Maggie,' he'd said towards the end. 'And don't spend all your time running after the kids either. You'll get over all this business, and I want you to go on and, well, I mean you've been so supportive of me, and there's time for you to do all sorts of things.' The business he talked about was his dying. 'Don't live in the past,' Peter said. But overall it had been a past worth living in.

Margaret wasn't accustomed to eating alone. It made her slightly self-conscious, and more aware of other diners. The talk, the demeanour, of other people drew her attention when she lacked the absorption of a conversation of her own. Two men at a nearby table discussed difficulties they were having in getting building permission for a lakeside subdivision. Although they responded in conversation, she was surprised how little attention they paid each other. One man, athletic and bald, seemed absorbed in burrowing into his plate, and the other stared through the window as he spoke, watching passers-by in the still bright evening sun. Margaret noticed how his gaze followed women rather than men. When women talked to each other the words were accompanied by eye contact, by emotional exchange of one sort or another: men seemed content to rely on simple meanings. 'If I'd realised there was going to be such a bloody rigmarole, I would've got onto it earlier. The lawyers will lap it up, of course,' said the window watcher. He glanced at Margaret with a mere passing flicker of interest. She would get used to it in time. A fifty-seven-year-old woman by herself, after so long with a husband, so long with a social position established by a partner.

Even the return to the motel was a reminder of that. Everything just as she had left it, everything her own feminine possession. No one present with whom to share her reservations concerning the meal, or her observations of the conversation of men. She rang Greta, and after a lengthy talk asked for the boys to be put on.

How similar their voices were, how cheerfully off-hand, and how preoccupied their attention with a forthcoming school concert in which they were goblins in brown leather suits. 'They sound happy, in great form,' Margaret said when talking again to her daughter.

'Kids are so resilient,' Greta said. 'They miss Dad, though. I can tell that. They're missing you even more, so don't stay away too long. They wanted to show you their costumes tonight. What's it like there?'

'It's still hot.'

'Drive carefully tomorrow.'

'I'm looking forward to seeing the old bach. If it's still there, of course.'

'Be careful driving into Christchurch,' said Greta. Admonitions, assurances, warnings given to your children are all returned in time as the roles reverse.

In the morning Promise gave her advice on the weather and clothing. 'Stinking hot later,' she said. 'That car of yours got air-conditioning I suppose?'

'Yes.'

'Cotton, or linen, that's the only thing,' she said. 'I drive a lot with bare feet myself. Your feet are great regulators of body heat I read somewhere. It's restful somehow in the heat.' She didn't say anything about sunscreen, or dark glasses, or a hat. Margaret imagined her in twenty years: even thinner, even darker, like a teak hat-stand. 'Why don't you call in on your way back?' Promise asked, as if extending private hospitality.

Margaret enjoyed the drive over the Lindis Pass and into the Mackenzie Country. Until his illness Peter had done most of the open road driving, destination always the priority. Margaret was more leisurely, letting the big car loaf along a little under the speed limit. Traffic was light, and most vehicles went past, disappeared and left her at peace to enjoy the landscape and her thoughts. She and Peter had never developed the habit of listening to the radio, or a CD, while driving, and even though without his company, she preferred not to have that distraction. He had been a good talker and receptive listener. Some of her friends complained their partners never listened, never paid them attention. Her marriage had had its stress points, of course, its deficiencies, but consideration and engagement were habitual. Neither of them had sulked, neither of them took pleasure in inflicting pain. Peter was socially adept, and his talk stimulating and well informed, in contrast to the banal exchanges of many people they knew. He said that one of the things he noticed overseas was the higher level of conversation among professional people: the energy put into it as a tribute to those with whom you talked. It was one of the things she missed, having her own opinions and experience tempered, but not overwhelmed, by his incisive intelligence. Only about feelings had he not a lot to say.

The dun landscape was considered barren by some, but Margaret felt at home there. Flat country with little evidence of stock, or people. Some wilding pines, nothing that reached up far, and so the great, blue arch of the sky seemed to take up more of the space of the world. Most of her life had been set in Christchurch and then Invercargill, but her father's family had owned a fishing bach at Lake Alexandrina, where she had often spent holiday time before she left home. As she headed there again, turning off just before Tekapo village, and driving at the foot of Mount John, she experienced a strong sense of return. Not much seemed to have changed — the road was still unsealed and the land unimproved — but her response arose from more than that. Since Peter's death she had felt a compulsion to revisit her past, emotionally as well as physically. It was a natural and healthy part of grieving, she told herself, and would pass.

The car swayed on the rutted dirt track to the cluster of baches and trees at the south end. She remembered her father and grandfather joining with others occasionally to make ad hoc repairs on especially rough sections of the road. She remembered wintertimes with snow lying over the bare country like a pelt, and water pipes frozen in the bach, but mostly it had been as now: summer heat and the burnished rose hips like gems in the scattered wild briar.

Margaret put on her peaked suncap, and walked to the lake edge. There were more willows on the shoreline than she recalled, but little change otherwise. On the still water she could see two dinghies, one close enough for fishing rods to be visible. No power boats were allowed on Alexandrina: that was one of the things her grandparents had loved about it. It was a quiet place and what sound there was carried a long way — the slap of oars, a voice from the baches, perhaps a car starting, or the discordant call of ducks, perhaps the percussion of a man clouting shoes together to dislodge dirt from the treads. Often no sound at all except that occasioned by the movement of the air.

And the smell of landscape and lake, not town, compounded of rocks and soil, plants, insects, and damp margins under sun, wind and rain, but always in keeping with the season it accompanied.

Their bach was in the second row, and little changed. Originally an army hut with a corrugated iron extension. It had been repainted, but in a shade of blue that would in time be bleached to the colour she remembered. A man of about her own age was pottering about a boat and trailer close by. Boundaries were indeterminate and the small buildings clustered on open ground. The man asked if he could help, and Margaret told him the blue bach had once belonged to her family. 'John and Georgina Simmons own it now,' he said. 'They're not here much, because he has his own electronics business in Christchurch.'

'The Wallace family had your place when I used to come for holidays.'

'I bought it from them fourteen years ago. She died while they were travelling overseas, and he's got past the fishing. He comes up just occasionally for old times' sake. A decent old bloke, and full of tales about the lake. My name's Philip, by the way.'

'Margaret,' she said. They didn't shake hands. 'Nothing much seems to have changed.'

'It's the regulations. No new places are allowed to be built because of the lack of a sewage system. They're tough as hell on making any renovations and there's still no electricity. It's a bit different at the outlet. Things are more upmarket there.' He was a tall man with an office face, and spoke well. He wore jeans and a light grey jersey with no shirt underneath. An accountant, or a dentist, she supposed, maybe a polytech lecturer. 'Is this your first time back for a long time?' he asked.

'Longer than I care to say.'

'There aren't many quiet lakes now. That's the thing we like about Alex. The power boaters, water skiers and tourists all hang out at Tekapo, and we're pretty much left alone.'

'What's the fishing like now?' Margaret asked.

'You still get some good rainbow. Great eating. The old guys say brown trout were a lot more numerous years ago, but now rainbow seem to do better.'

'I'm just going to walk round the place. That okay?' she said.

'Absolutely fine,' said Philip, exercising neighbourly authority. 'Nice to meet you,' and he turned back to the boat and trailer.

During their conversation they had remained a full twenty metres apart, but that seemed quite natural.

Margaret walked round the building. The rough tussock grass still grew to the sides, worn back only in tracks to the door. The long-drop outhouse was gone, no doubt replaced with a chemical toilet. Little else external had changed. The wooden door of the bach, large and with ribbed panels, always seemed too grandiose for the place, and had been bought from a wrecker's yard by Margaret's grandfather. There was a tin lean-to at the door, and on the enclosed side hung, or leant, the typical paraphernalia of the place — oars, rowlocks, thigh-length waders, rods and tackle bags at head height, kids' toys, parkas, a cane basket, faded sunhats with set creases, a small wooden box that had once held tea and in which messages, or oddments, could be left, and three rusted horse-shoes nailed high for luck.

The smell of the place was just the same: the smell of implacable sun on wood, tin and fabric, of a place closed up for much of the time, of the trees and grass surrounding it, and faintly of fish and stale food. She didn't press her face to the window, not because it might seem intrusive, but because she didn't want to see any change there that might conflict with what she'd known. Inside for ever would be the old sofa, the two crowded bunk-rooms with faded quilts, the stone fireplace and the wooden table with tatty, yellow contact on its surface. Her father reading by the window, his glasses well down his nose: her mother giving some implausible description of a stranger met on her lake walk, or wondering aloud what simple meal she could concoct. And Margaret with them, but having at times the strange feeling that she was already looking back, already being silently swept past them into her own life.

Philip gave a wave as she walked from the bach back towards her car. She imagined him mentioning their meeting to his wife.

Strangers were rare. He would say he met a woman whose family had owned the Simmons place, and who had known the Wallaces, and his wife would ask her name, what she looked like, say he should have found out the surname. All more to pass the time than any true curiosity. Philip's description would make no mention of clothes, apart from the sunhat perhaps. Men make a physical inventory, not all of which is passed on: assessment of age, figure, sex potential. His wife would be fashionable perhaps, as befitted the spouse of a professional man, and tolerating the solitude and remoteness of Alexandrina because she knew he needed the break. Margaret found herself speculating more about the partnerships of others since Peter died.

Tekapo village had altered more radically, though she was familiar with that from occasionally passing through. She had lunch there, saw the new buildings that increased popularity had encouraged, and watched the Asian tourists swarm out from the buses for their photo opportunity by the lakeside chapel. She checked a slight disdain. It was no different from her own overseas bus tours: traipsing in a temporary congregation behind the guide to see the tower at Pisa, the Cappadocian caves, or the Greek monastery on a rock, and being more vitally concerned with food and lavatories, the petty vendettas within the party, than the postcard views. The things that remain most vividly in mind are those trivial revelations and incidents not mentioned in the brochures at all. Like the young American who propositioned her at the Gare de Lyon, in Paris. She had been waiting by the cases while Peter went to find their platform. The American must have been twenty years younger. Tall, well built, but with a face rather devoid of character. He put his backpack close to his feet as he sat down. 'A madhouse,' he said, and Margaret agreed. Maybe he was Canadian: she wasn't good with accents. 'Would you like to fuck?'

he said. Whenever she thought about it, she was sure he said only the one thing before that, but perhaps the impact of the question blotted out a few inconsequential comments. He must have been on something surely. 'I was told every French woman fucked, and I haven't scored in a month,' he said.

'No. I'm waiting for my husband,' she said. He didn't speak again, gave her just a quick glance, picked up his pack and ambled away through the throng. She was amused rather than shocked, and told Peter when he returned. She could tell that, rather than being affronted, he found it arousing. He put a hand on her hip there amid the crowd, as if he wished to cover her immediately in an act of possessive sex. For most men sex is something of itself, with no necessary connection to love, trust, procreation, even familiarity.

As Margaret had her sandwich, lemon slice and coffee at Tekapo, she wondered if that was to be the way of it now she was alone: slipping into the past rather than engaged with what was around her. Once her grieving was over things surely would be different, and after all the whole trip was an exercise in nostalgia in a way. So better to let it flow and then be done with it.

Before leaving Tekapo she sent texts to her son and daughter. 'Make sure you check in, Mum,' Greta had said, 'otherwise I'll worry.' Margaret thought of the boys, the elder just at school. They would remember nothing perhaps of this part of their lives: her affection, the times together. That was one reason she needed a future. It was important to her that she have some place in their lives, leave an impression of her love that would be with them always.

In the late afternoon she came into Christchurch, the slanting sun and traffic making the driving unpleasant for the first time on her trip. The city was familiar, though, and she knew of a motel close to Deans Bush: off the main roads and not far from where they had lived when Greta and Andrew had been growing up. Motels were more convenient than hotels when you had a car in the city, and more private, once you had your key, your pottle of milk and the curtains drawn. She checked the bathroom, always her point of assessment — size, facilities, cleanliness, the quality and quantity of the toiletries. Sachets were inferior containers: she was pleased to see phials. Her only disappointment was the proprietors' names. The man hadn't introduced himself, but on the reception desk was a small stand bearing, in white letters, 'Janice and Bruce Roberts'. So far away from the exoticism of Promise.

The house in Puriri Street was more recent in her past than the bach at Lake Alexandrina, but when she went there in the still, warm evening, Margaret found it had altered more. The side patio had been enclosed to make an incongruous conservatory, the Marseilles tiles replaced with long-run iron, and the cherry trees mutilated by savage cutbacks. She parked a little from the gate and stayed in the car so she wouldn't attract attention by loitering at the entrance. As at the lake, she had no wish to go inside, and could furnish everything there from memory. Even in its existing form the house seemed brimful of her life, shimmering almost with barely suppressed experience. How could other people move and breathe there without awareness of earlier possession? The big windowed lounge late on Christmas Day with bottles of gift wine, chutneys and olive oil standing by a chair, a black bin liner crammed with bright wrapping paper, the ravaged plates of nuts, cherries and chocolates, the extinguished, floating candles on the stained cloth of the extended table, the strings of Christmas cards along the pelmets. Andrew's presents gathered together by another chair, not yet taken to his room. The lesser detritus from the crackers still lying on the carpet — cardboard coins and strips from their construction, the dice, miniature whistles, tiny yo-yos, and keyrings that constituted the gifts. Peter's discarded shoes and book, by the sofa he rested on. Greta watching clichéd television repeats. The pine branch Christmas tree drooping, but still spangled, the camera on the coffee table with images already drifting into the past.

Of all the places she had lived in, this home had the greatest significance. A time when as a family they were most inward and well knit, when she and Peter were most aware of responsibility, of their children's dependence, of Andrew and Greta having no one greater in their lives than their parents. It was a time of striving and clear direction, a hectic time, and only in retrospect acknowledged as the high point of cohesion, no matter what individual successes lay ahead. It was an ordinary house, and they had moved on to better ones in which more money and leisure had allowed dinner parties, and art works bought with an eye for investment. But Puriri Street would not be dislodged. She sat in her car a little down from the gate and savoured past fulfilment and past regret.

In the motel that night she dreamt not of family happiness, but of Bevan Sugrue, with whom she had put all at risk. She hadn't driven past the medical centre where he'd been a partner, and she charge nurse for five years and lover for one, but that dream came, perhaps because she suppressed the memory when awake. He was a small, nimble man with a bitch of a wife. His wife, overwork, his concern for his patients and fear of misdiagnosis, kept him in a state of nervous tension and unhappiness. He and Margaret became close not because of initial sexual intent on either side, but because they liked each other: because she felt he needed support, and he appreciated it. Cynics could roll their eyes, but it was the truth of it. Truth, too, that so often friendship and proximity lead to bed. They took no risks at the medical centre. He had a key to his sister's flat in Papanui and they would meet there less often than they wished.

Margaret was surprised by the urgency and passion of his lovemaking, the thankfulness he expressed afterwards, the detailed praise of her breasts and thighs. It was flattery that Peter had dispensed with, though still eager for satisfaction. Bevan was a noisy and abandoned lover, revelling in the release. They would lie afterwards on the single bed in the small flat, his hot head on her belly like a cannon ball still reeking of the muzzle's powder, and reassemble themselves. There was guilt, of course, that sometimes after lovemaking led them to decide to just be friends: a decision rescinded when their bodies had been a few days apart. There was for Margaret the specific guilt on those occasional nights when she simulated a pleasure with Peter that had been spontaneous with Bevan earlier in the day. The unforeseen and greatest loss was in her own sense of moral authority within her family: how could she expect principles if she betrayed them in her own behaviour? So as Bevan and she had swung out from friendship to the extreme of being lovers, so they swung back again within the year, not repudiating their love, or the sexual experience, but regaining the stability of a relationship open to examination. Relief was greater than regret, relief that his needs were no longer her responsibility.

Margaret's motel dream, though, had nothing of overall exposition. It was a sudden, inexplicable and utterly convincing visitation. She and Bevan in his sister's sheets, the tight dark hair on his compact chest, a sheen of sweat at the base of his neck, the light above her seeming to sway although it was the bed that rocked, that wet slap of protracted sex. 'I could fuck you for ever,' he was saying when she woke, her breathing quickened.

Years after she and Peter shifted to Invercargill, she heard that

Bevan had divorced his wife and moved to Brisbane. It was the right thing for him surely, and Margaret retained affection for him, but never regretted staying with Peter. Lying in the impersonal motel room she knew that all of that was past: the physical thing with men, sometimes routine, sometimes flaring with an unsettling and dangerous power. There were more important and enduring matters. She would ring both Greta and Andrew before preparing for the drive to Nelson. She would cultivate the ability to look ahead, to accept that her satisfactions in the future would have nothing to do with sex.

She was packed soon after eight, but waited in her motel room until after nine oclock so she would avoid the work rush of traffic as she left the city. There was a faint smell in the alcove kitchen she couldn't place, until she opened the door of the microwave oven and found the inside had been sprayed with a cleansing foam and then forgotten. She resisted her first inclination to finish the job herself, but only because the same faint smell would then be on her hands and with her in the car on her journey. Margaret had a keen sense of smell. Fragrances and stenches were powerful fixing agents in the memory. The most evocative of all the senses, the psychologists said. Peter had a poor sense of smell, but great sensitivity of vision, especially the subtleties of colour. He blamed the rugby he played as a boy, said that at primary school he had gained a reputation for heroism by being the only kid who would tackle Pug Morrison head on. Pug was in the special class and bigger, older, less tractable than other youngsters. Divided septum, broken nose, claimed Peter, and it had never been picked up, even when further damaged at secondary school. There was no visual evidence of injury — he had quite a distinguished profile — but it did for his sense of smell, he said, so that he could make only gross distinctions.

'Now it's my turn,' Peter had said in the hospice room, on one of those days so like others there: when whatever was outside — sun, rain, wind, cloud, light or darkness — made no difference whatsoever. 'I'd hoped for longer, Maggie, but that's the bloody way of it. I know you'll do the right thing for me. I'm counting on you. Always have.'

'Greta said she'd bring the boys in later.'

'There's nothing for them here. They're bored silly, poor kids. And they make me cry because I love them, and then that upsets them.'

'We'll see.'

'Could you take home some of these flowers?' Peter said. 'I know people are kind, but they crowd out such a small room. When I wake up I feel I'm in my bloody coffin already.' He gave a laugh meant to cheer her. 'It's not as if I can smell them much anyway.'

'But people who sent them will expect to see them when they come. It's rude otherwise.'

'But I'm allowed to be rude now,' he said. When she kissed him before leaving she was conscious of the sickening decay on his breath, and his teeth seemingly enlarged. Barely could she keep her tears back. She deliberately inhaled his breath as proof that the organism does not represent the spirit. Love inflates a world: grief makes the earth flat. 'I'm sorry it's all fallen on you,' he said.

'So where are you headed this morning?' asked the woman at motel reception. She was fullish of figure and her dark hair had recently been cut and coloured in a style that suited her well.

'Nelson,' said Margaret.

'Lovely at this time of year. I always say the top of the south has the best weather of all.'

'I haven't been for several years.'

'Enjoy,' said the woman, as if granting dispensation.

Driving a long distance on the open road can be a form of justified idleness, and Margaret treated it that way. In the weeks before Peter's death she had felt as if she was being wound up so tight that eventually, like a clock, she wouldn't tick at all, and now the travelling, the time alone, even the dreams perhaps, were bringing some release. She didn't have to hold herself together, to maintain strict coherence to reassure others: she could allow her mind to flit, past and present to flow without heed. Sometimes she just enjoyed the landscape; sometimes she was preoccupied with thoughts without any conscious trigger in the present.

As she passed by the few buildings at Cheviot she found herself thinking of discomforted Dr Cairney giving her the news that Peter wouldn't live much longer. He knew she had worked in hospitals, had witnessed recovery and death, and the pronouncement of both: knew she understood he would give his prognosis, and then go to lunch, or ring his regular squash partner to confirm a playing time, or visit other patients and laugh with them on delivering an optimistic report. Professionalism was the euphemism, she supposed. No, no, unfair. She recalled Dr Cairney's gently voiced opinion and the awkwardness that proved he cared. Margaret's experience and training should have made it easier for her to understand and accept what was happening, yet knowledge had been no protection. It's quite different when it's you, or yours.

Along the coast, however, coming towards Kaikoura, she found herself thinking of her jewellery. She had decided to have it all valued when she got back from the trip, and wondered if there was anyone in Invercargill sufficiently qualified to carry out the task. Rings were her particular love, and each had a special and personal provenance. It relaxed her to think about her rings, the origin of each, and whom she would gift them to when the time came. Well, before the time came: she'd have to see that all was clear and in writing. Not counting the mere dress jewellery, she had eleven rings, and surely the total value of those would be over $50,000. She became absorbed again with the comforting task of bringing each to mind in colour and and detail, and making calculations. Those bought overseas were the most difficult to assess, and most likely to have appreciated considerably. And there was inflation to be considered too, so that real values were compared. Peter had advised her to get everything valued professionally, but she had quite enjoyed the anticipatory guesswork, although not greatly concerned with money in other ways.

Six of the rings were gifts from him, but she had rings from her mother, including a Victorian diamond solitaire in a claw setting so raised and liable to damage that she was afraid to wear it. It had belonged to her grandmother, and Margaret wouldn't contemplate any alteration of it. The most precious of her rings were not necessarily those of greatest monetary value. The engagement ring had been purchased when Peter had the least money of their time together. There was her Istanbul ring with emeralds, diamonds and rubies channel set, which evoked the happiest of holidays, and a hotel room, overlooking the Bosporus, in which Greta was conceived. Just to wear it was imaginative passport to their closeness, their commitment, and the almost exultant confidence they shared in the future.

Margaret liked Kaikoura. The site had character and called for a settlement. When she and Peter had travelled north with the children during the Christchurch years, they had usually stopped there. Maybe the café she had her lunch in was one of those they had visited years before. It was another exercise in eating alone, but she would become accustomed to that. She told herself she was lucky: good health, family in the same city, friends, no lack of money. She could probably find work if she wanted to: nurses were always in demand. Another man could be found just as easily, even at fifty-seven. She wouldn't say it to anyone, but she knew she looked younger than her age. But she didn't think she wanted another man, not in the way they would want her. Maybe later, when Peter had been dead for much longer, that would change, but she didn't think so. Friends and family, that would be the way of it for the future. People died too quickly anyway, at her time of life.

She thought about those things, but not in any particularly morbid way. In fact she felt quite chipper in Kaikoura, sitting with a view of the sea and with bright sun, as it had been each day since leaving home. Widow was an old-fashioned term, and most of its connotations irrelevant in a modern world. She would do all right, she decided. She would make a full life for herself.

Not far before Seddon there is a small lake shrouded by trees. Margaret pulled off there to have a few minutes out of the car. There was a dirt track through the willows to the lake, but no clear walkway around it. She watched ducks and black swans some distance away. It wasn't a recreational place: nothing, as they say, improved on nature. The water was still, but dark, and there was a lot of insect noise from the fringing branches. Peter would have been mildly impatient to be on the road, and would not have suggested the stop at all. There was no hurry now, no business appointments, or deadlines, that bustled you through life. In his way he had been an ambitious man, but not from selfish motives. Comfort and security for her and the children were his largely unexpressed concern. When Andrew and Greta went to university Margaret thought they should take student loans and so learn the value of money, but Peter disagreed. 'It's something we can do to give them a better start,' he said, and worked the harder to provide it. In Greta's case he was probably right; in Andrew's certainly wrong.

As Margaret went back to the car, through the few willows, she noticed something she had missed before. A pig's head in the cleft of a tree. Some hunter must have disembowelled and decapitated the kill there, for even she could recognise it wasn't a domestic pig. A head darkly hairy, narrow snouted and palely tipped. It was another of those random and incidental things that nevertheless would stick, like Promise as a name, like the idling boy shredding catkins as Peter was dying, the burnished rose hips of Alexandrina, or the shop no bigger than a bathroom in the Istanbul market where they had bought her ring with diamonds, rubies and emeralds. She wondered by how much time she had avoided the dismembering of the pig. Maybe it had happened elsewhere, and young guys, drunk and happy, had driven with the head leering from a window until they tired of it, and left it in the tree. She would tell Melanie about it when she reached Nelson, and Greta and Andrew later. She would make an anecdote of it to prove she was capable of light-hearted involvement with the world.

The autumn brown of North Canterbury and Marlborough was a surprise to her after Southland, and the source of more childhood memories. In Blenheim she stopped only for petrol. She was keen to reach Nelson, find her motel and have the later part of the day to herself before Melanie's party. She ran through the names of Melanie's children in her mind, so that she could ask about each and not become confused, for old friends expect familiarity with their lives. Melanie had said there were to be no presents, but Margaret had ignored that of course and bought a lampshade of multi-coloured glass so attractive she had been tempted to keep it for herself. Just a few years more and she and Peter would have been would have been celebrating their own fortieth wedding anniversary. She consciously shifted attention to the country she drove through: the boutique wineries and new buildings superimposed on pastoral farming, the shingle-bed creeks and rivers.

'Come round now. Come round straight away,' said Melanie when Margaret called. 'I'm cross you wouldn't stay here. Where are you anyway?'

'You've got lots of family. You'll be flat out, but thanks. We'll have plenty of time when the party's over. You'll get sick of me soon enough.' She was standing in the bathroom of the motel at Tahuna, having checked it out. Sachets unfortunately, but there was both shower and bath.

'Come round early then,' said Melanie, 'and don't get all dressed up. It's informal, just family and friends. You'll know lots of people. Liz isn't coming now though, her husband's had a turn for the worse. It's really disappointing: havent seen her for, oh, ages.'

Margaret wouldn't go early, although she didn't say that. Better to have time with Melanie the next day, when the whirl of preparation, and the party itself, were both over. Melanie and her husband were using their own home, but having caterers in to do the entrées, the smorgasbord dinner and carry trays of drinks. Margaret walked with the mobile phone from the bathroom into the main room of the motel, stood by the glass sliding door. She asked Melanie about her family, using the name of each member and showing awareness of situation. Is Rachel still considering going back to university to study medicine? Have Shaun and the Irish girl decided to marry now they have a child? Is Melanie's mother still able to recognise her when she visits her in the home?

In the courtyard of the motel a man was washing a blue car with a hose, just as Peter would have been. Why bother, though, until she's home again. Melanie told her about the preparations for the wedding anniversary, and Margaret was interested and supportive. As they talked, Margaret resolved to be outgoing at the party, make an effort to relate to others after several days spent in her own company. Peter had despised people who inflicted their tragic, or despondent, moods on others. You just have to button it, he would say. Suck it up and get on with your life. He had faced a personal grievance case brought by a secretary fired from his firm, a highly efficient young woman who had nevertheless caused disruption in the office because of her mood swings. Her case was upheld, the business had to pay thousands in compensation, but she didn't return to the job. Peter was unrepentant. He wasn't going to be pussy-footing around his own office, he said, just because she'd had a row with her partner, or it was the time of the month. He had been equally pragmatic about his illness. He admired discipline and rationality.

'Anyway,' said Margaret, 'I'll let you go, and see you later. You'll have heaps on your mind.'

'Come as soon as you like,' said Melanie. Margaret remained at the glass sliding door for a time, watching the man chamois the water drops from the blue cars bonnet and roof. It comforted her. It reminded her of Peter, although the man in the courtyard was short and overweight.

Melanie's house was high up, with a view over the sea and the highway from Blenheim. An expensive and attractive home, but without much parking space because of the hill. Margaret knew to leave her car on the road, and when she arrived several vehicles were already there. The evening sun was still strong and the sky clear. She would go in alone, no longer with a husband to talk with if the first people she met were strangers. She felt the oddity of that rather than any apprehension, for she had never been a clinging, dependent wife. It was a sign of alteration, however: an indication of the fundamental shift and loss that death brings. As she approached the door she consciously quickened her step and smile so that she would match the party mood.

Melanie was on the lookout for her and took her through the other guests to the kitchen island bench where her husband had set up the drinks. Selwyn gave Margaret a kiss on the cheek and held her hand for a time: actions that expressed his sorrow. He said nothing about Peter's death. He was a surgeon, and knew how such things were, and that you didn't discuss them at a party. 'What will you have?' he said in a voice quiet with compassion. Melanie had disappeared, but then came back with Cheryl Struthers, who had been with them in nurse training and a friend ever since. And divorced, so constituting a suitable companion. Melanie would have organised it, wouldn't she: told Selwyn that when Margaret came he was to look after her until Melanie found someone Margaret liked. 'What can I get you?' Selwyn asked Cheryl, and when he saw they were busy talking, he excused himself and went to offer drinks elsewhere.

The speeches would begin soon she thought. The jokes about the longevity of marriage and personal idiosyncrasies, and the acclamation from those married themselves, and those divorced, single or dispossessed. Cheryl was talking about her father whom they had recently had to admit to home. Three nights before she had received a call from the staff there saying her eighty-five-year-old father had run away, and when she went round she eventually found him hiding behind a copper beech tree in his soiled pyjamas, weeping in the moonlight. It was like being called to school for a naughty child she said. Old age could be so unfair. Cheryl herself was beginning to be proof of it. Her upper arms were heavy, and her neck had a quilted texture. She said she was going to have a second hip done.

The growing noise in the rooms made their conversation difficult, and they went out into the warm dusk of Melanie's patio. Three men were smoking as they leaned on the stone wall and talked in the unhurried way men do. Margaret and Cheryl took light, fabric-backed chairs and sat by the french doors. As they talked, darkness came gradually, so that the garden first and then the men became indistinct: just the waxing and waning of the cigarette tips and the murmur of their voices, companionable laughter. Margaret had a sense that all outside was fading away, even as the party behind the glass grew brighter, more intense. She would go in later and join the friends she recognised among the crowd there, but not for some time. She liked talking with Cheryl in the warmth of the summer night. But even as she listened, responded, talked herself of her grandsons, the visit to see the old house in Puriri Street, the pig's head in the tree by the lake, the farm at Ladbrook, nursing days many years before, a deeper current of her mind carried thoughts of Peter.

'Help me through, Maggie,' he'd said, before he went into the hospice. 'You're a nurse and know what comes now. You know what to do.' She did. She knew that often in cases such as his, death was sadistic: that despite the reassuring platitudes of the profession concerning palliative care, suffering would be immense. Love may bring obligations greater than any of society's ordinances. 'Help me through,' he said, 'as you've always done.' Life can be a buffeting, bewildering journey, and joyous as well. There is plenty of malice and stupidity walking in the world, but luck, radiance, wonder and love are experienced there too.

'I think it's great you've come all this way by yourself,' said Cheryl. 'You've always been so strong, so positive.'

Margaret decided there was no guilt: no guilt and no true death until the last of those who love you dies.

COMING RIGHT

'Jesus, though, am I sick of not having money. Other people have money except us. I see more stupid people than us with money, uglier too. Almost everyone I went to school with has done okay, except for the odd druggie and suicide. Jill Summers as was, has baches at Wanaka and Kaikoura better than our dump, and we only rent it.'

'Yeah, her husband's a real estate agent, though. It's a licence to print money,' said Ian.

'Why haven't you got a licence to print money?'

'Because I haven't got the qualifications.'

'Tell me about it,' said Noleen. 'Shit-hot at school, weren't you. First fifteen, first eleven, stuff all over your blazer pocket, and now guys that were nerds then are sitting behind the desk when we go in to beg for a mortgage. What a good laugh they must have.'

This was an argument they had often: well, not so much an argument as complaint from Noleen and deflection by Ian. On Noleen's side it was more a lament than a vindictive accusation. They sat in the car at Lumney Point, ate Kentucky Fried and watched the waves come in at an angle. The windows were misted up because of the takeaways: several years ago the reason would have been different. 'No, but it's a bummer, and it's not even as if we're hanging in there for a pay-off down the line, like Kate.' Kate and Martin lived next door, and Kate worked a ten-hour day at Hassell's Dry Cleaning while Martin finished his law degree and pumped petrol at night.

'Maybe he'll flunk out.'

'Nah. He'll be in a suit before you know it, and playing squash at the club at lunchtimes. They'll get a three-bedroom, brick place in one of the hill suburbs, and flick friends like us.'

'Good riddance then,' said Ian, 'if that's all they care about.'

He didn't consider himself a failure. Okay, he hadn't done much academically, but he'd been a prefect and sports captain: even won the singing cup, which would have resulted in jeering derision for most other recipients. From the seventh form on he was able to get sex fairly often with a variety of girls, and how can a guy be a failure when he's getting it regular. 'You're bloody hot. You know that?' Asplin Newby told him as they lay on some patio squabs in her parents' basement. Ian still thought about that sometimes when Noleen was going on. Okay, Asplin went on to varsity and became a microbiologist or something, but that doesn't change what she said.

'We need to get ahead somehow. That's what I'm saying. We don't have to be fucking world beaters, but we need to be on the up. I counted up the other day, and out of our friends only Anna and Frieda don't own their own homes, and Frieda isn't even married.' The recollection caused a gust of discontent, and Noleen wound down her window, and tossed out a pottle still containing some mashed potato and gravy.

'Yes, some whopping bloody mortgages, though,' said Ian.

Ian had a job at Central City Tyres and Mufflers, where he fitted and balanced tyres, and replaced mufflers. Five of them worked there, and he was next most senior to the foreman, even though he'd been there only four years. Noleen worked mornings at the Harbour Plantorama, though she hated gardening. Her job was mainly hand watering and responsibility for the portable displays outside the front entrance. She told Tony Bowden that she wanted to make deliveries, but he said if she wasn't satisfied with what they'd agreed, she knew what to do. 'You'd remember him at school,' she'd told Ian. 'Oily little turd who spent all break and lunchtime in the art room greasing round old Freetley.'

Noleen was quiet for a time, occupied with taking the skin off the chicken drums because that was what made you fat. Not having enough money was bad enough, but Jesus, imagine being fat *and* poor. Ian could eat everything he got his hands on and nothing happened, but if she didn't watch it she just ballooned. The sucking his straw made in the Coke container annoyed her, and his hand scrabbling on the cardboard for the discarded chicken skin. 'Well, it's what you pay for, isn't it? The seasoning or whatever is what you pay for, and you chuck it away,' he said. 'Anyway, we're not exactly starving, are we. We must have nearly three grand in the bank, we've got a good set of wheels and the landlord has to do maintenance on the house.'

He shouldn't have said anything about the car. Noleen reckoned it was a major reason they weren't getting ahead. A 1998 V8 Falcon repainted purple and with Zeon mag wheels and lambskin covers. It was a real guzzler, but Ian pointed out that he got a hell of a discount on tyres and exhausts, and mates' rates for just about everything else. That's the good thing about being in a trade. 'It's a bogan car, that's what,' said Noleen. 'When I went to Woolworths the other week, a skinhead shouted out something about purple and women.'

'I'd knuckle the bastard,' said Ian.

'For Christ's sake. That's not the point I'm trying to make.'

The point she was trying to make, but wasn't sure how to get there, was that she wanted to have a baby. Noleen liked kids. She spent time babysitting her sister's little girl, and enjoyed going there at other times just to play with her. And Ian would be a good dad, she was certain of that. He'd come from a happy family and didn't have any hang-ups about kids. Noleen talked to him about it that night when they got home. She told him she thought it was time to start a family, but it was no start to family life without a home of your own. 'You're the man of the house,' she said. 'It's up to you to come up with more. You know what that last bank guy said about a bigger income stream. Well, we need a bloody river, and quickly so that we can get a loan and into a place of our own. I could do afternoons as well, but that's bugger all more, and I'd have to knock off when a baby came anyway.'

'I suppose I could give up the Saturday games for overtime.' He played in the second grade as lock, and most people reckoned he could be still be first grade if he had time for the practices. Noleen felt a bit guilty when he said that. A good deal of his life had been sport before they married. It was what he was good at, and she knew you needed to feel good at something.

'I'm not saying that,' she said. 'You need time with your mates, I know. It's just that we're not getting on, are we. I don't see us managing getting a house and having a baby the way it is now.' She watched a bit more of the reality television programme in which people competed to lose fat. Normally she loved it, because all of them were heavier than her, but she couldn't concentrate with money worries on her mind.

'I dunno how so many other people do it,' she said. 'How, with just ordinary jobs, do they get so much money together for a deposit? How do they get the bloody loans? It beats me.' Ian was reading a *Wheels* magazine, but he saw she needed to talk it out.

'Often they get a kick-start from their parents, don't they,' he said. 'Like Rick. $60,000 from the old man, and only principal to pay back.'

'Yeah, well you and I'll be a long bloody time waiting.'

'We can't blame your folks, or mine,' said Ian. 'If you haven't got it, you haven't got it, and that's the size of it.'

'Something's got to happen anyway. That's for sure. Maybe you need to chuck that job and find something a bloody sight better.'

'We could win Lotto yet.'

'It's not funny, Ian. How can we have a baby on what we've got? You need to come up with something. I worry about it most of the time and it's getting me down.'

Ian knew it was, and being the sort of guy he was, he accepted her view that it was his responsibility to come up with the something. He didn't talk about it all the time, but he wanted to get on. He wanted to have a family and look after his kids well. His father had suffered a workplace injury in his early fifties, and money had always been short in the family, but they'd been happy almost all the time: Ian and his mum and dad, his brother Bruce. Noleen and Ian still went there every Christmas, and visited other times too. Noleen got on well with his parents and thought them good sorts, even if they hadn't set the world on fire. Her own parents hadn't done anything special, but they had a sort of covetous awareness, inherited by Noleen, of the lifestyles of those a notch or two above.

'Mr Menzies, I'd like to talk about my wages,' Ian said to the owner of Central City Tyres and Mufflers the next Monday. He'd waited until lunchtime and caught his boss just leaving the small glassed office at the front of the workshop. Mr Menzies showed no annoyance. He motioned Ian inside, closed the door and sat at his desk again, his hands steepled on a wad of invoices.

'Okay, shoot,' he said.

'Noleen and me are really keen to get a place of our own, and we're just not getting enough together to be able to make the deposit on anything much at all, let alone the mortgage we'd need.'

'Not easy,' said Mr Menzies, who still put on overalls from time to time and got stuck in.

'So I was wondering about a rise,' said Ian.

'I wouldn't want to lose you. I know you do a bloody good day's work. I tell you what, Ian. I'll give you an extra dollar an hour starting from today. I know what it's like getting some go ahead when you're not long married. That's tops, though. There just aren't the margins to pay more, and that's a fact. It's a cut-throat business and if I'm a few dollars dearer than the place down the road then I'm history.'

Noleen was pleased with the decisiveness shown by Ian and Mr Menzies. She gave Ian a hug and a kiss, and they went out the next night to the races, and actually made seventeen dollars, not counting the hotdogs and chips, but they both knew that fifty or sixty extra bucks a week wasn't going to make the difference they wanted. 'You need to think outside the square,' she told him. 'It's a pity you're not into computers. Seventeen- and eighteen-year-old geeks set up some website selling party poppers, or passing on police signals, and in no time they sell out for millions. You read about it all the time.'

Ian wasn't much on computers, but he was capable of thinking outside the hypothetical square. After a Saturday afternoon game in which his team had been given a bit of a lesson by Varsity, Ian and his mates had a few beers in their wooden clubrooms by the park. It was cold and they clustered round the radiant heater. Several of the wives and girlfriends were there, even half a dozen kids who watched the small television set, or scampered on the wooden floor among the chrome and plastic seats. Budgie, who was a useful half-back, was talking about phone sex with considerable familiarity, although denying he'd ever used it himself.

'It's big business, big money,' said Budgie. 'There's chicks making four or five hundred bucks in a couple of nights just gassing after washing the dishes and putting the kids to bed.'

'And not just women,' said someone.

'Absolutely,' said Budgie. 'Don't you worry about that. No travel, no bodily fluids, no bruises, no hidden cameras, no risk you see.'

'And no real shag at the end of it,' said the skipper derisively.

Ian agreed with that, but Budgie's claims for the money impressed him a good deal. That night at home he looked at the personal ads in the newspaper, while Noleen watched a programme in which people competed for 100,000 US dollars by comparing their terminal illnesses. 'Chat live with Kiwi babes one on one 24/7: fantasies come to life', one ad promised. The charge was $3.99 a minute plus GST. You paid by credit card and there was a 0900 number. Even if the babes got only half of that, it was bloody good money for just talking dirty to a phone. Ian didn't see any ads offering a chat with studs, but supposed they were out of place in a family newspaper. Ian wrote down some 0900 numbers. He didn't hunger for fantasies, but he did need money. You did what you had to do, didn't you, like the woman on the television at that moment who was writing with her teeth to show how little function her extremities retained. The live chat babes were probably not at all like the small photographs shown in some of the ads: they'd be home-bound, lank-haired women with their own desperations.

When Noleen went to a chick film with Frieda on Tuesday night, he rang a 0900 number. The answer was pre-recorded and confusing. He reached Beverley with his third call. Beverley said she hadn't had any guy ringing to offer services before, and wasn't sure of the procedures. She said maybe she could get someone to ring back, but Ian said he didn't want anyone to ring him at home. Beverley said maybe if he rang again in about an hour someone could speak to him about it. 'You sure you wouldn't like to talk to one of the girls now?' she asked.

'No thanks, Beverley. I'll ring back.' She was still there when he phoned back, and passed him on to Nick, who asked him if he was married, and told him that he had the wrong idea if he thought that he'd meet up with all the girls this way. 'I'm just looking to make some money by doing a good job,' said Ian.

'Well, we don't hire anybody over the phone,' said Nick. 'You come and see me on Friday afternoon if you're interested,' and he gave Ian a time and a place.

Ian told Mr Menzies that he had a dentist appointment on Friday. He took his best shoes and jacket in the car, and put them on before going up the narrow stairs to Nick's rooms above the local MP's electorate office. On the frosted glass panel of the door were the words Eureka Communications. Ian wasn't specially nervous. He could handle himself in most circumstances. If it didn't work out, then it didn't work out. He'd never had any trouble talking to women, and there was no guilt in talking: nothing to threaten what he and Noleen had, though of course you couldn't expect her to understand that. He loved Noleen and wanted to make her happy.

Nick was younger than Ian expected. He was short, slim, wore a dark suit and glossy black shoes. He couldn't have been much more than thirty-five. 'The chat stuff is only a part of what I do,' he told Ian a little defensively. 'I started with telephone polling and canvassing and let it develop in response to client need. Now people are much more comfortable with personal calls, and that's certainly grown. There's more money in it, that's for sure. People don't realise the extent of self-regulation, of course. There's some pretty nasty traps if you don't have that. You done anything of this nature before, Ian?'

Ian said he hadn't, and Nick went on to explain about some of the rules behind what might seem an anything goes arrangement to outsiders: about establishing adult status of callers, about never revealing details of location or identification, about never agreeing to meet personally with callers, about not making emotional attachments and never asking for extra money, or favours, about strict confidentiality. 'We're in the business of therapy, that's what it is,' said Nick, who was a very easy talker. 'People get a sense of release, of relaxation, from the social restrictions on conversation between the sexes in everyday life. Just a couple of weeks ago a guy who's responsibile for forty-three female staff told one of our women that if it wasn't for her he reckoned he'd be in police custody. There you are, you see. Therapy.'

Ian knew that Nick wasn't talking just to explain the sex chat line business, but as a way of sussing him out. After fifteen minutes or so, Nick came round to business. He said that most callers were men wanting to talk to women, of course, but there was a demand the other way around. He said Ian's voice had possibilities, had a certain timbre, and the suggestion of rough trade without threat. He asked if Ian had ever done any singing, and was pleased with himself to be proved right.

'It's all in the voice, see. Not so much what you say — Jesus, there's only so many parts, practices and positions, aren't there — but how you say it. Particularly with the women. Women are especially sensitive to a wooing voice. Basically they just want to be wanted.' Nick talked about that, about the approaches and language he'd found most effective himself. Maybe with a few pointers Ian could be given a chance, he said. Maybe he could be a professional sportsman, say, seeing he had that background, or the owner of a fishing boat.

'I couldn't work at home at all,' said Ian. Nick said most of the women did, but he did have booths in the other room, so that needn't be a problem. 'Officially I'd be doing that polling and survey stuff you talked about,' said Ian.

'Sure,' said Nick, 'but early days yet. We'd have to give you a trial and see how you went. People think it's easy, but it's not.'

That's how Ian started as a pollster at Eureka Communications. Noleen was chuffed with his initiative. 'Good on you,' she said. 'Just don't ring people right on teatime. That's bloody irritating, that is, to be rung right when you're getting the meal and asked about your banking habits, or how many times you've had a tropical holiday in the last year. Yeah, right, I tell them. What is it you ring about?'

'Politics mainly,' said Ian, 'and it's all later at night when people have settled. I quiz them a bit about their positions on the issues and what would make things better in their lives. How they'd like to see themselves in the future — stuff like that.'

'Someone's got to do it, I suppose, and at least you're sitting down.'

He started with one night a week, eight to ten, sitting at Eureka in a booth soundproofed with Pink Batts and unpainted chipboard. There was a sheet on the wall with twenty-three of Nick's rules of engagement typed on it. Ian became Russell, who'd played league in Aussie for the Bulldogs and was skipper of an orange roughy boat. Most of the calls were far less hard core than he expected: a good many were from curiosity only, and often he could hear smothered laughter from other women in the background. Nick's main advice was a parody of the mantra of real estate agents — compliment, compliment, compliment. Above all the women wanted to be flattered, to be the centre of smooth-talking male attention, even at $3.99 a minute. The number of regulars grew as time went on. He judged by their voices and conversation that most of those were older women. Two said they were widows, and one he worked out was a prominent lawyer. Conversations were risqué rather than pornographic, often surprisingly confessional on the caller's part. Everyone likes to be flattered, to be wanted. Ian didn't despise the need, or abuse it: he tried to give fair measure without shame on either side. It gave him insight, even sympathy, into the world of women.

'I must say you're a bit of natural,' Nick told him, 'and you seem to have a knack of avoiding the pitfalls. Guys more often than the women end up making dates with callers, and that can come to all sorts of grief.' He gave Ian a greater share of the $3.99, and Ian could work most nights he wanted. Some weeks he made $350 or more. Noleen was thrilled with his success, and showed it by being particularly supportive. She took a lot of trouble with their meals — Ian just loved a roast, or a rack of lamb — and washed his footy gear with cheerful care.

'I'm proud of you,' she said. 'Jesus, we're just forging ahead,'

'Yeah, well don't tell everybody, or they'll be all be down there at Eureka Communications asking to do it.'

'I never thought there'd be such a good business in phone surveys and selling. You never know, do you.'

'It's the convenience of it,' said Ian. 'People get used to doing everything with computers, or phones. Nick reckons that in twenty years there'll hardly be anything on the roads except freight vehicles, because people will be doing their work and recreation all without leaving the house.'

After five months Noleen arranged a meeting with a loans and mortgage officer at their bank. It was a piece of cake, she told Frieda later. She and Ian had three income streams between them, and a minimum deposit. They were lent money to buy a villa several blocks back from the beach, and two months after they moved in, Noleen was pregnant. It suited her: she became less concerned with the lifestyle of those better off than herself, and more thankful for her own situation.

Ian continued in good standing at Eureka Communications, and could pretty much work the hours he chose. He thought a time might come when he left his job at Central City and set up for himself in a workshop specialising in customised suspensions, which had become quite the thing with the petrol heads, but he didn't say anything to Noleen, or Mr Menzies, about that. He didn't want to get ahead of himself and come a cropper. Once he'd got on top of the mortgage, though, he promised himself.

They had a boy, and called him Thomas. Ian was there at the birth and a bit rocked by it all, but tried not to show it. He felt an instant love for the little guy. Tears of relief and joy from Noleen, enthusiasm from friends and both sets of grandparents. Frieda brought a three foot-high blue monkey, and said she was determined to get married herself. 'I wish your lovely man had a brother,' she told Noleen.

Frieda was there at the hospital on the second day, as Noleen and Ian prepared to return home. The blonde nurse came to say goodbye, and as she went away, Noleen said she was the one who'd said she liked Ian's voice. 'Said you had a cute, masculine voice,' Noleen said.

'Well, he has too,' said Frieda. 'All that singing you used to do, I suppose.' Ian just laughed and took one of the cases and stood in the corridor.

'He can sing to the baby then, can't he,' said Noleen, 'but not any nurses.'

'No, but seriously, you're dead lucky with Ian,' persisted Frieda.

'I will say he's been bloody good over the house and baby, but don't you say so and give him a big head. We talk a lot more about stuff now. He seems more switched on and understanding about women's things than he used to be. We share a lot more stuff now, and he's really chuffed about the baby. We're closer somehow. I could've done a bloody sight worse I have to say.'

'He wouldn't touch another woman I reckon,' said Frieda.

Ian couldn't hear them, but even if he'd been able to, he could have said with a clear conscience that he'd never touched another woman since marrying Noleen. A guy had to take his responsibilities seriously, set his mind to getting ahead and coming right for the sake of his family.

HOWELL

Even the most plebeian of families has some jewel in its history: a grandmother whose early talents surpassed those of Baron Rutherford when they were primary kids together in Brightwater; a Pitcairn cousin related to Fletcher Christian; an ancestor who fought as a fusilier at the Battle of Waterloo, losing an eye, but retaining a brass button to pass on; a Viennese landlady who tended Ludwig van Beethoven in his deafness.

My neighbours in Palmerston North could trace themselves in unbroken line to a Dutch paymaster who came to England after the crowning of William and Mary in 1689. Ted Gilley, who was custodian at the Foundation for the Blind, had the middle name Unpeas, which the eldest male of the Gilley family had been given for so long that everyone had forgotten the provenance of it. Noleen Browne told me that her great-great-grandmother was frightened in pregnancy by a carriage horse, and the child was born with a chestnut mane all the way down its neck. Hec Liddey, who played senior rugby with me, claimed that on his Maori side he was descended from Tuhawaiki, the Bloody Jack who beat Te Rauparaha. Certainly, no one liked to take Hec on when his temper was up.

My family has one touch of richness in its tradition. My grandfather was a Welshman who came out to New Zealand for the Better Life of the colonial dream. An ex-insurance agent and foundry worker, he was served up a bush farm in the Hokianga that gradually broke him, and then reverted to its natural state. Perhaps that experience made him all the more devoted to the story of our lost birthright.

Our late eighteenth century family had owned a colliery in south Wales we were told. In the retelling of the story my father often felt obliged to point out, with a scrupulousness which enhanced credibility, that coal mines then were not the huge concerns of later years, and often privately owned. A colliery nevertheless; a basis for family industrial strength over generations to come. Howell was the one son of three who developed a fine, early Victorian conscience about the treatment of miners in the family firm, and when fierce argument with his father and brothers failed to achieve better conditions, he repudiated his stake in the business and moved to Middlesbrough where heavy industry was booming. All of which is part explanation for a later Welshman with a Yorkshire accent hopelessly felling bush in the Hokianga.

The touch that I best remember my own father dwelling on, was that for Howell's lifetime his profit share was religiously put aside for him year by year, and he as religiously refused it. My father's tone was a mixture of wistfulness, resignation and quiet Methodist pride at an exercise of principle at the expense of us all. He often talked of Howell and Gladstone in conjunction, so that when I was a boy I thought they were known to each other, and only gradually realised that the thing in common was their rectitude.

Youth has little patience with nostalgia, and apart from a brief selfish reflection that I would have preferred Howell to have been less rigorously moral and more concerned for his progeny, I didn't care for family history. My father, though, had it close to his thoughts, perhaps because of the struggle he remembered in early years. As young men he and his brothers had worked on the roads in the Depression, and he hated to see a light on in an empty room.

I suspect that, in his more indulgent moments, he imagined some rock-solid Swansea dynasty willing to make amends: saw himself gravely accepting his due as Howell's heir. Money would have been welcome, but even more a scarred shield from the time of Owen Glendower, with the family crest inlaid: three boars rampant on a gold field perhaps. Despite the Depression, my father had a streak of bookish romanticism.

As an adult I became more interested in the sense of personal history, and in my turn passed on to my wife and children the saga of Howell, with a self-righteous stress on the theme of sacrifice. It wasn't until I was in my late forties that I had the inclination to begin research on my family background, and I expected to recover the full Howell saga from the mists of family folklore. Instead I destroyed that sustaining belief, for our Howell was listed in an early census as a fifteen-year-old miner at Blaenavon, South Wales, and his father as a bit carpenter in the ironworks there. He shifted to Middlesbrough sure enough, and signed his wedding certificate soon after with a cross: hardly an indication that he was a member of gentry descended from the Princes of Powys.

There must be something that began the petty legend, a brother who stayed behind and prospered perhaps, or a determination during a Welshman's courting to enhance the family's social standing. I regret having found poor Howell out, though the claims were not necessarily his own.

I never told my father. Several times before his death I heard him again tell the story of our lost birthright. It had an almost biblical fitness and balance: a story that had accompanied our family for generations, and embodied a good many precepts.

'I believe,' my father would say, 'that at the end of every year the family set aside that portion of the colliery's considerable profit due to Howell, and that each year for the rest of his life he refused to accept it because of the abominable working conditions for the men they employed.' I dare say Howell knew those conditions well. 'Had it not been for his stand on principle, we wouldn't be in this country today,' my father would say.

I haven't written off the story altogether. Maybe more intensive research will show a sound basis for its persistence, and anyway, belief has always been more powerful than actuality. Howell certainly existed, and made the break from Wales that led first to Yorkshire, and in time, for some of his descendants, to this country, carrying in their imagination at least, some honour of lineage.

Rather than diminish Howell, I have decided for the future to increase his stature and significance, partly in memory of my father, partly because the family is short on impressive ancestral achievement. I shall weave in claims for an imposing physical presence, an evangelical crusade in the tenements of industrial Middlesbrough, and a misplaced deed of transfer recording his donation of the signet ring from the line of the Princes of Powys now displayed in the historical gallery at Harlech. Every family needs a hero.

TRAVELLING IN EDEN

I have a blank concerning my entry into the Palliser Centre, and little recollection of the desperate weeks before, which made attendance essential. My conscious history there begins with an interview with Dr Austen. Academics always assess an office, for it reflects not just something of personality, but of the incumbent's position within the hierarchy of the institution. More generally, it speaks of the corporate body itself: the function, the largess and the degree to which staff are valued. Dr Austen's second-floor room was small and the furniture nondescript, but the one large window overlooked a neat lawn with an oblong garden of staked, yellow roses. Better a small office with such a prospect, than a large one above the kitchens with a view of pig barrels, lavatory louvres, a heap of discarded heating radiators and a shed for ride-on mowers.

Dr Austen talked to me about the aberrant behaviour induced by alcohol, and the physical damage of prolonged abuse. I could still pull out of it, he said, without irreparable harm. I must have met with him before, but that's my first clear recollection of us together: sitting in the small room with the shadow of the building stretching towards the roses, and Raymond Austen moving side to side a little on his swivel chair as he talked. He had a benevolent face the colour of mild cheese, and a pronounced furrow below his nose on his upper lip, like a well-formed miniature roof tile. I wondered what I looked like to him, and assumed an expression that I hoped was as amiable as his own. 'Are you feeling okay?' he said.

He told me he didn't believe in being prescriptive, that he wanted to lay out the options available to me and let me take responsibility for a choice of treatment. 'As in so many things,' he said, 'a lot of the success you achieve comes from the personal conviction that you will achieve success. But you know all that, I'm sure.'

He was right, of course, both in the proposition and my acceptance of it, but one of the effects of alcoholism is inattention, and as he went on to discuss programmes, I was distracted by figures on the lawn, in a sunlit patch between the shadow and the rose plot. Two thin, middle-aged men, and the bald one was leaning forward, talking to the other, patting his upper arm for emphasis, and the other man was responding with bursts of laughter loud enough to be heard faintly in Raymond Austen's office. Talk, pat, laugh, talk, pat, laugh, talk, pat, laugh: the pattern was duplicated so faithfully that for a moment I feared I had suffered some brain default that registered as repetition, but then I realised that, despite the counsellor's similarly repeated swivelling, his speech had a normal progression. He was talking of the methods coming into vogue in America for treatment of what is termed competent alcoholics. Middle-class people, achievers, people with a stake in their societies.

'There's a recent Johns Hopkins paper on how the bar has been raised in terms of what we regard as achievement. It's titled "Alcoholism and worthlessness in times of affluence". Excellent, excellent,' said Raymond. 'I must remember to let you see it. Two generations ago, to be able to provide for one's family was a sufficient source of self-respect and justification for existence. Food on the table and pride withal. The grace said before eating was an endorsement of that. Gone, you see. All gone. Now such basic provision is taken for granted by educated people in countries like ours, and so much more is expected. You've got to excel, be in advance of your peers, above all gain some celebrity status within your field at least. Competence is failure; the norm is failure; lack of distinction is failure.'

Beside the roses the bald man still recounted his anecdotes, and his companion responded with laughter, but the touching had stopped, and they began to walk slowly over the green lawn. Soon they passed out of the view framed by the office window, and there was just the grass, the shadow line on it and the yellow blooms to be seen. Only when neither of them was visible did it occur to me that the laughing man reminded me of my father: very tall, and generous in response to the efforts of others to entertain him.

Raymond Austen's enthusiasm for his profession was admirable, and his familiarity with contemporary medical literature reassuring for a patient, but I had so often been on his side of the desk that I knew that his explanations were as much for his benefit as for mine. How many times in discussion of a thesis had I taken the opportunity to live again some visit to an antiquity, or lay out the ideas for a journal paper I was considering. And when the graduate students left, I would have little memory at all of their own views, but feel a spike of renewed interest for my own.

How salutary to be a patient, an inmate, to be the recipient of treatment, to have the inferior role, when you aren't accustomed to it. Once you pass beyond wounded vanity, there is such valuable understanding gained. To be kept waiting outside the official door, to have your own conversation brusquely interrupted, or patronised, to be reprimanded by the cleaning woman for stains on your locker, and by the under-gardener for picking a tulip, to be ignored by young women, and surpassed as a raconteur in the therapy group by an unemployed country and western singer of no education whatsoever. To realise how ordinary a person you are, once the trappings of a profession are removed: to undergo submission.

'We are learning all the time,' Raymond said. 'Certainly accusation has no place in modern treatment. I myself see social change as equally important to effective pharmaceutical intervention, but there's no silver bullet, of course. Ah, no silver bullet.' He was free of extravagant affectation, though he did have a small hourglass in a wooden frame on his desk, like an egg-timer, and would reverse it to begin an interview, and run a finger down the pronounced indentation in his lip. He began to explain to me what he had to offer in the absence of the silver bullet, while I imagined the jocund swirl of brandy in a globed glass.

After lunch that same day there was a group therapy session. It was held in the far end of the dining hall because the carpet of the dayroom was being professionally cleaned, and the television lounge was being used for choir practice. Notice was given of choir practices many times, but during the weeks I was there I heard no singing, and no recitals were given. Maybe it was a euphemism for something more closely related to elusive health.

Aromas of mince, pasta and washing detergent still drifted in the air of the dining room as we gathered some of the wooden chairs to form a circle. The clothes we wore, our body language, were deliberately casual, but there was nevertheless an air of mild anticipation. Personal revelations were sometimes made, aspirations and failures revealed that were of interest to others, skirmishes for personal ascendancy in the netherworld of our pitiful society.

Eugene Dodd convened the session, and began as usual by asking new arrivals to briefly introduce themselves. One was a young man with very thin, tattooed arms and a vestigial goatee beard. Lloyd. 'My search is for the redeemer,' he said. 'We'll never be free of the drink until we have a greater salvation.'

'This may be the place,' said Eugene firmly.

'Let it be so,' said Lloyd. 'Amen.'

'There's religious blokes, ministers, who'll visit if you want them,' said Roseanne. She wore slipper boots, and had a left cheek tic if other people talked too much.

'Let's put that on one side for just the moment,' suggested Eugene. I heard that he'd originally been hired as office manager, but gradually moved into areas of treatment, where there were always shortages. 'Also this afternoon we welcome Caroline,' he said. Eugene wasn't a highly intelligent person, but had authentic compassion for others that survived a flow of needy and recalcitrant personalities. It was humbling to realise my own inadequacies by comparison, and simultaneously irritating to suffer his trite commentary.

'Nuffin would've stopped me if only I could've been able to learn another language,' said Caroline. 'I was going with a friend to teach in Korea if only I could've picked up the lingo quicker. She done very well for herself and I was left here with nuffin really.'

'How often drink sabotages our ambitions. You'll find all sorts of talents here, Carol.'

'It's Caroline.'

'Sorry. Caroline. You'll find all sorts of abilities here, Caroline,' said Eugene. 'Many of the brightest people fall into the arms of drink.'

'It's scientifically documented,' said Roseanne. Sometimes her tic was like an exaggerated wink, more often just a fleeting tremor.

'It's an easy way out,' said Bobby. 'That's what it is, whether you're bright, thick as two planks or nutty as squirrel turd. And it always works, doesn't it, more's the pity.'

'More's the pity,' echoed Roseanne.

'Down, down you go,' said Eugene.

'The slippery slope,' said Bobby, who always sat with his thighs splayed to accommodate a beer gut.

'In the end I rung up the help line,' said Caroline. 'The guy I was living with got shitty, but you know, don't you, when you need to turn your life around.'

'God reaches out,' said Lloyd.

'You've come to a turning point,' affirmed Eugene.

'There's a hell of a smell of mince or something in here,' said Roseanne.

'I can't smell nuffin like that,' said Caroline. 'I had my nose broken twice in domestics and now everyfing smells like milk gone off.'

'We are in the dining room after all,' I said.

'Who pulled your chain?' said Bobby.

'Now, Bobby,' said Eugene in a tone of both admonition and reasonableness. 'You know the rules of group discussion.'

'Do unto others, Christian charity, people in glasshouses, Jesus is always listening,' said Lloyd.

'Well, those things may well apply as well,' agreed Eugene.

'I just seem to make bad choices in my men,' said Caroline. 'I mean you don't like to be lonely, do you, but it's no fun getting biffed all the time either. I won't fucking put up with it.'

'Now, Caroline. Rules of discussion re language,' said Eugene, and Roseanne gave a dramatic twitch because she had been out of the conversation for so long. She started to speak, but Caroline overrode her.

'If only I could've got to Korea with a language with my friend Amber, everyfing would've been okay,' she said.

'Today,' said Eugene firmly, wanting to bring the group 'on task,' as he termed it, 'I thought we would talk about our parents. Share some of the influences of conditioning — causal links, prejudice, respect and so on.'

So we embarked upon our topic. I contributed nods and brief phatic noises; I inhaled the persistent and sad odours of the dining room, while keeping my thoughts to myself.

My mother and father were both similar and yet distinct. I realise now that both of them were studies in disappointment, but dealt with that quite differently.

Brian had wanted to be a doctor, but couldn't maintain his grades and finally became an industrial chemist in the paint manufacturing business. He was a considerable success there. So much so that that he outgrew practical science and ascended into administration. He was offered promotions to Australia, but turned them down and became a keen mobile home traveller. He started with a Volkswagen campervan and ended, after successively larger vehicles, with a house truck so big that the driveway had to be enlarged to provide parking space. He christened it Eden, and the name was scrolled professionally in gold metallic paint on both front doors. At the rear end of Eden was a special rack for a 50cc moped.

Dad provided the height in the family. He was six foot three and thin with it. He tended to stoop towards people in conversation, which gave an erroneous impression of condescension. Travel and drink were means of assuaging his professional disappointment, and he was happiest when the two combined to give him a double hit.

My mother was called Eve, and was undisturbed by the references that this provoked. When in a light humour, she sometimes called my father Adam, and he would call her the apple of his eye. Eve liked to tell of her first meeting with my father at a disco party in Lower Hutt. They had gone with other partners who became besotted with each other and disappeared together quite early in the night. Brian and Eve were the rejects who attempted to maintain their self-esteem by dancing with great animation and finding favour with each other. She said he was a temporary convenience who became a habit; he said that, apart from the besotted girl, she had the loveliest hair in the world.

Eve was a geography and history teacher, but saw her true calling as poetry. She did university extension classes, attended festival readings and published in small booklets co-operatively funded by their authors. She said that teaching prevented her from achieving literary success, that it drew from the same emotional and intellectual wells as her writing, but my father's income was enough to support the family if she'd wished to give up teaching. My mother had a very pleasant face, but steadily put on weight until she became one of those stately women who seem to glide on castors like theatrical scenery.

My father was a jovial man, skilled at superficial acquaintanceship. He could hold up his end in conversation with anybody, and told me that often on their travels he would strike up transient friendships while my mother remained inside the mobile home reading Elizabeth Bishop or Lauris Edmond. Like most school teachers, Eve had for so long confronted resentful ignorance that she assumed it universal. 'Dear God,' she would say, 'just to have some time to oneself.'

Maybe that's why she, as well as Brian, seemed happy to spend an increasing amount of life in the mobile homes, despite their differences. Movement and change gave my parents the illusion of progress, I think, and shielded them from the disappointments of not being a doctor, or a poet. Life on the road may well have protected them a little too, from the burden of an alcoholic son.

I rarely saw them during their retirement. My visits then were almost always to their empty house, where I would air the rooms, check appliances, collect the mail and carry out perfunctory tasks in the section. It was unusual to find my parents at home. Rather I'd receive the odd text, or phone call, from Blueskin Bay, Motueka, or Rawene in the Hokianga. And when they were in residence they seemed to be incessantly unloading their lives from the mobile home, or stocking it again. Finally they expanded their peripatetic lifestyle overseas and would fly to Vancouver, Cairns or Helsinki and hire mobile homes there for extended wanderings.

So the house was usually forlorn when I went there as an adult, and filled more readily by memories of childhood. The living room had an expensive suite in white leather to replace the black one I had defaced as a boy, nestled there picking at the leather surface absently as I watched television programmes of aliens, sophomores and hard-bitten cops, until at the very end of the sofa armrests the skin had been worn away to expose the softer, grey nap.

An electric heater had been installed in the fireplace, with the false flicker of moulded logs, but there was still the faint smell of pine resin, and small burns on the rimu hearth surround. 'Put a decent shovelful of coal on, for God's sake,' my father would say, but Eve never did because she wanted to use the wood ashes on the garden. 'Can't we put ourselves before the garden?' he'd say.

'Only to view it,' mother would reply. Yet I never read a poem of hers to do with Wordsworthian nature. Rather they were resolutely domestic and she favoured the twee device of shape replicating subject. She won second prize in a local competition with a nostalgic poem on the theme of old dresses in her wardrobe. On the page the words formed the shape of a clotheshanger.

My bedroom became Eve's study and sewing room, but the transition was incomplete. Her computer surmounted my desk, but my single bed was still beneath the window in case of overflow guests, and closely populated with soft toys in pastel colours. Most belonged to my sister, Rachel, though I recognised as mine one worn, ginger bear who could still be forced to emit a slight, terminal groan. A few of my own textbooks stood with Eve's more contemporary collection on the wall shelves, and the squat, greenstone trophy I won in inter-school debating still did duty as a bookend. The walls were repainted, but there was a minor blemish between the door and the corner where I'd put in an uncouth nail to hang a portrait of Pope Benedict XV as a typical student irreverence. I bought it at a garage sale together with a broken metronome housed in walnut, and a brass artillery shell cut down for an ashtray. All had parted company with me at some forgotten time over the years of student flats.

Even the laundry had its memories, although the appliances had been updated several times. There was no winking computer display when I was eleven and saw, through the almost closed door, Alby Wigram humping his sister on the sheets and pillowcases strewn on the floor. The two of them had stayed for a weekend while their parents looked at a grocery business in Hokitika. They can't have thought it a worthwhile proposition, for both Alby and his sister remained in Wellington. After seeing them in the laundry

I was surprised to find that they continued to look like all the other kids ahead of me at school. It was a lesson to me in the ambiguity of the ordinary.

Despite my father's love of travel, he was ritualistic, as if the repetitions could hold back even time itself. He whistled the same tunes for forty years — have you noticed how few people whistle now? He sat in the same kitchen chair and the same lounge chair; each night he took the change from his pocket and arranged it as a small pyramid on his bedside table; the car bonnet was inevitably the last panel he washed; he always cut and drew out the string holding the corned beef before carving it; whenever it started to rain he would lift his face to the sky and say, 'Send her down, Huey.'

He knew the experience of epiphany, and sometimes I would see him struck dumb for a moment, and with an expression of blank absorption. Only once did he attempt to communicate anything of that to me. We were walking by the rocky point of Abbey Bay when a great seal broke through the swirling kelp and surf only a few metres away, reared, gaped soundlessly, then subsided utterly. 'I feel as if God has just taken a photograph,' he said quietly. When a small boy I would hear him walk past my bedroom at night on his way to urinate and blow his nose on lavatory paper.

Children have difficulty sometimes in distinguishing between fact and fiction, and I find myself increasingly in the same predicament. In the midst of conversation I hesitate, struck with the suspicion that what I'm about to propose as having happened, is a recollection of a dream. Undoubted experience has become almost unbelievable at such remove, and places and incidents from reading, or imagination, have overwhelming persuasion.

Being a drunk has exacerbated this tendency I know: there are things of mammoth incongruity that are nevertheless indisputable, and happenings that seem essential in my life, but have been proven illusory.

Something of all this made me cautious when Eugene asked me for a contribution to our group discussion in the dining room. 'And what about your parents, Malcolm?' he said. 'Were they positive and supportive people?'

'They seemed to be always travelling,' I said.

'Uh-huh,' said Eugene encouragingly, but I didn't wish to say more, and Caroline began again about the sect her parents had belonged to in Wanganui.

I wondered what my father and mother talked about during all those hours moving through the world together. Maybe they didn't talk at all. Two disappointed people endlessly journeying in the Eden of a house truck, rather than admitting defeat.

THE DON FERNANDO MOTELS

It was Don's idea, the name, copied not from literature, but from a trotter that he'd consistently backed in the late nineties and that had consistently won. And he'd been attracted to the horse not by lineage, or form, but because it bore his name. Men have this thing about the perpetuation and profile of their name. There was Don junior too, their son. He moved to Perth, and joined a boat-building firm. He said his father should have been in dairying rather than slogging on a hill farm, and that he'd have rather been christened Justin, or Ben.

So when Don senior and Yvonne moved into the city, Don Fernando was the name he wanted for the beachside motels. The advice was to choose something beginning with A or B, so you were high in the order of the travel guide lists, but Don wouldn't be swayed. You don't give up on your luck, he said. Not when it was as rare a visitor as he found it perhaps.

The Don Fernando motels had fourteen units arranged around three sides of a courtyard, with the fourth side open to the road, and then the dunes and marram grass before the beach. The Spanish theme was dutiful rather than convincing: pink stucco with murals of cacti, and the motel sign in the exaggerated shape of a Mexican sombrero. The plastic key tags were inscribed Hacienda 2, 3, and so on. The persistent afternoon easterly blew sand and detritus across the road and into the courtyard. On summer days the cars of surfers congested the sides of the road, and all year round at night cars nosed into the dunes — quietly if they contained courting couples, raucously if filled with a boozing group.

The occupancy rate was a disappointment. Don had been keen on motels because of his handyman skills developed over decades of farming, but most of the work was cleaning, and dealing with people, and Yvonne did that. The thing was, Don said, that the council had given building consents open slather, when there weren't the visitor numbers to justify it. He spent more and more of his time in Hacienda 1 watching sport on television, or tinkering with the faulty lint trap in the laundry room. Despite his interest in games, he developed an intense dislike for male sports teams as customers at Don Fernando. 'May as well have pigs in,' he'd say, as Yvonne cleaned up the vomit and scouted for the glasses. She knew they couldn't afford to turn away anyone. She knew it was touch and go, because she did the books as well. Don Fernando was proving no El Dorado.

Right from the start, Yvonne thought there was something odd about Digby R. Savant. A pseudonym like that was an arrogance in itself — on the one hand hiding your identity, on the other flaunting the disguise. He arrived in a taxi during the third day of a stint of persistent, drifting sea drizzle. He kept the taxi waiting while he established with Yvonne that she'd consider special rates for long stay. 'A couple of weeks anyway, and then I'll decide whether to stay on,' he said. Well, in winter Yvonne wasn't in a position to drive a hard bargain.

Digby piled his gear in the small office, dismissed the taxi, and then began an inspection of the vacant units. There were eleven. Despite the soft drift of rain that settled on his babyish hair, he looked at each one, before choosing Hacienda 14, which was upstairs, closest to the road and overlooking the beach and the sea. 'As much as possible I'd like unit 13 to be left empty,' he told Yvonne. 'It's winter and I don't imagine you'll have that many bookings. I'll be doing a good deal of work inside.' Yvonne helped him take his gear up, and gave him a small bottle of blue top milk. 'I'd like green top in future,' he said, 'and the larger one. I'm a bit of a white coffee freak when I'm working.' Yvonne asked from politeness what his work was, and he said he did editing for academic journals. 'Mainly palaeontology,' he said, 'but also physical geology.' Yvonne didn't believe a word of it, but wasn't much interested either. He might stay some time, and he didn't look the sort to trash a room: those were the important things to begin with.

He did stay longer. When the two weeks were up he negotiated an even better deal for three months. Well, it was a relief just to have at least one unit earning every day, Yvonne told her husband. 'Bit of a wanker, if you ask me,' he said. Don didn't take to him because although he was often making niggly requests, he wasn't interested in having a decent talk about sport, or farming, or the deficiencies of the government. Yvonne went in twice a week to have a tidy. Digby set up his computer and associated gear on a card table that he borrowed from her. On the very few occasions he wasn't in when she went, there was no evidence of his work on his table. Digby was secretive concerning his own affairs, but inquisitive about certain things pertaining to other people. He often asked Yvonne about folk passing through, sometimes he approached them directly in a surprisingly affable manner and chatted with them, which miffed Don all the more. Several times Yvonne saw him in the dark looking into the windows of other units. For some reason travelling folk pull the curtains less than they would in their own homes. And once she saw him over the road, crouched behind a Ford Mondeo, and listening to a group of young guys and women who had built a fire at the edge of the dunes.

No visitors ever came to Hacienda 14, and Digby had no regular pattern of departure. When he did go out, it was almost always with a small, blue backpack. Yvonne met him a couple of times in the supermarket, and there were many cans in his rubbish bag when she emptied it. He was keen on pineapple, mashed corn and beans with small sausages. A couple of times when in adjoining units, she heard him talking: not so much a single flow, but as if he took both parts in some conversation. It was no business of hers. What was her business was ensuring he paid each week. Digby wanted to settle up at the end of his stay, but Yvonne was adamant. She made a good many concessions to Digby, compromises because of his long stay, but jibbed at that. Digby paid with little grace and always cash. He seemed to need to accompany the payment with some compensatory trivial complaint, or request. The laundry pipe had overflowed again, or could he have a Sunday paper delivered as well as the weekday one: the group in Hacienda 9 had kept him awake all night, or would Yvonne get the sand out of his coir doormat.

Digby developed a special interest in Barbara, the postie. She said he never got any letters, but was often at the box when she came to Don Fernando, and must have been watching her progress from Hacienda 14. He asked a lot of personal questions, she told Yvonne. Things like how she spent her time when not working, and if she had a place of her own. Barbara had very attractive, well-muscled legs, but Digby wouldn't have been aware of that in the winter, and she had separated from her husband because he made fun of her family and didn't want children. Barbara had been a top netballer in her day, and wasn't afraid of men. She said Digby was a bit weird — wanting to know stuff, but never asking her out, or saying much about himself. 'I reckon he could do a flit if you don't watch him,' she told Yvonne at their Wednesday Pilates class. 'What sort of a name is Digby Savant anyhow? You'd never see him again would you. Not even a car registration number.'

'I've got him paying every week,' said Yvonne. 'Cash. He talks to himself inside the unit and eats mostly out of cans. He wouldn't know a fresh vegetable.'

'I don't like his hair,' said Barbara. 'All bum fluff. And he's so soft looking, isn't he? Hardly a muscle in his body, I reckon. He asked me the other day if I was interested in the occult, and I told him I didn't want anything to do with cults. I hear about the things that happen to women there.'

Digby Savant stayed the winter at the Don Fernando Motels, over four months in all. Only two people had stayed longer: a Wrightson's manager and his wife on transfer who were waiting to move into a new house, and a German expert on port freight equipment who was advising the harbour board on its expansion plans. Digby left in a taxi, as he'd come, and with no discernible increase in his luggage. His last comment to Yvonne was that all the haciendas needed to have heat pumps installed. 'What's there is very drying on the skin,' he said. He stood in the concrete courtyard, and the breeze agitated his longish, baby hair so that it danced on his forehead. 'So I guess this is au revoir, sayonara and auf wiedersehen to the Don Fernando Motels then,' he said, with false and exaggerated regret.

The assured income was the only thing Yvonne and Don missed, and Barbara said she was glad to come on her round and not have Digby idling at the box. Months passed, and he'd been almost forgotten when Yvonne noticed an article in the features section of the Sunday paper. It was in the book pages, which she never bothered about, but the photograph caught her eye. It was Digby receiving the prestigious Mooncutter Literary Award and People's Choice sash from the Minister for Arts and Culture. His novel, *El Hernando Motel*, was a runaway success for the hitherto unknown author. An auction was to be held for the film rights. The article exulted in what it termed a grim exposure of the underbelly of New Zealand society and the ambivalent duality of contemporary societal attitudes. Subtle allegory and existentialist flourishes, it said. An excerpt was given in which Digby wrote of the filmy curtains in the upstairs motel unit flowing inward from the open window like ectoplasm, while the vast breakers sounded bell-like in the distance and the grey sand scuttled ominously across the road towards the buildings.

It was their place, no doubt, Yvonne told Don. She bought the book the next day. It was about this famous author who comes to the El Hernando Motel suffering from writer's block and the effects of a failed relationship. His curiosity in the world is awakened by the oddity of the proprietors and the passing faces of the caravanserai, and especially Sally, the postwoman, an ex-athlete whom he comes to befriend, and eventually love. Sally has become drawn into a satanic cult dominated by the charismatic bikie leader, Bennyboy, and the hero witnesses her violation and murder in the dunes while helpless to intervene. The climax comes when the grief-crazed writer confronts Bennyboy on the cliffs of Nugent Point, and after the two grapple violently against a sky seared by flashes of lightning, they both fall to their death on the rocks below.

Don didn't read the book, but when Yvonne told him the story, he was more despondent than usual. 'He was pretty much a prick when he was here, and now he's done for us. Who's going to want to holiday here now? People will take it for gospel, won't they?' He was right about people soon recognising the setting, but Yvonne saw the advantage in that. Women have the ability to see more options than men.

She changed the name of the motels from Don Fernando to El Hernando. The president of the provincial moteliers' association said that Digby would sue, but Yvonne replied that what was sauce for the goose was sauce for the gander, and having taken so much of theirs that was true, he couldn't complain about relinquishing a little of his fiction. She put up net curtains in all the haciendas, and let the sand accumulate somewhat at the motel entrance. At dusk one evening she and Don went over to the dunes, and he hammered a waratah into the ground of a small hollow near the surfers' track, and Yvonne attached one of those cemetery arrangements of artificial flowers. She didn't put a name, just a plastic postal code tag.

Digby's book was on the bestseller list for twenty-three weeks and published in eleven countries. The El Hernando Motel was almost always full, even in winter, and Yvonne charged double rates for Hacienda 14 because of the ambience. 'Whatever that is,' said Don. People often came just to gawk, and many went into the dunes to have their photographs taken by the waratah and flowers, and shed a tear or two. Yvonne kept copies of the novel in the office which she sold on commission for one of the locally owned bookstores.

Newspaper and television journalists pestered Don and Yvonne to talk about their connection to the book, but they never did, and Digby wouldn't confirm or deny their motel as the setting for his novel. And he never contacted them, never came back to the seaside there, never sent an anonymous cheque to Barbara, or apologised to Yvonne for the printer refill ink that soiled the carpet in Hacienda 14. Both had benefited, though, Digby through creating art by distorting life, and Yvonne by altering life to reflect art. Quite a satisfactory quid pro quo you might think.

MICHAEL

As long as I endeavoured to maintain the deception that I was a good person, I was never at ease. I feel more comfortable now that I admit a good many shortcomings. You must become more tolerant of yourself as you go on, otherwise regrets and guilt become incapacitating. Michael used to say that the trouble with me was I'd had things too easy for too long.

He and I were such old friends that I can't point to a specific origin. We went to the same primary school, maybe even the same kindergarten, though memory strains that far back. We swirled with our contemporaries — a shoal of sprats. The sprats gradually formed into coteries, one of which contained us both. Our friendship had its fluctuations over the years. It was strongest when we had need of each other, when occupation or proximity drew us together, when neither of us had an obsessive conviction, or ambition, when we were least focused on the women in our lives. We never lost our friendship entirely, however, and the longer it lasted the more life and incident we had in common, and the more natural it seemed. Close friends become like family, with whom courtesy may be disregarded without affection being questioned.

Flattery was not one of Michael's skills, or intentions. He was cynical and pessimistic by nature, also loyal and possessed of a sort of dogged courage. He was a tight arse as well, never more pleased than when paying less than his fellows. You didn't put one over Michael, or if you did you didn't repeat it.

As adolescents we must have seemed an odd pairing to a casual observer. I found sport a bore, and Michael was senior champion in discus, shotput and javelin. But his success came not from dedication and a consuming interest, but natural physical advantage and a quick understanding of technique. He couldn't be bothered with the training demands of team sports. From an early age he was very broad and strong — and intelligent. In the courtroom he was an intimidating figure: had he been poorly dressed and in the dock, rather than suited and counsel, he might have been termed hulking.

In all the years before we went to university, I seldom went to his house. Michael preferred to come to mine, or we would meet in town, or at school. 'Mum doesn't keep well,' he'd say. I realise now that what she suffered from, and so what the family suffered from, was the antipathy between herself and her husband. Maybe it's not a terminal sickness, but it's a debilitating one. I remember best a rare overnight stay when I was a sixth former and my parents travelled to Sydney for a wedding.

Mrs Chute — pronounced shoot — worked as receptionist for an optician: Mr Chute was an engineer with the council. They'd known me for ever, but seemed rather surprised when I turned up for tea, and with a small duffel bag for the night, though they must have agreed to host me. When Mrs Chute talked, her husband looked at his plate with a reduced, disparaging smile, ready to change the subject as soon as she finished. When he spoke, Mrs Chute busied herself with small, distracting tasks, picking lint from her sleeve, touching the flowers in the centre vase, or reaching past her husband to gather plates. Sometimes a quick, exasperated laugh, when nothing but exasperation could account for it.

There was never a suggestion of any physical violence, or even vindictiveness, and I suppose they assumed an agreed partnership was presented. Mr and Mrs Chute were rarely together, and that's why I hadn't noticed their predicament earlier. I can't remember any other occasion when I was with Michael and both his parents. Perhaps I overstate the situation; maybe it wasn't so much dislike they shared, as indifference. Whatever had drawn them to marriage had passed long ago, and they were stranded together, with Michael and his small sister, Penny: they were like strangers seated together on a long haul flight and barely maintaining civility.

I offered to help with the dishes as my mother had instructed me, and, as Michael and I dried, his mother talked to us quite freely about the teachers at our school, some of whom she'd recently had discussions with at a parents' evening. Mr Chute was watching television, but when we went through later, and Mrs Chute remained in the kitchen, he showed an equally friendly side in advising us on political questions quite outside our interest. Neither of them made any reference to each other then, or in all the years I knew them.

I've realised since that their marriage wasn't unique, but at the time I had only my own parents for comparison. Their relationship was one of gracious compromise, quiet affection and mutual support. The example set for me was so much better than that for Michael, but I didn't profit by it.

Michael married early and divorced early. I was best man, but never knew Frances well. He and I were living in different cities then, both working hard at our professions and seeing little of each other. Frances was a lawyer too, and I remember her as a dark, slender woman always coming, or going, rather than sitting down to talk. I never asked him what went wrong, and all he volunteered was the comment that he had colleagues at work and needed more than that at home. I consider that the two of us were close in the way men are: Michael was honest in what he said, but his nature wasn't confessional at all. Guys don't like to download emotionally: you can become a sort of hostage to personal revelation.

When I shifted to Auckland we spent a good deal of time together again, as single guys: not much in the clubs, but leisurely meals at smaller restaurants, and companionship at the movies, or theatre. Some evenings we'd just sit in his lounge, or mine, with a bottle of wine and put the world to rights. He'd talk quite openly about his cases, as I would about the business world. We trusted each other's confidentiality. He was into politics, and I preferred classical music.

Michael had a house set in the native bush close to Titirangi, and I have a more modest place in Mount Eden. Neither of us lived as monks, and quite often we made up a foursome and went to a gallery opening, or festival session. Katherine Broughton was the woman with Michael on these occasions. She was a legal secretary at his work: as dark and slender as Emma, but more demonstrative and more relaxed.

Once four of us flew to Australia for the Melbourne Cup, although I cared nothing for racing. We had a couple of nights in Sydney too, and went to see *Death of a Salesman*. I became accustomed to Katherine's distinctive and attractive laugh: sudden and often at things only she found amusing. She wore her hair long, and I admired the dark sheen of it.

Another trip we did together was to Wanaka and Queenstown. Four of us flew to Dunedin and hired a car for a summer week.

We spent a lot of time talking as we travelled, as we visited wineries and restaurants, as we sat in motel units. Katherine knew interesting stuff about Japan, because her father had taught at an international school there. She said that we don't realise that there's an entrenched traditional class system in Japan that still has enormous influence, but it's not apparent to outsiders. She thought that in the end it would be the oriental races that controlled the world. I don't remember what the woman I was with talked about. Katherine had a distinctive perfume — faint, but lingering.

Michael liked a drink, especially beer, but seemed impervious to any effect of alcohol, not so much because of muscle mass, I think, as the power of his will. I've known few people with such implacable self-control. He hit me once, but it wasn't a lapse, just full intention. We were at a party in Mission Bay, not long after I came back from establishing an outlet for my company in Singapore. The hosts were a couple rather older than us who ran an employment agency and bred Siamese cats that skulked, with the occasional strangulated cries, in the shrubbery at the edge of the paved barbecue area.

You have no experience of yourself as the complete drunk: no personal recall of the point of extremis. That's one reason you tend to dismiss the extent of your offensiveness. I remember only brief frames: one was the effort to skewer a cat with the barbecue fork, one reducing a silly woman to tears with loud argument, one a confrontation with the indignant hostess, one being punched hard in the ribs by Michael. There was the pain of the blow, and the pain of having it administered by a friend. There was the moon on the water as he drove me home round the bays and refused to talk to me. There was the vague, sour guilt the next morning, and two more people whom I hoped not to meet again.

I rang the cat hosts and apologised. The woman's response was icy brevity. I also rang Michael. 'So much of what we do in life is involuntary,' I said. 'I blame those bloody Siamese cats. The noise of them would drive anyone to drink.'

'You're not funny, or clever,' he said. 'You're a sad fuck who hurts himself, and other people as well.'

'I've just hit a rough patch.'

'You need to take stock of things before it's too late,' Michael said. 'Time to stop playing silly buggers.'

He was right, but that didn't influence what life had in store for him. What's fair has little to do with what happens, and that's fortunate for most of us, but not Michael. Two weeks later he was the victim of a hit and run driver while jogging on a gravel road through the Waitakere reserve. He lay in a ditch for thirty-six hours before being discovered. The coroner concluded he would have been alive for some of that time. The driver responsible was eventually found, but that didn't seem important to me. Michael was gone, that was the thing. The best and oldest friend, the one most casually treated and most valued.

Michael's father was long dead, but I met his mother at the service in Tauranga, and went back briefly afterwards to that same house in which I'd stayed for a single night while in the sixth form. I hadn't seen Mrs Chute for many years, and Penny only a couple of times since school days, when she and her husband came north to visit her brother. 'I can't make any sense of it at all,' said Penny outside the crematorium. 'Just can't see why someone with such talent and strength would have that happen. And Mum shouldn't have had a religious service. You know Michael wasn't religious at all. It was hypocritical, but nothing I said would talk her out of it.'

At the house Mrs Chute took refuge in duties as a hostess, bearing plates of club sandwiches, and spotting mourners who had no tea or coffee to console them. But when you were close to her, a quivering rigidity could be seen in her face.

She put her hand on my forearm. 'I've put some photos on the other table,' she said. 'There's some of you together at varsity, and you're in the wedding ones of course. I've heard nothing from Frances. Not a line, not a phone call. I don't suppose you've kept in touch?'

Mrs Chute had placed the photographs in rough chronological order, so it was possible, in a circuit of the dining room table, to have a haphazard overview of Michael's life. Because he was a physically imposing guy, it was especially difficult to realise that now he filled no space in the world at all. There were the formal shots of the wedding, graduation, Michael being called to the bar, and candid pictures, including one of us both on the Honda 350 he had when we flatted in Patiti Crescent.

Katherine came to the house after the service, but her relationship with Michael was unknown to his mother. 'I'm just someone from the office as far as the family's concerned,' she told me. She was pleased to find me there, as she knew hardly anybody else. Katherine, too, was surprised that Frances hadn't appeared. 'I met her once briefly at work,' she said. 'It was after the divorce and over some division of assets stuff. I think Michael pretty much gave her everything she asked for.' I almost said that was out of character from my experience, but it wasn't the time for that sort of comment. Katherine didn't stay long, and after looking at the photographs, slipped away. Together with Mrs Chute and Penny,

I suppose she was the most affected by Michael's death, but I was probably the only one there who knew that. Perhaps her grief was augmented by not being able to declare or share it, by not appearing in any of the snapshots of Michael's life. As I waited to say goodbye to Mrs Chute, I saw through the window Katherine going down to her car alone. Dark clothes, dark hair and neatly slim. During our conversation we hadn't said anything significant of our loss.

'Did you like the the vicar's words about Michael?' Mrs Chute asked me as I was leaving.

'Very moving,' I said. After all a eulogy, the whole business, is more for the benefit of the living than the dead. Michael couldn't give a stuff.

'He'll live always in our hearts,' his mother said.

To be honest I think my feeling after Michael's death, initially at least, was weariness rather than anger, or sorrow. There was a pointlessness about so much that I'd assumed significant before. But that would pass, I told myself. It's a predictable emotional response and then equilibrium is restored.

Katherine rang me a fortnight after the cremation.

She wanted the chance to talk about Michael, she said, and we met during lunchtime in a small sushi bar not far from her work. She was there when I arrived, and I sat on a high stool beside her and ate sushi, although it's not my sort of food. Katherine had only a herbal tea. 'How are you managing?' I said.

'I'm feeling rotten.'

'A sudden death like that. It's such a shock, and there's no chance to say goodbye, is there? No preparedness at all.'

'You don't mind talking?' she said.

'Of course not.'

'I'm feeling rotten because he's gone, and because I'm pregnant,' Katherine said. Her voice was quiet, composed, but a declaration of pregnancy has an intrinsically melodramatic element somehow, and for just a moment I was aware of that, and just as quickly ashamed of the response. Maybe because a man never faces pregnancy, there's always an element of make-believe, or amused complacency — even deus ex machina.

'Did Michael know?' I said.

'Oh yes. We'd been talking about it a lot before he was killed. He wasn't keen on having it, although he said he'd support me in whatever decision I made. I don't doubt that at all. You know what he's like.'

'Were you going to get married?' I wasn't embarrassed to ask Katherine such a question — after all she'd come to me — but there was a sense that I was intruding into Michael's life when he didn't have one any more. He'd made the decision not to tell me of the most important thing happening to him, and now it was being revealed to me in a way over which he had no control. Michael and I had come to value privacy in our friendship.

'He didn't want to get married,' Katherine said. 'He had that experience with Frances, and I think his parents' marriage was pretty unhappy. Not that he talked about them a hell of a lot, but it was a sad family in many ways, I think. There wasn't any neglect, or abuse, or anything, but an absence of warmth I suppose.'

I looked at the counter trays of sushi, so many different compositions that seemed the same at a glance. I remembered the separateness of Michael's parents within their marriage, and the brisk personal ambition he and Frances showed when they were together. 'What are you going to do?' I asked.

'I need to talk to his mother. She should know that Michael's left a child shouldn't she. My hope is that she'll welcome it — a grandchild to make up just a bit for Michael. That's my main reason, but also I think I'm entitled to some support from

Michael's estate. He was going to buy an apartment for us and see to things when I couldn't work. You know he was quite well off by ordinary standards, and my job isn't highly paid. I stayed there at the office mainly because of him. Everybody there knew.'

Even in that situation, having lost the man she loved, and left pregnant and unmarried, Katherine could show sensitivity to the feelings of Michael's family. I admired her a lot for that. She could have gone in guns blazing to get what she could for herself and the baby, but she had concern for Mrs Chute, Penny and Michael's memory. She had never met his family until he was dead, and wanted my advice, my assistance as to the best way to make an approach. She didn't want to go there with demands, she said, but as someone who had loved Michael as much as they had, and with a living part of him to share. 'I don't think I can do it on my own,' she said, 'but you've known them for years.'

'Well, not really. I saw a bit of them when we were at school and varsity, but bugger all since.'

'At least they know who you are.'

'Katherine, I'm happy to do everything I can,' I said. 'You're in a hell of a position, and the family needs to be told for all sorts of reasons. It'll work out.'

What a situation for her, but I never doubted her sincerity. I'd seen them together, I knew the loyalty of Michael's nature, and in an age of DNA testing there was no swiftie to be pulled regarding paternity — not that I mentioned that to Katherine. Did we make a comfortable couple, sitting on our high stools in the sushi bar and talking confidentially? She looked as slim as ever to me. Who could guess that we talked of a road killing, personal and family grief, an unborn child, and money. Michael had come to the best time of his life, and not been allowed to prolong it. 'At first,' said Katherine, 'I thought of ending it for both of us as well, but I snapped out of that.'

I rang Mrs Chute and said I'd like to come down for a chat about Michael. I didn't mention that Katherine would be coming with me, because that would lead to questions I didn't want to answer on the phone. The Sunday we went was a cloudless day, with the blue sky like a great suction cup that threatened to draw us from the surface roads, shelter belts and green dairy farms. Katherine and I talked about the trip to the Melbourne Cup, and the Central Otago trip, and she asked me about Michael when he was younger. She was surprised when I said he had something of a reputation as a tightwad, and hated to be taken in over anything to do with money. She said he was always wanting to buy things for her, and often left money in her office desk. She was surprised too that he'd been so good at sport, and said he'd jogged and gone to the gym only for health reasons. Recently he'd become interested in local government through his work, she said, and I remembered his talk about what was needed to preserve the lifestyle he enjoyed in the Waitakeres.

Katherine wasn't feeling great, and we made two comfort stops before Tauranga. She was going as the pregnant girlfriend to visit the unsuspecting mother of her dead lover: enough to deal with surely without having morning sickness. The paleness of her face accentuated her dark hair, and she had small emerald studs in her ears. There was a symmetry about her as a woman that was especially attractive. Everything seemed to be in keeping. 'How do you think she'll take it?' she asked as we neared the Chutes' place.

'Whatever the outcome, you've got nothing to be ashamed of at all.'

Mrs Chute hadn't gone to any trouble for me. She was in her gardening clothes and wielding secateurs when we arrived. I think she assumed Katherine was my girlfriend, and didn't seem too put out by her appearance. The three of us sat on white plastic chairs on the verandah, the overhang of which reduced somewhat the blue, expansive sky. Mrs Chute said she was finding the section a trial, and was thinking of selling and moving to be closer to Penny in Palmerston North. She remembered that Katherine had worked for Michael's firm, and she said she'd had a very nice card from the partners and staff there.

It seemed to me that the longer Katherine and I left telling her the reason for our visit, the harder it would be, and I didn't want Katherine to have to do it. When Mrs Chute went into the house to get coffee for us, I followed her, and stood by the bench as she prepared the tray. 'I hope you both won't mind instant,' she said. 'I've got used to it now there's only me. I don't bake now either.'

'Katherine was Michael's partner,' I said. 'They were together for over two years before he died.' Mrs Chute was feeling the side of the jug to judge its temperature.

'Well that's all over now,' she said. 'Michael never mentioned anything to me, but it's very sad for her. Maybe she'd like to visit the crematorium gardens and see the plaque. I had it put on the natural stone terrace wall, quite close to his father.' I think that was the first time I ever heard her refer directly to her husband.

'She's pregnant with Michael's baby.'

'I don't know anything about that,' she said. 'Nothing's been said about any pregnancy, and Michael's gone, hasn't he.' I suppose I had expected Mrs Chute to show signs of shock, or dismay, or even joy perhaps, but she didn't look directly at me, kept fiddling with the tea things, the kettle, the cellophane on the chocolate sultana biscuits. Just the way she had found distraction when Michael's father was alive. There wasn't any easy way to drive things home to Mrs Chute. I told her there wasn't any doubt about the baby, and what a wonderful thing it could be for all of them. On the other hand there could be an appeal to the court for recognition of parentage and support from Michael's estate, with all the publicity for the family that entailed.

'Michael loved her very much.' I said. 'He often told me.' He hadn't, but it was true nevertheless.

'Why didn't they get married then?' asked Mrs Chute.

'Ask yourself what experience he had of marriage,' I said. 'What he saw of marriage here, and then with Frances. Why would he want any of that again?'

It was abrupt and cruel. I knew that even as I said it, but there wasn't time for sensitivity. Katherine was waiting on the verandah, alone and pregnant. I expected Michael's mother to fire up at what I'd said, but she turned to me, gave a sort of smile. 'But you've never been married have you?' she said. She was looking directly at me: for the first time I noticed how dark were the irises of her eyes in comparison with the hollow paleness of her complexion and her hair from which age had leached out the vital colours. 'Never mind, never mind,' she said after a pause, as if I'd made an apology. 'I'll go and talk to Katherine. What's her other name again?'

'Katherine Broughton,' I said.

She took the tray with the instant coffee and bought biscuits, walked from the kitchen down the passage. I didn't follow immediately. The rest was up to them. It was women's work: sons, lovers, pregnancy, babies, families, compromise. When I did go to the door I could see them farther down the verandah, talking steadily, or listening. Mrs Chute's stained gardening gloves were still on the round table, but she didn't fiddle with them. I stood far enough out from the door to enjoy the porcelain sky and a glimpse of the sea, but not close enough to overhear Katherine and Mrs Chute. I imagined Michael as a boy in that house. His physical strength, and the indifference to other people's opinion of him that never left him. I remembered him telling me that his mother didn't keep well, and now she was making vital decisions, and he was dead.

Everything that I heard about matters after that visit came from Katherine. I've never been in touch with Mrs Chute, or Penny, again. Katherine said that Penny was by far the more understanding of the two, and she was the main benefactor of Michael's will. Mrs Chute didn't put up any obstacles to a fair settlement, but she showed no great interest in the baby girl when she was born, while Penny was supportive and wanted her own children to grow up knowing their cousin. I know that was important for Katherine. I like to remember that on the way back to Auckland that day, Katherine told me she didn't think she could have gone down to see Mrs Chute without me.

I helped Katherine find a house to buy in Mount Eden, and Michael's firm did all the legal work for her on that and the settlement without charge. If there was any heavy lifting to be done with furniture she'd give me a call, and I visited her in hospital when baby Alice was born, and in the months afterwards I'd sometimes take them for a drive in the weekend. Katherine said she felt stir crazy from being inside too much.

I don't see much of them now. Katherine married when the little girl was two. A geographer from the university whom she met at the gym. A lucky man. He seems a nice enough guy, but I don't call round. It could be awkward: some male friend of the child's father hanging about in an undisclosed capacity. They have a baby boy of their own now. I get a Christmas card, and I've been twice to dinner parties. The geographer asked me for share market advice. Little Alice looks just like her mother, and she's fortunate in that. I tell myself the best of Michael is bound to be there too.

Maybe I'll go to Tauranga one day and see Michael's plaque in the crematorium, maybe see if Mrs Chute is still in the same house, and ask her why she's not interested in his daughter. No, I'll never do it. So much about people is difficult to understand. There were a swag of possible outcomes to the friendship Michael and I had, but this is the way it turned out, and nothing can be done about it now.

SOJOURN IN ARLES

Sometimes these things begin in casual ways that give no indication of the final significance. David wouldn't have been at the party in Monaco but for an Italian rail strike that prevented him travelling on. He stayed an extra day in Nice with the Ramages, who were close friends of a close friend of his at home. The Ramages had expected their hospitality to be at an end on the Monday, and so had accepted the party invitation. 'Don't worry about me a bit,' said David. 'I'm quite happy to stay here. It's kind enough of you to put up with me for an extra night. I could go to a hotel, or a B and B.' The Ramages hadn't been captivated by David, but they were polite people and dutiful hosts. They rang their Monaco acquaintances and were assured that an extra guest would be okay.

David didn't speak French, but most of the party goers were ex-pats, or possessed several languages. Monaco is that sort of society. He didn't get introduced to the hosts, as the Ramages were distracted at the rather splendid tiled entrance by an assortment of potted plants. Helen Ramage was a potted plant enthusiast capable of distinguishing fourteen varieties of fern. Cóte d'Azur parties are different from Kiwi parties in several ways, one being that those attending don't expect to know everybody. David had canapés with two South African men on a yachting voyage to Crete, goats' cheese and filo with a local couple who marketed antique curios, and spilled a little vin rouge on the dress of a tanned, elderly woman before he could find out much more concerning her. In retreat from that débâcle he skirted the pool and found a stone bench behind tubbed cypress trees from which the Grimaldi castle was visible against the darkened skyline. How warm the air was, how pleasant the fragrances.

It was there, as he was finishing his Beaujolais, that he was joined by a man whose insignificant body seemed just the necessary bearer of a large and pleasant face. 'Attlee Kellor,' the man said.

'David Wilson.'

'Do you mind?' Attlee said, and he sat down beside David. Even seated the height difference was apparent, although David wasn't quite six foot. 'My hearing's not so good now in a crowd, especially for French, or German, and I get tired because of needing to concentrate. I take a little time out every now and then. I'm not disturbing you?'

They told each other what they did, and how they came to be there, which is what you do at such gatherings. Attlee said he was a futures broker and financial adviser: the host was his client. David explained his local government work as an events manager, and his decision after his wife's death to have an overseas trip. 'I don't know the hosts at all,' he said. 'I'm an acquaintance of a friend.'

They got on well, perhaps partly because they had no shared

past and no likely future . . . The very randomness of their meeting encouraged them to openness and surmise. Attlee discussed the impact of the spread of the Euro currency, his prostate concerns, and his philosophy in giving financial advice. 'My clients are successful people,' he said, 'so I ask them what course they think is best, and then encourage them to take it.' David talked about the balance of delegation and supervision in team leadership, the use of most of his savings for medical expenses before the death of his wife, the nature of living alone.

'I've always wanted to see Italy,' David said. 'Tomorrow the trains are supposed to be on again, and I'm heading for Venice.'

'Ah, Venice.'

'Then Rome. A couple of weeks in all, and then I might come back and go on to Spain for a bit if the money holds.'

'I have to go to America quite soon. The south, Florida, on business, and then back to London where I spend most of my time.' People stood on the patio only metres away, strung lights showed glimpses of coloured dresses between the slender cypresses, and voices carried. The stone of the seat was still warm to sit on. 'I have a place in Arles,' said Attlee. 'It's where I'm staying at present. Why don't you spend some time there when you come back to France? Days, a few weeks: I feel better having someone in my places when I'm away.'

'A house sitter?' said David.

'I suppose so, yes.' Attlee took a few steps out to be in better light, fossicked in his wallet, and then came back to the seat. 'Here's my card. Email me, or ring, if you want to stay, and I'll tell you how to get the key.'

That was the sort of place it was, the sort of party it was. Where people of substance and judgement were accustomed to making decisions quickly and with confidence. Where no big fuss was made of such an offer. Attlee said he meant it. 'You'd like Arles,' he said. 'It's a good hub, a historic place and not too big,' then he went on to talk about other things. They parted when the hostess rang a bell, and everyone went in to eat: fifty or sixty people standing about the tables, drifting through the rooms, eating their main meal at almost eleven o'clock at night. David heard Attlee talking to others in French, and didn't see him again.

'Attlee Kellor?' said Paul Ramage the next morning, when David had already packed. 'Attlee Kellor is a very rich man. Travels the world and has places in New York and London.'

'And Arles,' said David.

'I believe so. He's a high flyer is Kellor. Someone told me that he was born Hungarian and changed his name for business purposes. Interesting guy.'

'I thought so,' said David, but he didn't mention anything about the invitation to stay in the place in Arles. He didn't want the Ramages to think he was the sort who bludged his way around Europe, and he didn't expect to take up the offer anyway. The disparity between his situation and Attlee Kellor's was too great to make acceptance easy, or risk rebuff if he made contact.

In the end he did take the risk however. He came back from Italy with many memories and very little money. He didn't feel he could impose on the Ramages again and they hadn't pressed him to return. If he had to pay accommodation, he couldn't stay much longer before flying home, and he doubted if he'd ever be back. Time in Arles could be the special cap to his travels. David took the train to Marseilles, and stayed in a backpackers' hostel close to the station. He felt like a grandfather there, solemn among the quick movement and flirtatious laughter, although he too was in good humour most of the time. Not all the backpackers were travelling in couples, or groups, but their youthful sociability made him doubly aware of being alone. He found an internet café and sent a message to Attlee asking if the offer to stay in Arles still held. He signed himself David from the Monaco party. 'Absolutely,' said the brief reply and gave him a name and address, wished him well.

The railway station at Arles was surprisingly small, and few people got off there, even though the tourist season was barely over. There seemed to be no bus service, and David took a taxi to rue Molière and the workplace of Madame Desmarais. He expected to meet a lawyer, or an estate agent, but Madame Desmarais was a florist, and busy behind sprays and bouquets wrapped in coloured cellophane, or pale gauze. Her English was surprisingly grammatical, but spoken with a strong accent that baffled David at first. Yes, she knew about him, yes, M Kellor had said he was to be allowed the key. Madame Desmarais must have been in her sixties, but her slender figure, pampered skin and arched cosmetic eyebrows allowed her to retain a certain feminine glamour once sexual radiance was gone. She took David's arm and manoeuvred him to a chair at the side of the counter. Soon she would herself take him to the house she said. When she finished with the one customer remaining.

'A gypsy,' she told David with a touch of disdain. They watched him leave the premises: a stocky man in an expensive suit with bold stripes, and gold on his fingers. David found the gypsy's obvious pleasure in the flowers he bore appealing, but said nothing. Madame Desmarais hung a small sign at the door, locked the shop and set off briskly. 'Rue de la Monnaie,' she said. It was more of a walk than David expected, and he was thankful that his case had wheels, which clattered over the concrete and cobbles, but people were used to that.

Rue de la Monnaie was in the old town, not far from the river, and David's guide stopped before a high wooden door in an even higher stone wall. Within was a small courtyard, the cobbles humped in places because of the roots of a large, dark-leafed tree in the centre. Beneath the tree was a small fountain with water flowing from the throat of a bronze bird. The three villas that formed the other sides of the courtyard had elaborate carvings on the lintel stones of their main doors. That's how it used to be hundreds of years ago — beauty and privilege hidden behind high, blank walls.

Attlee Kellor's home faced the gate, and Madame Desmarais took David into every room on both floors, advancing into each one with a sweeping gaze as if taking inventory. The kitchen was modern, and all else wonderfully preserved, with shrouds suspended above the beds, unusually high, patterned ceilings, and relief picture wallpaper of fêtes, market days and wars, all in grey on white. David ran his hand lightly over it. 'So old, so old,' said Madame Desmarais, 'but I must return to my flowers.'

They stood for moment on the steps. 'The Benoits are on your left, and Madame Lefevre on your right, but she's in Paris at this time of year,' she said. 'Do you want someone to come and cook and clean?'

'No, but thank you,' said David.

She gave him the large key for the gate and one barely less large for the door. 'I come to collect the mail each day,' she said. 'Leave a note there, or come to my shop if you need to ask me anything. There is an electricity switch beneath the kitchen bench.' She seemed to have no curiosity concerning the length of his stay, and went away without looking back. David made himself coffee and stood at a window of one of the smaller upstairs bedrooms. Despite having been empty, the house was warm and surprising sweet-smelling — something of wood and fabrics and flowers. The climate accounted for the warmth: David supposed Madame Desmarais responsible for the freshness. From the window he could glimpse the narrow rue de la Monnaie beyond the wall and the curved orange tiles of lower houses. He would sleep in that small bedroom, he decided, and not Attlee's room, which had silver-backed brushes and silver-rimmed photographs on the inlaid and gold-scrolled dressing table. He had difficulty in recognising his absent host in any of the photographs. The men in them were young, with the sheen and shimmer of young men so that they seemed to fret slightly within the frame, and anyway David had spent time with Attlee only during that one evening of the party, and already his appearance had dimmed. David remembered that he was short, that his face was lined and his longish hair was grey: just a generic description of an older man. And yet there was David standing in his house at Arles, touching his brushes, looking at photographs that must have chronicled some part of his life.

At dusk, David went cautiously into the old town and had a light meal at the first restaurant he came to, because he didn't want to get lost in the dark. The meal wasn't a good one and the wine was a poor rosé sold to tourists, but he didn't mind, for on other days he could find better places. He went back to the house, taking pleasure in using the two keys, and went to bed early. He was tired, but he lay for a while on the hard, clean bed, with the shutters still open, and looked at the wonderful figured wallpaper that had plentiful small signs of long wear, but none of abuse. How much better than the backpackers' in Marseilles he thought, or the shabby cell of the Rome hotel. Many generations of affluent and civilised people must have lived in the house, minor family oligarchies waxing and waning. How his wife would have loved it, and thinking of her he fell asleep.

Before noon the next day, David crossed the small courtyard and knocked on the door of the Benoits. M Benoit seemed taken aback slightly by the neighbourly visit of introduction. A tall, shy man who was polite, but showed no curiosity about David. Perhaps his diffidence arose from his limited English, though David felt he considered the visit slightly transgressed custom. He met M Benoit and his wife only occasionally afterwards, passing in the courtyard, and they would smile and give soft greetings in their own language. After lunch he found a bunch of dried lavender on his step, and thought Madame Desmarais must have collected the mail. Most mail days afterwards there were flowers of some sort left for him, although he saw her only on his occasional visits to the shop in rue Molière.

During the first week or so David developed a routine of exploring Arles in the mornings, eating out as inexpensively as possible, and then returning to the house to read, or record his experiences. He had begun his journal as a way of capturing material for his emails and letters to his daughter, Anna, but increasingly it became his way of working through his life — youth, career, marriage, ambitions, and the death that put all of them in question. Attlee had a small study on the first floor, looking out to the courtyard. The desk was heavy with computer, printer and related equipment, there were framed pen and ink drawings of Provence on the walls, but very few books on the shelves. It was for Attlee only an occasional home, of course, and there would be more evidence of his character in London and New York.

David visited the Roman amphitheatre and baths, the old bridge, he strolled the walkways alongside the Rhône and through the park on the Boulevard des Lices. He saw the gargoyles on the Musée Réattu and found cheap restaurants in the back streets close to quai de la Roquette. He became accustomed to the supine, begging dogs with the card beside them — pour vivre merci. In her fragrant shop, Madame Desmarais gave him directions to the

Vincent van Gogh display, and said that during the mad artist's stay the citizens of Arles had taken up a petition to throw him out of town. A nice irony that now the association is trumpeted in tourist publicity. And in the afternoons David would relax in the lovely old home behind the high wall, and make his notes, reflect, and enjoy whatever flowers Madame had left on her last visit to collect Attlee Kellor's mail. And he would try not to be sad.

Towards the end of the first week, he had the first telephone conversation with the woman in Barcelona. He had had the occasional call from people who spoke no English and so disconnected in confusion, or people who rang off just as quickly when told Attlee Kellor wasn't there. The woman from Barcelona was the only one who hung on determinedly. 'But you're an associate of Mr Kellor's, right?' she said, when David explained he was a guest in the house at Arles. David told her he had a cellphone number and an email address for Mr Kellor that he could give her. 'I'd be very obliged for your advice as an associate,' she said. 'I don't want to bother him if it's not necessary. It's just straightforward advice I'm hoping for.'

It would have been an embarrassment for David to explain his relationship to Attlee, the charitable reality of his presence in Arles. He allowed the Barcelona woman, Mrs Collingwood, to think he was a business associate by not denying it. What she wanted was advice concerning investment in a Russian energy company. She was a lawyer specialising in contracts and had been offered the opportunity by a Spanish colleague. Her husband used to do a good deal of business with Attlee. 'Mr Kellor gave me advice once before,' she said.

From the study window David could see the shadow cast on the courtyard cobbles by the central tree, and the juggling glint on the water jet from the bronze bird. He remembered from the party in Monaco, Attlee's dictum concerning financial advice — find the client's opinion, and then support it. What harm could he do by following that? And the woman's voice was pleasant, and yes, he wished to prolong the conversation just that once. So he encouraged her to talk of the company, the offer, the confidence she had in her Spanish friend, and then said he thought she should invest, as long as the amount wasn't essential to her livelihood. 'I much appreciate your views,' she said, 'Thank you.'

That was the end of it, he thought. He continued his quiet exploration of Arles, and took those excursions he could afford: to St Rémy, for example, and the walled town of Aigues-Mortes.

Increasingly he spent time writing of his life, and that became more a private letter to his dead wife than to Anna, though he continued to tell his daughter of his experiences. He sat in the wonderful house in rue de la Monnaie and wrote about his ordinary life in New Zealand, the happiness as well as the subsequent grief and despair. He found himself closer to his wife, better able to express the love and loss, when he was on the other side of the world. It was gradual release to write freely about their marriage, in which affection and loyalty had been strong, but more tacit than he would have liked, looking back. He wrote at length, haphazardly, about incidents and times especially warm in recollection. Their restoration of the home in Hataitai, the camping holiday in the Maniototo when Anna was twelve, the trip to Sydney when he was promoted to events manager at the council. Now that his wife was dead, their life together seemed caught in tableaux of poignant chiaroscuro.

Mrs Collingwood rang again from Barcelona during the fourth week of David's stay. She was very pleased with the outcome of the earlier investment, she said, and wondered if he could advise her concerning a substantial forward currency purchase she was considering. 'Give me your best assessment of the pros and cons,' said David, and knew that he would again apply Attlee's philosophy in his reply. As he listened to her pleasing, Oxbridge voice, he looked at the ink drawings of Provence on the study walls, some white flowers that were Madame Desmarais' latest gift, and then his attention was caught by the Benoits' thin cat with a lizard in the courtyard. Mrs Collingwood asked how he was enjoying the time in Arles, and David talked a little of his visit to Les Saintes Maries and of the great variety of colourful pottery in stalls along the seaside promenade there.

'I'm leaving quite soon,' he told her, and she thanked him again for his help and wished him a safe journey home. 'I've enjoyed talking to you,' he said. 'Good luck in your life and work.'

His conscience wouldn't let him stay longer in Attlee's house. Five weeks or so of such freedom and comfort were fortune enough, especially as he'd had no reply from the last email sent to London. Good things must come to an end. He would tell Madame Desmarais that she would soon have the keys back: maybe she would need to go through the house before he left to ensure all was in order, the silver brushes still on the inlaid dressing table in the master bedroom, the silk wall hangings in place, the lock intact on the wine cellar.

David arranged his flight from Paris to Auckland via Singapore for the next week, and on his way back from the travel agency called in to see Madame Desmarais. There had been drizzle when he set out from rue de la Monnaie, and heavy rain on the way to the florist shop. He shook his umbrella at the door, and noticed the wet toes of his light, leather shoes. He wasn't used to rain in Arles. There was no one in the shop, and David went to the entrance of the small annexe that held a wooden work table, and stored flowers, greenery and boxes. Madame Desmarais was putting newly delivered flowers into deep metal trays with mesh covers to support the stalks. 'So you have heard from his people in London,' she said, when David told her he'd made his plans to leave in three days.

'I haven't heard from Mr Kellor. I sent an email, but didn't get a reply.'

'M Kellor is in hospital in London,' said Madame Desmarais. 'His son rang yesterday to say he's very ill. He wasn't able to talk to me.' She no longer looked glamorous. She looked the elderly woman she was, standing in the annexe, stripping lower leaves, while the rain made a timpani of the low roof. Guilt was David's reaction: guilt that he was in possession of Attlee's house while the man was sick, guilt that he had no understanding of the emotional history between his benefactor and Madame Desmarais that would enable him to properly express commiseration.

'I'm so sorry to hear that,' he said. 'I'll send an email. Maybe a letter would be better.' Madame didn't reply, and just nodded when he excused himself and went back through the shop.

Despite his umbrella, his trousers were quite wet by the time he reached the small courtyard, where puddles accentuated the uneven paving stones, and the cascade from the mouth of the bronze bird was at one with the falling rain. His socks had begun to absorb the dampness of his shoes, and he changed his clothes before going into the small study and sending a message to Attlee, wishing him a complete recovery and thanking him for his kindness. 'I'll never forget my weeks here in your home and in Arles,' he said. 'The place is everything you described when we talked in Monaco, and it's been a time of both peace and rejuvenation.' Would Attlee Kellor ever read the email? Maybe his son would would open it and wonder who the hell this guy was living in the house at Arles.

David then made himself a salad in the modern kitchen, and ate it there, watching the rain clouds moving away to the north.

On the day before he left, David found a letter on the doorstep as well as a final bunch of dried lavender left by Madame Desmarais. The envelope had blue and orange hachures at its edges and was addressed to David, Associate of Mr Attlee Kellor. There was a note of thanks from Mrs Collingwood and cash of 1000 euro. Her thanks seemed rather more formal when not invested with the natural warmth of her voice, but he put the letter in his journal: one more thing explicable only in terms of his time in Arles.

David tied the dried lavender above the kitchen window the next morning, and had a last walk through the house to ensure he left it as he had found it. Nothing of himself remained behind, although he would take so much that was intangible away. He locked the door below the stone lintel with the carved ships, and the heavy wooden door in the wall that gave access to rue de la Monnaie, and wheeled his suitcase clacking along the narrow streets to the flower shop: past restaurants he'd eaten in, façades he'd admired, past the small business selling fans and kites, and past the begging dogs — pour vivre merci. The day was bright and warm, and David hoped for that weather in Paris, where he'd be in a few hours.

There were customers in the shop, and for a time David waited while Madame Desmarais prepared flowers for them. 'He's no better and no worse,' she said, when there was the chance to talk. 'He can't speak to anyone, and the doctors have warned the family.' She seemed to have regained something of her brittle glamour, but her hands had a quiver he'd not noticed before.

'I'm really sorry,' said David. He gave her the large keys, and a bottle of Château Haut-Bailly he wouldn't have been able to afford if not for the money from Barcelona. He thanked her for her help, during his stay, especially the flowers left at the door on mail days. 'I've had such a special time,' he said, 'and Mr Kellor's so trusting, isn't he.' It was a presumption to use his Christian name when she, who was so much closer to him, did not.

'Ah, M Kellor is a judge of character, and we've had our spies,' she said. 'Madame Benoit misses nothing, and there are reports around the town.' So he had been observed even as he observed others. Maybe in the mornings of his absences M Benoit, or Madame Desmarais, had come into the house with another key to ensure that all was well. Maybe they had appraised his one case of very ordinary possessions, maybe read something of his journal on the study table.

Two smartly dressed women came into the shop, and Madame hurried her words to ensure privacy. 'We know you needed your time here,' she said, and 'Au revoir', as she turned to her customers, and he took the handle of his case again. So, at the very end of their acquaintance she used her own language, and he replied with it.

'Au revoir. Merci beaucoup, Madame.'

He took a taxi to the small railway station, and waited there with other locals and tourists. The station was in the newer part of the town, and already he felt that he had left the Arles that mattered to him. He was glad to be going home to his own country, his daughter, friends with whom he had a known history, but he took with him a sense of the richness that comes sometimes from the spontaneous and passing friendship of strangers.

PAULIE TALLIS

'Alas, poor Yorick! I knew him, Horatio: a fellow of infinite jest; of most excellent fancy —' Paulie was declaiming in Chappy's Chippy in the main street of Te Tarehi. It was hosing down outside and nearly dark. Paulie had a captive audience of three who waited with numbered chits for their orders. Well, five as an assembly if you include the fryer man and the Samoan guy working there. The fryer was a wizened man like an overbathed jockey and had no teeth. He shook the wire baskets in the fat, and showed his gums as he laughed at Paulie. They all thought Paulie was pissed, no doubt, and when he was in full flow he gave that impression. Except that the words were always true. Oh, he'd had a few ales, but what fuelled him was the heady mix of desperation and art. He flagellated himself with the irony of quoting the bard in Chappy's Chippy while the patrons chortled in contemptuous incomprehension and the street lights jittered and gleamed on the wet asphalt. He, Paulie Tallis, with the best part of a BA, and poems published in two literary periodicals. He, Paulie, who for three months had been the face of Prefit Homes on Australian television.

Paulie's an actor, but you won't have heard of him. He does mainly stage work at a bottom feeders' level. He's thirty-seven and still spends most of his time at school, touring with a co-operative that offers Shakespearean excerpts and elementary stagecraft workshops fitted around the drama syllabus for NCEA. The troupe doesn't get any support or endorsement from the department, despite Paulie's solicitations. He also made approaches to established theatre groups, but they weren't keen. Some didn't even respond to his request to operate under their 'auspices', as Paulie expressed it in his letters. A lot of fuckwits who couldn't act their way out of a paper bag, had no more understanding of commitment and integrity than a pig's arse, Paulie said, but not in writing.

There's four of them in Paulie's Bard Words troupe. They travel in two rooted vans: one a Bongo and the other a something or other. The badges were nicked at a co-ed in Dunedin. Even with two vans there's barely room for the four of them because of all the props and stuff they carry. There's Elsinor Castle battlements that have to go lashed to the roof rack of the Bongo wagon. Paulie is the director and administrator. Conrad is the young, disorganised one who did a drama course at some provincial polytechnic, and is always paid last, if at all. Matt is the oldest guy, nearly fifty, and not with them all the time because he's also a beekeeper in a small way, which has priority. He's not paid at all, happy to be fed and housed on their short tours. He's fully amateur is Matt, and takes most of the humorous roles without needing to put a cushion under his tunic. He used to do a lot of local musicals, but started forgetting the words as well as missing the notes. Doing comic bit parts in Paulie's troupe means he can ham his way through when he dries. Extreme caricature and visual innuendo go down well with adolescents, and Matt has some practical skills as well that are useful to keep the vans going and the scenery together.

Justine is the only woman, but all woman, and that's what matters. Justine is twenty-nine. She once had a part in *Shortland Street*, and sometimes gets to act in television ads that pay damn well. She has a degree in dramatic practice and theory. While the others scurry about to set up in school halls, common rooms and auditoriums, Justine composes herself in some ad hoc dressing room, sometimes even the Bongo van. Despite being full-breasted she has an ethereal air upon the stage. Off stage she has a ferocious talent for self-advancement before which even Paulie sometimes wilts. She gets the greatest cut of proceeds, and as well an under the table extra of thirty dollars a performance, paid by Paulie without Conrad, or Matt, being aware of it.

Aha, you're thinking, Paulie as director and paymaster gets to shag her, but I have to disappoint you. It's a misapprehension common among males that a woman's libido is necessarily commensurate with her looks. Justine feels a hundred phantom hands upon her when lightly clothed as Ophelia on the stage, but the audience as a single entity is her preferred lover. It's not that she doesn't have sex, it's just not a pressing need. Useful at times of financial stringency, of course, and there's a married, high-profile Christchurch QC who's tapped from time to time. She's no mug is Justine.

It was Justine who hit the horn on the Bongo van to remind Paulie that they were waiting outside. They could see him dimly, posturing in Chappy's Chippy. 'For Christ's sake,' said Justine, 'I'm freezing here, aren't I.'

'Yeah,' said Conrad.

'Doesn't he ever stop, for Christ's sake,' she said.

'Nah,' said Conrad. He had very limp, fair hair, and used a lot of Fudge to try to give it some height and body. Paulie said people expected their Shakespearean young men to have a good head of alert hair. Actually, Conrad didn't mind sitting beside Justine in the van. Better if it had been daylight, then people could see them both more clearly and envy him sitting with such a babe. He usually managed to be in the same van as Justine, leaving Paulie and Matt together. The downside was that Justine always insisted on driving, so there was considerable peril attached.

'If I never do another gig in a school gym it'll be too bloody soon,' said Justine. 'They expected me to change behind a pile of canvas mats. Jesus. And the smell, eh.'

'Tell me about it,' said Conrad.

'No way, Jose, I told them. Those kids were feral I reckon. There could be cannibals in those big schools and nobody would have a clue even as the roll went down.'

'Yeah.'

'How the fuck does Paulie do it month after month?'

'He loves the lines, doesn't he. He just has to be saying the lines,' said Conrad.

'It is now high suppertime, and the night grows to waste.' Paulie had his paper parcels and stood in the entrance of Chappy's to give his exit lines. He held the door open with his back and gesticulated with wrapped shark and chips in one hand, and snarlers and spring rolls in the others. 'O for a muse of fire, that would ascend the brightest heaven of invention.'

'Dude, shut the bloody door,' the Samoan said.

'A kingdom for a stage, princes to act.'

'You deaf or something?'

'Think, when we talk of horses, that you see them printing their proud hoofs in the receiving earth.'

'Just as you say, mate,' said the fryer, 'but time to piss off now, okay?' He smiled at the three patrons still waiting to emphasise the extent of his tolerance.

'You hear what we're saying,' said the Samoan guy. 'You go rap somewhere else now, and close that door for us cause it's winter.'

You don't argue with Samoan guys that big — even armed with a prologue from Shakespeare, you just don't argue. Paulie let the door close behind him and headed for the van Matt was sitting in. In his light, slip-on shoes he skipped about to avoid the worst puddles. A small man waiting for his burger order came to the window of the takeaway and put his fists on the misted glass to form binoculars in an attempt to watch Paulie's progress. Maybe the wonder of poetry had quite undone him; maybe he expected Paulie to dematerialise once he was without an audience.

The next morning Paulie and Justine went to see the dean of humanities at the teachers' college. Paulie had sent a letter to request a meeting. He took the battlements from the top of the Bongo, and wore a blue velvet jacket and white shirt with ruffles. He knew, though, that nobody was going to be looking at him with Justine along. She demanded to be paid for such meetings even though they created no direct income. 'Justine Preminger, latterly on *Shortland Street*, is our company's leading lady,' said Paulie in introducing her.

'And understandably,' replied the dean with enthusiasm. He was quite young, and had his hair combed straight back in 1930s retro style. He wore a gold ring with a large, dark stone. Why did Paulie bother with a theatrical troupe and audiences at all? Ten minutes in the broom cupboard with Justine, and the dean would produce what cheque was required of him. But life is no longer ordered in such a way.

'Ophelia and Cordelia are wonderfully realised in her repertoire,' said Paulie.

'Special favourites of mine,' said the dean. 'Shakespeare never fails, never fails. I think I can persuade my colleagues that we need two sessions. One for the pressure-cookers, and one for the degree people. You sent me a list of scenes, I know, but is it possible you could do a bit from *Titus Andronicus*? We may well tackle it for our own end-of-year production.'

'We're open to suggestion,' said Paulie.

'I'd quite like to see the facilities,' said Justine. Her legs were crossed. The dean's work brought him into contact with many young women, but Justine was a match for any of them. 'We need a suitable changing room, and preferably a stage,' she said. She'd told Paulie after that visit to an Anglican primary school that she couldn't stand the bloody kids virtually under her feet when acting. 'Do you have a specialist drama teacher on the staff?' she asked as the dean took them to see the auditorium.

Performing at the teachers' college was the top end of Paulie's gigs. He called a rehearsal at Matt's packing shed in Lincoln to cover the scene from *Titus Andronicus* the dean was keen on. Even though the sun shone, and Matt offered each of them a two kilogram pottle of clover honey, it wasn't a success. Conrad was spaced out from a prolonged pot session, and Justine bitched about finding herself doing her lines among Matt's antiquated machinery: feeling the insect husks and rat droppings underfoot, and looking up to see, in the chinky light from the tiles, Matt's old pushbikes suspended from the rafters.

'These fucking conditions are just not on for professionals,' she told Paulie.

'It's this one time, for Christ's sake, Justine,' he said. Their normal selections were so habitual no rehearsals were needed, and performance was honed before their junior audiences. 'You think you're the only one here that deserves better? For Christ's sake. Just because you got good tits and legs you think you act better than everyone else?'

'I hear a moooooo cow,' said Conrad idly. He sat on an apple box in the sun and from the shed door looked over the paddocks.

'Friesians just there,' said Matt.

'There's a level below which I don't go, Paulie. Not as a professional I don't. There's a self-respect you have as a professional artist, you should know that.'

'As a fucking artist you do what you have to do,' said Paulie. 'You don't get up yourself about your occupation.' Did he need Justine to be instructing him on the self-respect of the professional actor? Shit. He was thirty-seven, wasn't he. He'd been in fringe theatre in Sydney and San Francisco. He'd drunk beer with Russell Crowe and David McPhail: separate occasions. Was he ecstatic to be in Matt's packing shed with cobwebbed bikes swaying on baling twine above his head? Was he unaware of ambition unfulfilled?

'I like a mooooo cow,' said Conrad as he toked a joint.

'Dairying's bloody everywhere now,' said Matt. 'It's white gold.' He and Conrad took no part in the flare-ups between Paulie and Justine. They knew their place. They'd had their own conversation about driving Matt's honey business to success when the troupe failed. All such groups were acknowledged to be transient.

'I can hack it. Don't tell me I haven't paid my fucking dues,' said Justine, 'but there's a limit and I reckon Bard Words has just about reached it over the last couple of months.'

'This is a good place,' said Conrad dreamily. 'I was born in country like this. I've roots in country like this. Maybe you're right about the two of us of making a go of beekeeping.'

'This gig at the college is the real thing. The audiences there will know acting when they see it. They're not just hormonal cretins sitting there to get out of maths, or chemistry. It's a bloody good earner too.' Paulie wondered why he bothered to hold them together, bothered to do all the extra work needed to keep Bard Words on the road. All he ever got was whining complaint, or incomprehension, or disrespect. Wasn't it Sartre who said that hell is other people?

'I reckon we could make a team, Con boy. The business needs two people to really make it hum,' said Matt. Moving whole batches of hives around the countryside was getting too much for him, and he'd been diagnosed with diabetes — but he said nothing of that.

'Can we go over this scene just fucking twice?' said Paulie. 'Is that too much to ask of actors, that you actually take the trouble to find out when you walk on and what the lines are? Jesus.'

'I'm just saying, aren't I,' said Justine.

'Well Con and I are sitting waiting,' said Matt.

'Bring it on, dude,' said Conrad, with assurance that came only when he was whacked.

The dean let them leave both vans in the two visitors' car parks quite close to the auditorium. The three guys carted in the scenery and props, while Justine composed herself in the piano practice cubicle, which doubled conveniently as a dressing room. She and the dean had a spirited discussion about Elizabethan clothing, during which Justine said she never wore a bra when doing Shakespearean roles. 'So right, so right,' said the dean, 'from a historical point of view.'

'And much better for voice projection.'

'Absolutely,' said the dean. He swivelled slightly on the piano stool, and drummed his fingers lightly on the scarred lid of the instrument.

'I'm not one for constriction,' said Justine.

'Freedom, possibility: it's how great art works. It's how life should work,' said the dean.

The morning's audience was made up of the second- and third-year degree course students, most of whom were women. Paulie had made a selection of Bard Words strongest pieces, plus the shortened, under-rehearsed scene from *Andronicus*. Apart from Matt's overacting the gig went off well. Justine once again achieved an ethereal presence while revealing physical charms; Paulie chimed and timed the big speeches with undeniable professionalism; even Conrad, inspired by an appreciative and adult assembly, displayed a nimbleness of movement and effervescent delivery that disguised essential pig ignorance.

For the afternoon session the audience consisted of the pressure-cookers, many of whom were mature people making a career change, and not much accustomed to poetry and theatre. A good many of them had trade experience, and some thought teaching an escape from the prison service, welfare caregiving, or fish splitting. Their concentration was fitful; several made a quiet withdrawal between scenes; one large guy wearing stock boots reacted to Matt's performance as Falstaff by calling loudly, 'Get rid of fat guts and bring back the babe.' There were, however, no farcical collapses of scenery, no outbursts of booing, no particularly noticeable confusions on the stage. Just an atmosphere of patent mediocrity, and the lack of that frisson which makes acting worthwhile. It's how it is sometimes: how it was a good deal of the time for the members of the Bard Words troupe. Even the dean's animated thanks at the end of the performance fell a little flat.

The three guys loaded the scenery back into the vans and, as they finished, Justine appeared with a cheque from the dean. Paulie was offended: as director and administrator it was his right to deal with finance. 'Oh, get over it,' said Justine. 'Here it is. We were just chatting and it made sense to bring it, didn't it. For Christ's sake.'

'There's protocol,' said Paulie, aware he sounded petty.

'Oh, for Christ's sake,' said Justine.

'I thought the morning gig went okay,' said Conrad.

'We really should spend something on the vans,' said Matt. 'Neither of them has a warrant, and the Bongo's due for registration.'

'Actually, I may have to pull out of the troupe,' said Justine. 'The dean's really into drama, and thinks there should be more emphasis within the programmes here. He wants me to apply for a full-time position combining drama and responsibility for counselling and harassment issues. He says my university qualifications and theatre experience are ideal.' She tried to keep her voice matter of fact, but she stood very upright and her face was almost luminous. An academic position, a substantial pay packet every fortnight, professional colleagues, and the freedom to do freelance acting in her own time. There'd be an office with her name on the door.

'Oh, right,' said Paulie, and Matt and Conrad turned away a little, as if dazzled and also belittled by the rise in Justine's fortunes. They were nothing without her. Even Paulie had to admit that to himself. Without the slight lasciviousness of her presence they were just loser poofters to the school kids. They were the dust beneath her wheels. You had to have a leading lady. 'Well, we'll have to chat about reorganisation,' said Paulie. 'Yeah, good for you. Best of luck and all that.' Paulie wasn't going to beg: an artist has more pride than that. But she'd sold out hadn't she, gone for the bourgeois security of teaching instead of following the star.

Paulie loaded the last cane basket that contained the props he called baubles — crowns, sceptres, rings with glittering glass gems the size of gannet eggs, a dagger to be seen before, some embroidered and bead-encrusted caps for married women, belts with embossed buckles, bold brass bracelets and necklaces of counterfeit gold. Normally each of them gave Paulie an indirect charge from the dramatic thrill of scenes in which they were required. But after Justine's news how tawdry they seemed, how dilapidated the two vans, how desolate the winter asphalt of the teachers' college and his own future. Paulie was determined not to give way to bitterness. 'You'll do a bloody good job, Justine,' he said. 'You go for it.'

After Justine's appointment and the dissolution of Bard Words, Paulie sold both vans, and was appalled by the small sum he received. 'I might as well have given the bastards away,' he told Conrad as he handed over $286.44 from the final divvy up. Most of the scenery and props he sold to the Ashburton Repertory Society. He burnt the battlements of Elsinore to keep warm during an especially cold snap in August, and kept just a few costumes and baubles for personal appearances.

Paulie, Conrad and Matt had a final drink together at the Carlton, and ended in the darkness of Hagley Park doing a bit of *Coriolanus* by the duck pond. Paulie felt indeed like 'one that converses more with the buttock of the night than with the forehead of the morning'. The full moon appeared fitfully like a great coin among the heaped clouds, and the wind shivered the oak trees. Conrad and Matt soon tired of their own performance: they had begun the emotional transfer from Shakespearean actors to entrepreneurial beekeepers. Already they felt embarrassment at Paulie's obsessive devotion to an art that demanded so much sacrifice.

'See you, Paulie,' said Matt in the car park.

'Yeah, good luck, mate,' said Conrad.

'If we do meet again, why, we shall smile,' quoted Paulie. He set off first on his 50cc step-through and was overtaken by the other two in Matt's small truck. Matt sounded the horn, Paulie shook one arm in the air, and they parted forever, unless coincidence should bring them together. It's how things are, Paulie thought in the sudden glare of passing moonlight. People are in the forefront of your life for reasons of expediency, and then ricochet away.

Paulie decided to move to Auckland and see if his talent was better received there. He was offered one last gig before leaving — at the inter-denominational hospice in Avonhead. Fourteen people on the way out, and Paulie was to serve up his best blank verse after they'd had their lunch and medication. An unusually thick mist was closing around the building, as if to smother them all. Some inmates were in beds wheeled to the back of the main lounge, most were well down in the soft chairs. Paulie was unfamiliar with embalming fluid, but there was a waft which somehow brought that commodity to mind.

'Professor Aardvark's here, you know,' said Matron Dutton. 'He used to give readings himself before it got too much. Talking's beyond him now.' Paulie remembered Aardvark from the university, as did whole generations of English students. A tall, glaring man with prodigious memory for quotation, and vowels that would do a chicken proud. And there he was, still and pale, like a carved candle in the front row. It was a form of leave-taking for them all, with Paulie's destination perhaps less absolute than that of the audience.

Have I told you that he's not bad-looking, Paulie, with goodly nose and chin, that he's had his share of admiration, though there's this intensity, almost obsessiveness, that keeps him apart. Maybe it was the presence of the professor, but Paulie felt a special resonance in his own reading. His one-man performance was predictably centred on the great soliloquies, and he made them a farewell in his own way — a farewell to the Bard Words Troupe, to Canterbury, to the old pricks of the hospice, to a certain naïve expectation in himself as well. But it served also as defiant fealty to his love of language and theatre. The fog came pressing at the windows, gradually swallowing up the greenery outside and the neat assembly of clay planters. Time and place met in focus.

It was hard to distinguish in Paulie Tallis' audience those who were rapt, those asleep, those who had expired. One small, bald woman sang quietly of love, but as Paulie gave his considerable best from the tragedies, he experienced a sense close to exultation. He was convinced, too, that Professor Aardvark's lips shaped some of the lines, and that he nodded when, after the performance, Paulie leant down to his ear to whisper — 'Yes, you old bugger, "Our revels now are ended. These our actors, as I foretold you, were all spirits, and are melted into air, into thin air."'

BLUNDERER

That night I had gone back to work quite late. The campus never completely dies, but it had by nine o'clock reached a point of feline somnolence: the trees black fur against the paler sky, a few office eyes glowing yellow, and from no distinct direction the subdued purr of air-conditioning exhalation. My walk on the bank path, passing in and out of the more intense shadow of the willows, was a familiar one. Mallard ducks were in small clusters on the grass bank, and clattered uneasily as I went by. The humanities and media studies block forms one of the darker quads, but campus topography is second nature to me. Perhaps a gardener's trolley, or a Papua New Guinean man trap, was set on the neat asphalt path, but we manage life by evaluating risk.

On the second floor a window was lit: that of Alan Scadding. No doubt he was pushing on with his book. A work on post-glacial landforms, specifically pluvial deposits. He'd be putting the hours to good use, while I drifted in one of life's more persistent eddies. He'd be rattling up the pluvial word tally, or sending ingratiating messages to those people who might be helpful in the future. A born distance networker, and assiduous in working a room.

The green, electronic eye of acceptance winked at me, when I wielded the swipe card. I didn't bother turning on a light at ground-floor level, or for the stairwell. A glass wall at the top of the stairs let in a fading glow, which glinted on the illustrated posters advertising forthcoming academic courses, as if they were theatrical productions coming to the city. Hist 307 The Johnny Reb Story. A Southern Perspective on the American Civil War: Media Stud 222 The Peter Jackson Phenomenon. A Personal Impact on World Cinema: Geog 312 Cometh Global Warming: Fem Stud. Fashion and Sexuality.

And in defiance of departmental regulation, the more urgent and personal concerns of students were there too, sometimes obscuring the course posters themselves. Two female flatmates wanted, or a buyer for a 1988 Honda Accord as and where is, people interested in aromatherapy, AGM of the Hispanic Society, a mountain bike and a second-hand copy of *The Youth Age*, by Voltain and Spruiker for sale. And all sprouting the little scissored tufts with the contact telephone number, or torn edges where these had been.

I did light the corridor that gives access to my office, so I could see to use my key. The door has a pinboard for student messages on which I display cartoons that prove I'm not a teacher of unbending solemnity. Students these days resent any distinction, any formality. The vice-chancellor was told to shut the fuck up just a few days ago, while escorting a group of Chinese dignities through the library. It occasioned laughter in the common room, but it was the rueful laughter of a lost cause.

Once inside the room, I turned on the small lamp beside the computer, and the dragonfly of coloured glass that formed its shade cast rainbow lozenges across my desk. From habit rather than expectation, I checked emails. Janis Sozlly, Cerrpll Tohorhoi, Jamaal Werner, Leon Rameddan and Judath Lltp were all eager to make contact: all purporting to be people, but most likely personally enhancing pharmaceuticals in disguise. There were valid messages, including the usual student pleas for assignment extensions and a reminder from Scadding to provide a semester course description, but only one that interested me.

The University of Illinois had advertised the position of visiting fellow in urban geography, and I'd requested further information. The reply was full and friendly, as is the American way. A Dr Walley said he was aware of my book on origins and symptoms of inner-city decay, and thought an application from me would receive serious consideration. The attachment contained a dozen pages or so dealing with the nature of the fellowship and the university, though the most space was given to the recreational possibilities of the campus and city of Chicago. I imagined myself strolling in Hartley Gardens in the fall, wearing a shin-length, dark coat, a blue scarf, a slight smile, and jesting with American colleagues concerning the idiosyncrasies of the faculty head.

The tableau failed to console, however, not just because I knew the encouraging response from Dr Walley was probably no more than the habitual benign tone of the professional administrator, but the more essential doubt concerning the advisability of an application at all. Did I have any compelling wish to spend an academic year in Al Capone's metropolis, or was it rather that there was a dangerous thinning of the ice in my own city, my own life? I turned off the computer, and sat with the small coloured lamp still on, which draped a veil of bright harlequin colours across my hands and the papers on the desk.

The reverie was at the expense of tasks already more than once postponed, including preparations for the arrival of visiting academic, Dr Robin Blundeleir, and a session as supervisor with PhD student Adrienne Flowerday, who was completing a thesis on the societal effects of public transport. I could recognise in myself the malaise observed in several colleagues over the years — the failure of conviction in the significance of one's life's work. And even in the personal experience of that, one part of my mind was detached and determined not to succumb to such triteness. Psychological inertia is a grim destroyer of the professional academic, but there's a wimpishness to it that repels. All over the world people make a stalwart fight for water, food, love, family and employment, the right to their beliefs, the right to live. And insulated from such reality the intellectual pines in secure complacency for some greater frisson of purpose.

In defiance of that I read almost one hundred pages of Adrienne's competent scholarship, and noted a pertinent article on age and gender differentiation within urban bus users of which she seemed unaware.

I knew Ms Flowerday well, or had at least been in her company often, and as I read her work, her image was plain on the chair beside me, as her real self would be the next day: dark, clean hair drawn back from her round face, shoulders slightly hunched in concentration, Adidas trainers well planted in the carpet, and some deep ambiguity in her hazel eyes that was never expressed.

After leaving the office, I walked the corridor length and then switched off the light. The course posters and haphazard student notices were still ghostly at the top of the stairs, and I was confident of my footing because of the dim light through the full-length window. I could see the asphalt walkways like dark creeks among the night lawns.

But the release button however at the ground-floor doors wouldn't activate. Now don't you bugger me about, I admonished the genie of Murphy, who controls all such things. But the system wouldn't let me go. It wasn't the first time I'd been imprisoned within the building, and I knew of a possible means of escape — the ground-floor reprographics room was often left unlocked, and from its window I could drop into the garden below. Alan Scadding, still perhaps working in his room, would no doubt have had a more elegant solution, but I wasn't going to importune him. 'Donal, Donal, Donal,' he'd say, with humorous resignation and falling cadence. 'Always the world is in revolt against you,' and the electronic system would be obsequious in function for him.

Reprographics was unlocked, and there was space between the two main photocopiers to reach the window. I banged the frame to force it open, and began to squeeze through. I've never been athletic, although I've the height for basketball, and in your forties suppleness wanes. For a moment I became stuck, half in, half out, with the narrow aluminium sill painful at my ribs and the latch caught in my jersey. A final heave and I was tumbled into the viburnums and hebes. I lay sprawled on the dirt and amid the dark leaves for a time. All was very quiet. There was moisture at my knee and a crushed snail came away in my hand there. The moon behind uniform cloud gave a faint beatific luminosity to the sky. There was absurdity in it, of course: A forty–nine-year-old senior lecturer lying in the night garden like an alley wino.

The posture was demeaning, and my back painful. I stood up, closed the window, moved to the path where I checked for injury by a variety of small movements. The light went on in the copying room, and at the same time a voice, Alan Scadding's, said, 'All sorts of stuff in here.' He stood at the door, leaning in slightly as if the floor of reprographics had just been washed and he didn't wish to mar the surface. 'Rather untidy, I'm afraid.' His companion was large, assured and wearing an expensive suit. He barely glanced within.

It had to be Dr Blundeleir, arrived and having an informal tour of the department. Perhaps it was his condescension, perhaps it was my sense of ignominy, though unobserved, perhaps just that Scadding was his companion, but I took an immediate dislike to Blundeleir. Blunderer I christened him as I walked into the dark, holding my left hand with fingers extended. Some intestinal snail slime remained, and I didn't wish to use my clean handkerchief to remove it. 'What do you bet he'll be a complete arsehole,' I said in a challenge to the ducks beneath the willows.

I met Dr Blunderer at a staff meeting the next day. Scadding, as acting HOD and director of programmes, extolled his virtues, and so did Blunderer in his reply to the welcome. It was a pity none of the mallards had taken on my challenge. There were thirteen colleagues present, and I counted those that I would save from drowning if there were any danger to myself. Four, only four, and two of those were women to whom I was sexually attracted. I began to think quite seriously of Chicago. There was a song wasn't there. Frank Sinatra, was it? I sought the tune in my head while Blunderer entertained us with a detailed account of his speciality — architectural design and ethnicity.

'I seem to remember something of yours on decay,' said Blunderer, when it was my turn to be personally introduced.

'You seem to remember correctly.'

'Demographic, of course, not dental.'

'Of course,' I said. Blunderer continued to wait, perhaps in expectation of a compliment for his wit, or my reference to some work of his own.

'Toynbee is not now fashionable, I know,' he said finally, 'but I find in all large cities common patterns of development that are markedly organic.'

Blunderer is formed like a macrocarpa tree stump, with no discernible neck and a wrestler's chest so hirsute that he seems to wear a wolverine waistcoat. His family in Pennsylvania is very wealthy, having been providers of army uniforms and accoutrements since the time of the War of Independence, and although he laughs readily and shows teeth as dazzling as a sabre, I thought him contemptuous of the small scale of our lives. He often mentioned the historical significance of some of his forebears; he and his wife fly business class to Sydney to see the Russian ballet; they're active at city art auctions.

Blunderer was initially a visiting fellow, but before the end of his stay he was offered a longer term appointment, and became my office neighbour. He finessed the art of boring conversation to a level that was life threatening. His entry into the common room caused me to experience an uneasy sense of oxygen deficit, and if long in his company I would feel a growing compulsion to cry out — not obscenity at Blunderer, not words at all, but a sort of wailing, atavistic appeal for release. The noise that one hears occasionally in the dead of night from agonised beasts in a zoo. Usually I was able to contain it; once, however, I was overcome in a staff meeting during a particularly long discourse from Blunderer on the comparative merits of mean and median marks in course moderation. I managed to simulate a cramp attack, but the outburst was a jolt for colleagues, several of whom had been asleep.

There was also a tête-à-tête, reluctant on my part, in the tutors' room where I had gone to consult past copies of periodicals stored there. Blunderer came in for the same purpose, and hemmed me between stacks of *Our Physical World* and *Statistical Oceanography*. For thirty-three minutes he expounded on the influence of Islamic mosaic motifs on western architecture as a result of immigration. Because of Blunderer's chest capacity he has a particularly sonorous voice, as if speaking from a cavern. I tried to concentrate on the pin-stripes of his superb suit and the broader, colourful slashes on his equally fine tie. Blunderer dresses as a tycoon. I had an increasing sense of claustrophobia, both physical and psychological, and manoeuvred past him, excusing myself with the recollection of an appointment. 'Not at all. I'm happy to share my work with you any time. Feel free to ask me again, Donal,' he said. 'I've felt at times some constraint between us,' he added. 'I hope that we get to know each other better.'

'We'll be hunky dory,' I said. I hadn't used the expression for twenty years. It was perhaps an unconscious reaction to the formality of his own language.

'Hunky dory?'

'Right as rain. Good as gold,' I said, setting off down the corridor. It occurred to me that alliteration plays a considerable part in the formation of our idioms.

Blunderer was exceedingly noisy within his room, exclaiming often and apparently ramming the furniture together. I thought at first he was fornicating with students, or suffered from epilepsy, but after some Sherlockian deduction decided it was no more than endemic clumsiness. Perhaps after the spacious ease of his Pennsylvanian family home he found it difficult to contain himself within the cell provided for him by the university.

Not long afterwards there was the slight contretemps with Ms Flowerday. She was crouched on the blue vinyl chair in my study as I tactfully showed my disappointment with the lack of intellectual rigour in her most recent thesis work, especially a tendency to unsubstantiated generalisations concerning the maintenance of psychological distance in Japanese commuter trains. 'I'm sick of it,' she said.

'Sick of it?'

'I've gone off it,' she said. 'It doesn't connect with anything essential to my life any more.'

This is the type of graduate student that sits before one these days. People who go off things instead of buckling down to the sacrifice and grim drudgery of scholarship. 'I read Dr Blundeleir's book on Cambodian settlement patterns as interpreted through changing religious architecture,' she said, 'and I've decided to do something similar for Myanmar.'

'A year's work on the societal effects of public transport, and now you want to jettison all that and switch to Myanmar. There is a procedure involved in changing a PhD topic, you realise.' I retained a smile, I'm sure, a soft voice and reassuring tilt of the head. 'Quite a serious decision at this stage, quite a business administratively.'

'I've seen Prof Scadding and Dr Blundeleir,' said Ms Flowerday doggedly. Her eyes never dropped from mine. 'They say that in the long run it's what best for me, something I can feel a real commitment to. They said to talk to you about it and then come back.'

'They mean well, I'm sure.' Almost certainly Ms Flowerday knew my opinion of Scadding and Blunderer, and their similar regard for me, but nothing was said of that. 'I agree that you must do what challenges you academically.'

Ms Flowerday had a blue plastic watch strap and small zips at the leg ends of her jeans. Her eyebrows were plucked into high, thin arches. She still believed that success and fulfilment in life came from following a dream. 'Let's look at the sequence to make the switch as advantageously as possible,' I said. Nothing was to be gained by showing chagrin, or revealing to her that Professor Scadding was an opinionated, self-serving careerist, and Blunderer more so, and corrupted by wealth. I imagined Ms Flowerday on her research trips to Myanmar: her perspiring moon face and fixed hazel gaze, her digital camera clasped for protection like a cross, and her heavy sneakers, each with a spray of excessive shoelace, taking a good grip of terra firma. 'I wish you well, Adrienne,' I said. 'I've enjoyed seeing your work develop over the year.'

'I'm expecting Dr Blundeleir will be my supervisor if I change direction,' she said.

Blunderer's wife is very beautiful, outgoing and intelligent: quite wasted on such a man it seemed to me then. She wears clothes of exquisite material and cut, and moves as gracefully in them as if clad in a sari. I met her only at occasional university functions, as Blunderer never invited me to their home, as he did other colleagues. All because he discovered I was responsible for the corruption of his name that even other staff used on occasion, and because I banged on the office wall a couple of times after the constant noise from his room distracted me from my work. I rather hoped Blunderer would be adolescent enough to bang back, but he forbore. He came to my door and with restrained civility asked me not to knock on the wall again. 'If there is an issue, Donal,' he said, 'have the maturity to come and discuss it with me.'

'It's just the bloody din,' I said.

'What din?'

'The noise from your office,' I said. 'Continual banging and so on. It becomes distracting.'

'What banging? These partitions are very thin. You know that. I don't dance; I don't sing; I don't have a radio on. Goodness knows what it is you're on about. I have a chair on wheels that allows me to move from the computer table to my desk, that's all. What is it with you.' Blunderer filled all of my doorway, and the whiteness of his teeth contrasted with the dark expanse of his eyes. He increased the volume and reasonable tone of his voice a little, conscious that it could be heard down the corridor. 'All I ask in institutional life,' he said, 'is professional respect and toleration among colleagues. Not too much to ask, even of you?' and after a supercilious glance at mismatched oddments in my cubicle, he padded, bear like, the few paces back to his own room.

A few days later I had an email from Dr Walley in Chicago, concerning my application for the fellowship there. He said he knew Robin Blundeleir was teaching with me now, and that a brief testimonial from him would enhance my application considerably. Although Blunderer had never taught at Chicago, Walley said previous colleagues there held him in high regard, both for his scholarship and personal judgement. What ironies our own life provides for us. The deciding factor in making the application had been my desire to avoid Blunderer's presence, and yet I needed his support to achieve that end. Pride prevented me making any such request. I confess to pinning a dead mouse to his door. I'd found it behind the assignment drop box in the department office. It was flattened on one side, and seemed to have dried out quite without decomposition.

It's interesting the way a new personality in an established group is sometimes assimilated with very little effect on the whole, and at other times becomes a catalyst for a substantial realignment. Blunderer was deferential to nobody, but shared Alan Scadding's enthusiasm for change. Refreshment was the word of the moment. The academic programme needed refreshment, as did teaching practices, student assessment procedures and allocation of staff responsibilities. Blunderer's considerable weight and overseas reputation was thrown behind the acting HOD and refreshment swept all before it, like a Coca-Cola ad. I was becoming seen as a reactionary, a man out of touch with the prevailing culture.

Everything changed, however, between Blunderer and me, after I saved his life. The ambulance people made that grand assertion. It was a Thursday evening, a little after nine, and as I locked my room I saw light shining through the glass panel above Blunderer's door. I'd heard nothing through the wall over the last half-hour or so, and Blunderer wasn't one for working late. The corridor lights were out and I saw from a rim of yellow that his door was slightly ajar. Normally I would have walked on, but mewling sounds came from within, and when I knocked on the door it opened enough for me to see Blunderer sitting on the floor of his office with his back supported by the computer desk, and the contents of his case scattered before him. He had two expressions on a single face: one piteous, the other beyond his control.

Blunderer had suffered a terrible stroke. Odd that it had occurred with far less noise than his everyday and irritating movements. Such a heavy man that I had difficulty even pulling him far enough from the table so that he could lie face up on the carpet. 'You'll be okay,' I said. How fatuous are our comments in such circumstances. There was an umbrella in a plastic pouch hanging behind the door. I put it under Blunderer's head, which made his breathing less forced. 'Just take it easy. You'll be fine,' I said as I punched the emergency numbers.

It didn't seem right to be so obviously looking down on Blunderer, so I sat on the carpet beside him, tried not to let my face register alarm at the disarray of his: one side given way as if the strings of puppetry had collapsed. Blunderer made no attempt to talk, no movement except that the fingers of his good hand moved on the carpet as if to test its quality. 'They'll be here in a jiffy,' I said. 'No need to worry.' Blunderer was dying perhaps, and I was telling him it was of no concern.

They weren't there in a jiffy, of course, and there was great need to worry, but eventually I heard the siren and went to the main entrance to let the medics in. I do think that I showed a flash of foresight by taking care that Blunderer's door didn't snib shut behind me.

I helped the two ambulance officers carry Blunderer on the stretcher down the stairs, and then through the quad to the vehicle. He was very heavy, seeming even more so because inert. His hands were carefully crossed on the blue rug, and on the left wrist was his quite beautiful gold watch that caught for a moment the flashing lights. A tortoiseshell cat came bounding out of the dark, leapt briefly into the ambulance as we loaded Blunderer, and then fled again. The most unusual happening of the night, but apart from a snort of surprise from one of the medics, we paid no heed to it.

As Blunderer and I disliked each other, I thought it hypocritical to travel in the ambulance with him, despite an invitation. Also it could be seen as deliberate emphasis on the service I'd done him. When the ambulance had gone I went back to Blunderer's office, gathered up his papers, a packet of green tissues, two whiteboard pens, a muesli bar and a pair of manicure scissors. I took the case home with me, admired the rich suppleness of the leather and the gleaming brass of the catches. There was an embossed green and gold emblem in one corner that I took to be the trademark of his family firm.

I visited Blunderer in hospital two days later, and already there were signs of improvement, although he couldn't speak. Some people make excellent recoveries, the doctor said: so much depends on where the damage is and how much the brain can reroute. Blunderer filled up the hospital bed, and already had impressive beginnings of a dark beard to match the thatch that showed at the base of his throat. His wife was there. She was embarrassingly effusive in her thanks: tears in her eyes, and the light touch of her fingers on my arm. 'You saved Robin's life,' she said. 'The doctors said time was so very important.' Poor Blunderer, so superior only a few days before, and then felled, considered under obligation to an enemy. 'Not at all,' I said. 'I'm thankful I happened to be there.'

'Yes, you saved his life,' she said tremulously.

'I've brought his case from his room,' I said. It's difficult to dislike a person who is so much in your debt. Difficult to refuse a heroic role offered by a woman as beautiful as Blunderer's wife.

Blunderer's recovery was quite rapid, and surprisingly complete. He was back at work within eight months. His general health and his fierce determination were given credit by the doctors, as well as the location of the failure within the brain. The interesting thing is that he recovered a better person, and I don't know the clinical explanation for that. At a stroke, you might say, his vanity and self-obsession were wiped away: replaced by consideration and humour.

Blunderer and I often now walk at lunchtime through the trees and over the lawns to the staff club, where we have a pasta salad, and Blunderer will buy a bottle of Central Otago pinot noir. He's lost a good deal of weight as well as much prejudice and pretentiousness. We talk about our work, our lives, our colleagues, the tedious and incremental creep of administrative trivia upon our time. Blunderer is not anchored by the need of a salary, and is considering resigning to travel, research and write full time.

Blunderer has told me that he has recommended me to succeed

the retiring editor of *Geography Today*, a prestigious academic journal published in New York. Scadding's promotion to associate professor closely followed his success in having an extended article published in its pages two years ago. Blunderer and I were in a window alcove of the staff club, having hot chocolate after a tedious departmental meeting. Outside were four cherry trees, and with each gust of wind the pink-tinged blossom whirled in panic before the buildings and the sky, like a shoal of coral fish before a predator.

'I wouldn't have a dog's show,' I told Blunderer. 'I haven't published enough. I haven't been invited to enough conferences, given sufficient papers. My area of specialisation isn't fashionable at the moment.'

'I think you're ideal,' said Blunderer. 'I'm on the board there. Between you and me, I provide a substantial cash donation each year, which allows them to continue the full-colour format that's so important to them.'

'It would be blatant cronyism,' I told him. I imagined the stimulating intellectual challenge arising from editorial control of such a highly respected, well-funded publication.

'You could do it from here — right here.'

'Wouldn't it be morally dubious?'

'Not at all,' said Blunderer as the wind ruffled the cherry trees and petals whirled into the sky. 'It's patronage, not corruption. Much of the world's best art and scholarship has been achieved because individuals with power and resources made personal choices when giving support.' Odd how the new Blunderer, the post-stroke Blunderer, is far more succinct and persuasive in argument. 'Leave it to me,' said Blunderer.

I have a standing invitation to attend Blunderer's notable Sunday brunches: his wife rings most Saturdays to encourage my attendance. It's not the same without me, she says.

I'm there today. On Blunderer's patio, fringed with lavenders in giant, free-standing pots with a fiery glaze, I mingle with bankers, local politicians, an antique dealer minus a thumb on her left hand, and American expatriates. There is wine, a smiling Asian girl circulates with canapés, and the bright sun creates flashes like flying fish from the ripples on the swimming pool.

Blunderer's wonderfully attractive wife has just introduced me to a futures dealer as the man who saved her husband's life, and now draws me aside to talk privately. She says that her sister, recently widowed, is coming out from her estate in South Carolina to stay with them. 'Camille is the beauty of the family,' she says warmly, 'and so looking forward to meeting you. We've told her everything, of course.' There is not a cloud in the sky above Blunderer's patio. His guests are intelligent and candid, his wife a treasure for the eye and mind, his sister-in-law mine for the taking, his generosity sincere, and even his academic discussion has a new bloom since his recovery. From a distance I hear him praising me to the futures dealer, saying how much I have changed, apparently not recognising the transformation in himself. Dear Blunderer.

MID-CANVAS FIGURES

It was late summer when I went to Mrs Cullum's in response to her advertisement, and the sun was still able to reflect wanly on the windows of the small villa. I didn't realise then that in winter it would disappear almost entirely, and the valley become an enclave of permafrost within the city. No husband was in residence, or ever mentioned by my landlady. Mrs Cullum was sole head of house and firm overseer of me and Mr Ancaster. In Britain we would have been called lodgers; here we were boarders.

Mrs Cullum was a woman who drew attention to herself by an excess of manufactured fragrance and bold mismatched clothes. When she passed, even outside amid the Wellington wind, there was an additional gust of perfume, and the house reeked like a leopard's den. She retained something of a figure, but I don't think she wore a bra, and was thus slung low, almost to the waist. Her legs were her best feature: long and still well contoured, although marbled with bluish veins, and she liked to sit with her legs crossed and the free foot oscillating. She was fifty, Mr Ancaster told me, which I thought then very old.

My guess was that Mr Ancaster was a little younger: certainly he was a little shorter. But he too took a pride in his appearance, although he was a boarder with only a bedroom for privacy, no evidence of family, and a small, ruptured car that refused to start in winter. The last was no great hindrance to him, for he was employed at the botanical gardens, within walking distance. I never saw him in work clothes, and his small hands were scrupulously clean: just a faint yellowing on the smoking fingers of his right hand. Mrs Cullum once told me he worked mainly in the hothouses. He wore gaberdine trousers with pronounced cuffs and a knife-edge crease, a green Harris tweed sports coat, and ox-blood brogues that shone like chestnuts after their evening buff on newspaper spread on the tiles before the unused fireplace.

Dressed in such retro fashion he could have stepped from the pages of a 1950s menswear catalogue. To be fair, I think he had two pairs of gaberdines, because after prolonged observation I detected a slight distinction in their light colouring. I'm sure he had no other good jacket, or shoes. When it rained, he wore to work a clear plastic, calf-length coat that made him appear like a man in a bottle.

Mr Ancaster had a thin, Hitlerish moustache, and often brought home most splendid blooms, which Mrs Cullum would display in a square vase covered with miniature, multi-coloured ceramic tiles. She would make reference to them at mealtimes, saying such things as, 'I never seen such colour in local flowers, Mr Ancaster,' or, 'What heavy fragrance the hothouse brings out, doesn't it,' although her own perfumes always overcame it.

Mr Ancaster would give a small cough as a response to the compliments. This cough was his replacement for the phatic communication of others. It was a reduced, double cough generated in the upper throat, and nothing to do with being a smoker. He coughed as acknowledgement when addressed, as a response signalling concurrence in conversation, and as a prelude to speech. Yes, and his hair is another thing I remember well. He had a head of ash grey hair, short and upright, so that when close you could see the pale scalp beneath.

I realise now that Mrs Cullum's meals were peculiar indeed, but what is customary soon becomes accepted, and the three of us might sit down without comment in the Aro Valley to a dinner of beetroot sandwiches and chips, the bread beneath the heaped potatoes bright with the suffusion of the beetroot's blood. Maybe boiled sausages in chicken and onion packet soup, Yorkshire pudding with hundreds and thousands perhaps, or chickpeas and pears. I had not one day of illness in the two years I spent there, though I did have a scare concerning a communicable disease and a fat girl doing economics.

Mrs Cullum told me on different occasions that she had been a teacher of modern dance, a franchise holder for a portfolio of toiletries sold door to door, the charge hand at Lefroy's Baby Woollens, and an usher at the Regent Theatre in Cairney Street.

It's easy now to be selective in retrospect so as to make her appear almost a Dickensian figure, and myself an amused observer, but she was the confident presence in her own home, and Mr Ancaster and I obedient minions.

Gin was the spirit of choice in the Aro Valley. When I returned from lectures to the late afternoon darkness of Mrs Cullum's kitchen, there was often a bottle of Gordon's Special London Dry Gin on the table between her and Mr Ancaster. It occurs to me that

I've never lived with any group of people who weren't drinkers. Mr Ancaster took his gin neat, and our landlady favoured a modest addition of tonic water. My arrival was usually the signal for the tête-à-tête to break up. 'Such a day — these few minutes are all I've had. Absolutely flat out,' Mrs Cullum might say, or, 'No rest for the wicked, I've got things to do,' and she would take the bottle and bustle away. Mr Ancaster would cough, but stay at the table because the kitchen was the warmest room in the house. He would toy with a dark, bakelite ashtray, and smoke self-rolled cigarettes with intense concentration, turning them often in his fingers for inspection, as if their appearance there was a perennial surprise to him.

There were rare times when I was invited to have a gin, and although it's not a favourite of mine, I never refused, and the three of us would sit on the wooden chairs that had faded, flat cushions attached to their backs with tapes. These were the times I think when Mrs Cullum and Mr Ancaster had been drinking at the table long enough to feel expansive. Mrs Cullum would tell us of the significant events in the world — the neighbour's cat spraying on her washing, her certainty that someone glimpsed on the television was a former dancing colleague, the tragedy that a barely opened jar of strawberry jam had grown a mould thick as frog porridge. Mrs Cullum's perfumes were powerful enough to cover the faint fumes of gin, but the taint of various liquors clung often enough to my fellow boarder, and through the thin wall that separated our bedrooms I heard often the clink of bottle to glass, and Mr Ancaster's preparatory cough.

I saw her only twice after I left, years later when I was back from Europe and had a non-tenured position at the university. On the first occasion she was looking down at me through a bus window as I waited outside at a city stop. I had forgotten that her face was rather like that of a pike, her lips far forward and very bright with lipstick. I waved to her, and she glanced further back in the bus to see whose attention I wished to attract.

The second time was in a florist's shop where I was buying roses for Vicky to celebrate our daughter's first birthday. Mrs Cullum was a customer also, but didn't recognise me. I introduced myself, and she seemed pleased to remember my time as her boarder. 'Of course, you were an agreeable boy,' she said, 'despite the untidiness, but my God, one of the biggest eaters I ever had.' I would have eaten more had it been available. She was wearing high-heeled shoes to flatter her legs, had a yellow scarf over her shoulders, and fly-away hair dyed fire engine red. Mutton dressed up as lamb, my mother would have said. Some deep lines on her face gave her a set expression of mild affront, and her heavy scent overwhelmed all others in the florist's. I should have realised that, since she was buying flowers, Mr Ancaster was no longer in her house, but he was the only topic I could think of with which to continue the conversation.

'Absolutely no idea. None whatsoever,' she answered my query. 'I believe there was some incident with a member of the public in one of the hothouses. I gave him his marching orders.' Her pronounced lips tightened in indignation at the thought of Mr Ancaster's disgrace. 'I've boarders of an excellent calibre now,' she said. 'Of course property values in the valley have soared, absolutely soared.' And she began to tell me of the prices obtained by various neighbours, and of the lives of those neighbours, although I had no recollection of them, or their increasingly valuable homes. Only after I left the shop did I realise that not once during the conversation had Mrs Cullum asked any question at all about me. At least in the small space I had in her memory, I would remain an agreeable boy, rather than a drunk.

I never saw Mrs Cullum again, but drink united me with Mr Ancaster, in a sense. Drink is a convivial thing, according to conventional wisdom. Let's have a drink together and unwind, people say. But only the first few drinks are interested in community, and then the possessive demon takes control. In the end booze isolates you from people, even those you love, those to whom you have a duty, those who love you. It's a narrowing focus until there's just alcohol and you — then finally booze is you in some hapless symbiosis. The smell of it even, becomes intolerably provocative, as the scent of a woman to her besotted lover. The physicality of it, even: how the liquid weight of it surges from the bottle, the fluidity of it against the tongue and mouth, its mobile resistance to compression. The varied sounds and colours of it, even. The absolute necessity of it that no logic, or advice, can stand against.

So it was the aftermath of addiction in which I met Mr Ancaster again. In the Mather rehab centre, which was a long way from both the Aro Valley and the university. It was the practice at the centre for inmates to help in some way with the running of the place; voluntarily, of course, though not to do so marked you out as someone not in accord with the ethos of situ, as Dr Bigg liked to express it. The ethos of the place was never formally set out, but obviously included a collegial and cheerful willingness to reduce the overheads.

I was mailman during part of my stay at the Mather. Letters and parcels were left at reception, and some vetting was done by Trevor Staples the counsellor. A few people were not permitted to have parcels given to them, and had to open them in Trevor's presence. I would take the mail and go through the rooms and distribute it upon the beds. The bedspreads were of cotton, and all ivory, or pale green, except Greta Wallop's patchwork cover, which she brought from home because it had been made by her handicapped son.

Some beds received mail regularly, and some never. Some received a variety of envelopes with the address handwritten, and some just the occasional stale, official window envelope. Mail distribution was a manifest sign of life outside the place — of the steadfastness of support, or indifference.

After some weeks there was a reallocation of jobs. I lost the position of mailman, and agreed to help in the laundry. There were murmurings about bribery and corruption in connection with the changes, but there always are in such places. I didn't mind the laundry. It was warm in winter, machines did most of the labour, and my stint was just three hours twice a week. It was there, in the vaporous atmosphere and revolving noises of the laundry rooms, that one of those things you usually hope to avoid in rehab happened — I met someone who knew me. I was taking a second load of sheets to the drying room when I noticed a slim man sitting on an upturned blue, plastic bucket just outside the door, and smoking, with great concentration on the act. His grey hair was as stiff as a scrubbing brush, and he wore gaberdine trousers.

'Mr Ancaster?' I said. Sooner or later we were bound to meet. 'Gareth Siddup,' I said. 'I boarded with you at Mrs Cullum's for a couple of years when I was at varsity.' Mr Ancaster gave his signature cough.

'Yes, yes, that's right,' he replied reflectively, as if confirmation, even authentication, was expected of him. He'd got thinner, as alcoholics often do, and his skin had darkened with the nicotine and the drink. He had accordion creases below his eyes, and the apathetic passivity that those unfamiliar with the disease mistake for serenity. 'I'm supposed to be knocking off,' he said. 'They're down on it here, aren't they.' He meant the cigarettes. It went without saying that drink was out.

Mr Ancaster hadn't long been admitted, and had aged a great

deal. Originally all we'd had in common was Aro Valley and Mrs Cullum, but at Mather we had the additional connection of being alcoholics. We began to talk sometimes, especially on those visiting afternoons when I knew Vivienne wouldn't be coming; Mr Ancaster never had any callers. We complained of our fellow patients and the staff who tended us, but also we talked of our boarding days. Neither of us wished to say much about the subsequent and sometimes despairing lives that had followed. There was a north-facing window at the end of the second-floor corridor in Kotuku Block, and a form there on which we'd sit together when there was winter sun. Mr Ancaster would have a crafty fag, and drop the butts into the green agapanthus below.

'We were at it, of course, Sheila Cullum and me,' he told me as the sun came and went in a cloudy sky. There was a quiet pride in his voice, as if he needed that opportunity to inform someone that although he was an ageing and nondescript alcoholic who had shamed himself in a municipal hothouse, yet he'd once been his landlady's lover: he'd been the object of affection. I was surprised, because he'd always seemed so much an auxiliary in the house, and I'd never witnessed any affection from Mrs Cullum towards him, apart from her admiration of the flowers he provided from his workplace. 'It wasn't open slather,' Mr Ancaster admitted. 'Sheila was very careful about it all. She knew your lecture times to a tee, and we never went to each other's rooms in the night. But if my luck was in then before lunch sometimes. She didn't like to do it on a full stomach. Of course I wasn't on the sauce the same then.'

He'd taken care of his appearance then too, whereas in the Mather Centre his trousers were pouched at the knees, grimy at the pockets, and instead of polished brogues he had schoolboy shoes with thick, rubber soles. A scurf of dried skin particles would gather on the folds of his dark socks.

During another talk he told me that he'd paid the rates for Mrs Cullum, always supplied the gin, and helped her out with legal fees when her neighbour took her to court over spraying the boundary hedge with weedkiller. 'I could've done with the money for the car too,' he said. If he was telling the truth then I'd quite misread the household when I lived there, but that's so often the case. You think you know how the circumstances were in a certain time and place, and then someone recounts experience from a different angle and all the pieces change.

'It was the prostrate that ruined it,' Mr Ancaster finally confided to me. We were both sitting on bucket bottoms outside the laundry door, and lifting our faces to a welcome sun. 'I couldn't piss so they gave me the operation, and after the operation I couldn't get it up.' I expected him to tell me that after his prostate had been removed, Mrs Cullum had dumped him and sought a capable sexual partner elsewhere. We judge women to be as self-serving as ourselves, and she had seemed to me a decidedly unplatonic woman. She had shown understanding, however, and it was Mr Ancaster's own injured pride that had caused difficulties. 'I didn't like her touching me when nothing could come of it,' was how he put it.

I enjoyed the winter sun on my face and felt the bucket beneath me vibrate because of the laundry machines not far away. I postulated that Mr Ancaster had indirectly become a soak because of the swelling of his prostate. There are innumerable things that can trigger alcoholism. I could tell you about it. 'I still liked to talk to other women,' he said. I didn't let on I knew there had been some incident in the hothouse garden that had led to his disgrace. It was the final irony that his need to give an impression of manliness had led to his being accused of something beyond his capability.

'Somehow the booze got the better of me once I left Sheila's,' he said. This is how the alcoholic feels: the victim of a masterful force rather than personal decision. 'Remember the strange tucker she used to drum up for us. Jesus. One awful bloody night we had a carrot and blackcurrant pie. But she was a fine-looking woman, mind you. You have to say that.'

'She had good legs for her age.'

'She told me she used to be a dancer. She said too that she used to have her own business once, selling women's stuff.'

'Cosmetics.' I could imagine Mrs Cullum scouting business by inviting a small coterie of Aro Valley women to her house, and painting their mouths and faces boldly to advertise her wares, her own fish forward lips vividly glossed. 'Did she ever say anything about a husband?' I asked.

'Never a bloody word.'

'And nothing about children, I suppose?'

'Never a word,' said Mr Ancaster, 'but just once some sister of hers came, and they had a stand-up row at the door about family money. The sister kept on saying, "But who tended them at the end, tell me that then." I think maybe she called herself Mrs because it wasn't good to be single and have men boarders.'

Mr Ancaster discharged himself after just the month of July. He said nothing to me of his intention and made no farewell. Dr Bigg told me it was against his advice. I knew there'd been secret tippling. Nothing at the Mather Centre, certainly not my company, was able to withstand the siren call of mother's ruin.

I made his defection one more reason for sticking to my own resolve. He was the doppelgänger of my future self if I couldn't beat the drink. Some difficult nights in rehab I dreamt of him. He'd be holed up in some wretched room with an unpainted chipboard wardrobe and a metal fire escape, I told myself. From the window he would watch a pin-striped starling on the rusted rotary clothesline, and chickweed frothing over old tyres heaped behind the garage. The only greetings he would receive would be from checkout girls and Sally Army volunteers. He'd put pencil rings around menial job vacancies in a folded newspaper, and his hand about the neck of the bottle would shake. At night he would lie awake, listen to the mice in the ceiling, cough just to hear something human and familiar.

The burnish of his ox-blood brogues, the perfect crease of his duplicate trousers, profusions of hothouse flowers, the pre-lunch fragrant consummations in the Aro Valley boarding house — all memories of some high peak of his life from which he was inexorably descending, hand in hand with gin.

BRIAN AND BAZ

'He's late again,' said Brian.

'You know Baz,' said Jenny.

'He needs a bloody bomb under him.'

'He's always the same,' said Jenny. 'You know our Baz.'

Brian had the ex-army Bedford parked outside, with the long, double-axle trailer behind that held the sawbench. He sat at the kitchen table with a view of the street. In the lunchbox in front of him were some extra sandwiches and carrot cake for Baz. It was the same every working day, as if Jenny felt sorry for him; as if she wanted to show Baz, as a single guy, a glimpse of the substantial advantages of being married. It was a typical generosity, and Brian admired his wife for that. What got to him was Baz's disordered life; so laid back he was almost horizontal. After a year working together it was never a surprise, and never any easier for Brian to accommodate.

He watched Baz arrive in the even older Commer truck with high netting sides to hold in loads of firewood. Baz swung out of the cab and came up the drive in long strides, the steel-tipped boots cast like weights to stretch his step. His legs were lean and brown, he wore a blue tartan Swannie, his hair was black and unruly at the crown. His teeth were good except for a gap in the top left side. Jenny said he had a certain unreformed charm to him.

'Morning,' he said to them both.

'Hi, Baz,' said Jenny. 'Good weekend?'

'Living quietly,' said Baz with a grin.

'Hi,' said Brian. He took the lunchbox and parka. 'See you then,' he said to his wife.

'See you, Jenny,' said Baz.

As Brian and Baz walked out to the trucks, Brian asked if he'd filled up on the way over, and Baz said that he'd been running a bit late and would have to stop at the petrol station at the junction. 'Jesus, Baz. It's a good half-hour drive to McFedron's, you know. We need to get stuck into that windbreak today.'

'Yeah.'

'I'll start getting set up out there. Might pay to fill up the chainsaw can at the junction.'

'Okay. See you then,' said Baz. As he pulled away he saw Brian checking the sawbench trailer, tugging at each of the adjuster straps. Nothing left to chance with our Brian.

He was methodically setting up when Baz arrived at McFedron's. He wore his yellow, hard hat and the collar of the grey work shirt was turned up to protect his neck from the sun. Brian never tanned: just reddened and peeled over each summer. His arms were thick and his shoulders and chest filled out the shirt seams, though he wasn't a tall man.

As Baz began to help, he noticed that the big blade and the

chainsaws had been sharpened. 'I went up to the yard for a while on Sunday and did it then,' said Brian. He wouldn't have mentioned it had he not been asked. He looked back down the track towards the farm buildings. A ute was jogging its way towards them. 'Aye, aye,' he said, and cocked his thumb towards it.

Colin McFedron walked over and greeted them. Most cockies are interested in purpose-built machinery, consider themselves capable of putting together something that will do a job okay. Colin walked around the iron bench, noted the big front rollers that were detachable, the small tractor engine adapted for belt drive, the heavy safety guard of the blade. 'Well, she's pretty compact all right,' he said. He grabbed the metal guard to see how it was triggered. 'Everybody's so much more safety conscious now, aren't they? Jesus, some of those old get-ups, eh? And the number of guys hacking bits off themselves even with just chainsaws.'

'Makes you wonder,' said Baz. He and Brian kept getting the sawbench securely anchored with waratahs deep in the ground. If you stopped working every time a cocky passed the time of day you'd get nothing done.

Colin looked up at the straggle of trees on the slope. 'You'll have a couple of loads of slabs for me, I suppose?' he said. Baz smiled to himself. There was always a little try on, and Brian always held the line.

'Four hundred bucks for a piled load in the big truck: cheaper than usual because it's you, and we can dump it by the shed in passing.'

'I thought you might toss it in with the contract.'

'There's bugger all margin as is,' said Brian. 'The windbreak's never been thinned. Most of it's just firewood — bugger all sawn timber.'

'There's some old man macrocarpa in there as well as pine.' said Colin.

'Shits of things to bring down, aren't they, Baz?'

'Bastards of things actually,' said Baz.

'Does burn well, though,' said Colin. Brian was squatting at eye level, checking the bench was even.

'We can make sure your load has plenty,' he said.

Colin McFedron was happy with that. You didn't get anything for nothing from Brian Annit: what you did get was exactly what was promised. A fair deal and good measure. No one ever said he'd tried to put one across them.

When Colin had gone they went up to the trees and had a talk about how they'd fell them. It wasn't a big stand — twenty-nine mature, uncared for trees. Brian had counted and assessed them before giving his quote. He'd said he wasn't interested in the creek willows. They were hard to get at, never any decent timber in them, and the firewood sparked.

Baz and Brian raddled the trunks of those trees they needed to top, and began the job. As they'd only been setting up during the first part of the morning they didn't bother with a morning tea break. Although taller than Brian, Baz was good in the trees. He was supple and strong, climbing surely into the branches with the chainsaw on a leather strap across his shoulders. He had an economy of effort and endurance that Brian envied at times. The two of them worked high up and well apart in separate pines, picked out by the whine of their chainsaws, the flashes of safety harness, helmets and bright red ear muffs.

Brian came down first and sat in the shade of the Bedford to have his lunch. Then the noise of Baz's saw stopped and he came through the windbreak, his boots noiseless in the dry mulch of pine needles. Everything seemed quiet after the tempest of the chainsaws. Gradually the sounds natural to that landscape were able to assemble again, to provide the context of relaxation. The subdued noise of the breeze in the trees and the grasses, the calls of returning birds, the lazy barking of one of McFedron's dogs. Baz got a school backpack that held his lunch from the cab of his truck and sat down by his partner, his back against a wheel. Sweat put a sheen on his brown skin and darkened his hair further. 'Ah well, Jesus,' he said.

'Well, it's a start,' said Brian. 'What do you think we should knock over first?'

'Let's do that dirty big macrocarpa bastard at the bottom.'

'Okay.'

'I reckon there's some good timber in that,' said Baz. He was a good judge of timber was Baz, even though he hadn't worked with it as long as Brian.

'We might be in luck there,' said Brian. He pushed his lunchbox a bit closer to his partner, and with the flat of his hand indicated the amount of good food his wife had packed. Every day they worked together he made that unspoken invitation, and every one of those days Baz took nothing from him until the invitation came. Baz had been dragged up, but had innate courtesy.

'How come?' he said.

'Some guy rang up from this woodturners' and carvers' club. Said they were looking for close-grained macrocarpa blocks, especially with irregular grain. Good money too.'

'Good one,' said Baz. 'Can we deliver in one hit?'

'Wants us to keep it under cover until it dries out. He said there's other special wood they'd pay for too. Walnut and stuff.'

'Sounds a bloody useful contact,' said Baz.

He lay down with his hands under his head, and yarned a bit about a whitebait possie his brother had on the Coast. His brother was keen for them to team up. Brian remembered the guy he'd employed before Baz, who'd always had a iPod going so that he might as well have been in another world, and had to be tapped on the arm or shoulder to get attention. Could be bloody dangerous too if a quick reaction was needed. There was an ease about Baz, even when working, a disinclination to worry. Sometimes it irritated Brian, sometimes it was a restful counter to his own need to plan ahead. It might never happen, something will turn up, she'll be jake, no sweat, we can handle it, sweet as, Baz would say.

Brian kept his hat on even in the shade of the truck, but he undid his shirt so that he could feel the slight breeze on the reddish hair of his chest speckled with sawdust. He said he'd been seriously thinking of ditching the Commer and buying a Mack with only 87,000 on the clock that Menzie's Transport wanted to flick. Magpies were mobbing a harrier hawk above the windbreak, a single white cloud formed childish shapes in its movement, the newly sharpened edge of the big saw blade caught flashes of the sun. 'The old girl can't go on for ever,' said Baz.

Brian's cellphone went from inside the cab, and he answered it, took an order for a trailer load of dry pine and wrote the details down in an out-of-date diary with a vinyl cover. 'Before eight o'clock day after tomorrow, okay?' he said. He could drop it before picking up Baz. The order reminded him of another he'd promised before the middle of the week. 'There's that load to the Indian woman in Fountain Street too, isn't there.' He was talking as much to himself as Baz, but Baz replied.

'Did it yesterday afternoon,' said Baz. 'I filled the small trailer and took it round on my car.'

'Good thinking.' Brian felt a bit guilty then about chipping him for being late that morning. 'Thanks,' he said.

They rested in the truck's shade. The easterly got up and sang in the pines and the sharpened teeth of the big circular saw. Baz saw Brian check the pocket watch he kept in a leather pouch at his waist. A wristwatch got knocked about in their work. He knew Brian would get up exactly an hour after he'd knocked off. It was his finicky way, and even got to Baz sometimes so that he'd deliberately take a minute or two longer.

'Ah, well,' said Brian. He stretched his thick arms up and arched back slowly to relieve the muscles. He lifted his yellow hat and replaced it after fluffing his hair. 'Let's drop that big bugger,' he said, and took up his chainsaw. 'Don't forget your goggles,' he told Baz, who often did.

The macrocarpa came down like the end of the world: a massive noise and flurry of smashing limbs, dust and foliage. The great stump was left with a mohawk cut of splinters where the scarf met the back cut. Baz and Brian cleared the trunk first, each aware without the need to talk, glancing to see the other's progress, perhaps holding a hand up to signal that a big branch was almost through that might jar the trunk and so be a danger to his mate.

They didn't notice Amy McFedron until she was almost beside them. She stood in front of Baz and held up a supermarket bag in which she had four scones on a disposable plastic tray. Baz and Brian cut the motors, and Baz took the offering. 'Thanks for that,' he said.

'You shouldn't have bothered,' added Brian, but in a tone of appreciation.

New faces on the farm were an interest for Amy. The scones were her way of checking the guys out. She was a tall, full-breasted woman in her mid-forties, and confident with men. She told Baz she was glad to see the windbreak going, and that she'd persuaded Colin to replant English trees closer to the farmhouse. She'd had a trip to Britain and said there the farmland had a lot more trees and greater variety. The stock benefits too, she said. Neither Brian nor Baz had been outside New Zealand. 'We need to become a lot more conscious of replanting in this country,' Amy said. Both men nodded: their job was cutting down trees, but they were quite happy for other people to plant them.

Baz and Brian watched her walk back to the ute. She gave a wave as she drove away. 'There's still plenty of mileage left there,' said Baz. 'I wouldn't mind.'

'Yeah, if you want to get your head blown off,' said Brian. 'I hear Colin gets pretty toey about her.'

'Still got it,' said Baz. Brian thought so to, but as a married guy considered the opinion best kept to himself.

'Might as well have our break now,' he said.

They took the scones back to the sawbench and the trucks, got the thermos out. Brian had a policy of no beer until the end of the day. Baz thought it one of his nanny ideas, but there you are. Amy's scones, farm size and well buttered, were soon eaten. Baz was thinking about Emily Sanderson, who stayed over with him sometimes at his flat. Emily worked in the office of Nation Concrete, and liked a good pub rave in the weekends. He could do a hell of lot worse, couldn't he, and he wasn't the only one interested, he knew that. She was a bright cookie too. Baz didn't have much of an education, but he was shrewd enough, and liked quickness in others. Sex was hot with Emily when she decided to give it, but she was fun to be with at other times as well. And Baz didn't like a woman to be too possessive. He'd had experience of that, including a girl in Ashburton who threatened to commit suicide when he stopped going with her. Baz didn't want any of that sort of thing. Even thinking about it made him feel uneasy. He could do a lot worse than Emily Sanderson.

'What do you think of Emily?' he asked Brian.

'Who?'

'You met her when you came round to the flat with that meat a couple of weeks ago.' Brian remembered the meat: a half-hogget that Kel Weston gave him because he was pleased with the sawn timber for the new woolshed. Brian had kept the forequarter and taken the rest to Baz. Fifty–fifty for any perks was what Brian always said, a fair deal, and what he said he stuck to. He remembered the woman too when reminded. The name was forgotten, but he recalled a fair-haired girl with thin legs and a good figure. She'd talked sense in a loud voice. Brian didn't particularly like a piercing voice on a woman, but talking sense was more important.

'Yeah, yeah,' he said. 'Seemed a good sort to me. Nice-looking girl.'

'I thought of getting serious,' said Baz.

Brian didn't say anything for a while. It was important, what Baz had said. Baz didn't bring up personal things very often, and Brian wanted to do the matter justice, even though it was about time to get back to the macrocarpa log. 'Well, I don't really know her, of course,' he said, 'but she seemed a good sort to me. You've been seeing her a while now, haven't you?

'A fair while, yeah,' said Baz.

'Is she even-tempered?' Brian's brother was married to a woman of tempestuous moods, and Brian thought it a bloody tragedy. His brother said sometimes he felt like hitting her when she flew off the handle.

'She's pretty good,' said Baz. 'Throws a shitty from time to time, but usually I deserve it. But then we're not living together, so you're not sure are you?'

'Keep away from a moody woman, that's all I'd say,' said Brian. 'That's bloody important, I reckon.'

'You'd be right,' said Baz. He was thinking of the Ashburton girl.

Brian wasn't going to risk further advice on such a tricky and personal concern. He felt lucky in his own marriage, but never attempted to analyse it. He checked his pocket watch, and got to his feet. 'Ah, well,' he said.

'Yeah,' said Baz, and they picked up their goggles, hard hats and ear muffs and walked back up the slope to the fallen tree. Without any comment they stood for moment enjoying the view and the quiet before starting the chainsaws. The downs were patched with crops of different, subdued colours, and willows marked the snaking path of the creek. Some of the grass was shut up for hay, and the wind made soft, sweeping undulations in it. The late afternoon sun was close to the skyline made by the foothills, and already some groups of gulls were flying back towards the coast. Neither man had anything to say about the rightness they felt in working there.

They had the trunk lying free, and many of the branches reduced to firewood, before they knocked off for the day. Even though they were accustomed to the work, their arms were getting twitchy with fatigue, and that wasn't good when working with chainsaws. Brian lacked the natural balance that Baz possessed in physical work, and he was older, but he compensated with effort and strength. 'I'm about buggered,' he said.

'It'll be easier tomorrow on the sawbench,' Baz said. Brian had to push himself, didn't he: had to prove day after day that he could hack it. Why couldn't the silly bastard just ease up a bit? But Baz admired the tenacity of it, even so. Brian could work the arse off most guys.

They both put their gear into the Bedford. Brian took off his steel-capped boots and put on sneakers worn down at the heel. 'Fancy a beer on the way in?' he said. He took his cellphone from the glove compartment and clumsily rang Jenny. His voice was self-conscious. 'We're on our way,' he said. 'We'll stop for a beer at the Oaks. Shouldn't be long though.' A hundred wives might think differently, but Jenny knew one beer would be it, and so did Baz. Sometimes on these occasions he stayed on to drink and Brian went on home.

'I'll drive if you like,' said Baz.

'You've locked the Commer?'

'Sure,' said Baz. Who the hell was going to walk through Colin McFedron's place to pinch a dunger like that?

He knew that after work Brian liked to smoke one cigarette: a roll-your-own that was a survivor from a former habit put by. Brian smoked it as they drove back to the city. He had the window partly open, but Baz quite liked the smell. It relaxed Brian to smoke, so that pale radiating lines showed at the corner of his eyes and pale seams on his weathered forehead. The two men talked hardly at all as they headed for the hotel, and the silence between them was an easy one.

They sat outside at the Oaks because of their work clothes. There were long wooden tables and forms. From habit both Brian and Baz assessed the how well the wood was weathering, but didn't comment. There was a hedge that cut down noise from the road. Baz had a lager and Brian a dark ale. Baz had a peculiarity that Brian disliked of rattling his drink in his mouth before swallowing, but what did that matter really, he told himself. Baz had proved a bloody good worker: the best he'd had since he started the yard and mill. You didn't get guys prepared to slog the same these days.

'I'd like you to have a look sometime at that Mack truck I was talking about,' said Brian.

'Sure.'

'We'd be pretty well set up then. It's not been a bad year at all.'

'Good,' said Baz. He imagined that Brian would be squirrelling away a fair bit. Not a lot of impulse spending with old Brian.

'How would you like to come in as official partner?' said Brian.

'It's no big deal I know, but you do half the work. Fair's fair. There'd be more in it for you that way.'

It came as a surprise for Baz. He'd always worked for someone else; his family had always worked for someone else. He hadn't imagined the possibility of any other status.

'I haven't got the money to put in,' he said. It was true. A single working guy, he spent his money as he got it: spent it on drink, on his car, on takeaways and sometimes happy baccy, on Emily. He was thirty-three and paid rent for the flat in which he lived.

'We'd work out something about the plant,'said Brian. 'It's just a two-man business, isn't it: the leased yard, the sawbench and the trucks. No big deal. But fair's fair, and you do as much as me. Fifty–fifty down the middle. I don't want you going off with your brother whitebaiting or something. Seems to me we work okay together. Anyway, you have a think about it. And it could be a good thing if you're popping the question to Emily.'

'Thanks,' said Baz. He put a long arm across the table to shake Brian's hand and they held the grip for a moment. 'I appreciate it.'

'We'll have to put something on paper,' said Brian.

'I'm not worried about that.'

'Nah, we need something. Maybe you and I go in and see the accountant if you're keen. We should keep away from the bloody lawyers if we can.'

'Too true,' said Baz.

'If we both get stuck in then I reckon we can do well enough. We haven't got the overheads of bigger outfits, and they're not interested at our scale anyway. A niche market, the accountant calls it. And you should bring Emily around for a meal sometime. Jenny would like to meet her.'

That's all they said about the partnership that day. The two of them sat a while longer in the lengthening shadows. There was brief talk about how much time they reckoned McFedron's windbreak would take, and whether they had enough covered space at the yard to store the timber, then Brian finished the last of his beer and stood up. 'Better head off,' he said. 'Want to be dropped?'

'I'll stay for a while, I think,' said Baz.

'Okay. I'll see you in the morning then — a bit before eight.'

'Sure.'

'We should go to the yard on the way out and get that load of firewood done.'

'Okay,' said Baz.

He watched Brian go, slightly splay footed in his dirty sneakers, and with sawdust still flecked in his work shirt. A straight-up sort of guy, despite taking everything so seriously. Not a barrel of laughs, but he'd always played fair with Baz, and now he'd given him a bloody good chance to get ahead. Didn't have to do that. Baz wouldn't forget it.

As he left, Brian had a last glimpse of Baz, just getting up to go and get another beer: tall, loose limbed, yet with natural co-ordination. His dark hair, stiff with sweat, was like a cock's comb and the gap in his teeth showed. He might settle in for a session. Brian knew he had mates who drank there. He'd grow out of that, though, especially if he married his girl. The thing was he could work, not like so many young buggers. That's what you needed in a partner, someone who could graft, someone who wasn't stupid, didn't put you in danger. Someone who wasn't distracting you by yakking all the bloody time. They'd do okay, he reckoned, him and Baz.

PATRICK AND THE KILLER

'And how are you anyway?' said Uncle Blick when they met without design at the airport.

'Not so bad, not so bad,' said Patrick's father, who was dying of prostate cancer at the time. Afterwards Patrick asked his father why he didn't tell the truth. 'None of his bloody business,' his father said. 'He's always been a snooping sort of bastard.' Blick came to the funeral three months later, though Patrick put it down to a sense of family solidarity rather than callous curiosity.

'He went down so quickly,' said Uncle Blick sombrely at the chapel. 'I met him at the airport only weeks ago and he was fine, then wham. There's no way of knowing, is there, and he was three years younger than me.'

'We appreciate you coming,' said Patrick.

'Wham, just like that,' and Uncle Blick's face contorted slightly as if he felt the impact.

Patrick was unsettled by his father's death. He felt grief, of course, but also it forced him to evaluate his own life. He was thirty-eight, unmarried, and with a polytechnic diploma in small business administration. Unfortunately he didn't have a business of any size to administer. He worked as a salesman for Globus Aluminium Mouldings, and usually pronounced the name of the metal in the American way, because he thought it sounded more classy. In an endeavour to improve his circumstances not long after his father died, he asked GAM for a raise in salary and a better company car. Both requests were refused, and the manager said that in fact things weren't that good, and they'd have to let him go with a redundancy of just a week's salary for each year he'd been with them. 'It's something I hate to do,' said the manager. 'It's a hell of a thing, I know. To be honest, Patrick, we've had to give priority to those with dependants. You'll appreciate that, I know.'

To save a little face with family and friends, Patrick told them he'd resigned because he wanted to live in a bigger place with more opportunities. He moved to Wellington and rented a run-down bach at Eastbourne in which the sound and smell of the sea were always present. The owner intended bulldozing it and building a new place on the valuable section, but in the meantime, because the lease was only month by month, the rent was reasonable. Someone had gathered shells onto the small frontage over the years, and it resembled a giant child's sandpit. Someone had painted a green and blue parrot on the roughcast by the low back door, and the single bedroom smelled of stale sweat as well as the sea.

Within the first week, Patrick had a choice of two jobs: one was handling freight at the airport, the other was in a Johnsonville video store. He took the latter because it was closer to Eastbourne, and also because he was fond of films and videos. The guy who interviewed him said the staff were entitled to fifty per cent reduction on hire, but in practice if you took stuff home at lock-up time and had it back when you came to work, no one bothered about it. Just keeping your fingers out of the till was the main thing, he said.

Two of them were on at a time and Patrick was surprised how busy it kept them. Issues and returns were only part of it. He spent a lot of time sorting out those titles that were to be put out for cheap sale because of excessive wear, or because they were no longer in demand. There were thousands of videos and DVDs and a special computer program to keep track of them. There was a screened section at the back of the shop that held the porno stock, and Patrick soon noticed how many of the customers would add a highbrow art movie to their stack of porn, as if that made the average content morally acceptable. It wasn't a career, of course, and Patrick intended to find something with better prospects within a few months.

All that changed the day he met the killer at the petrol station in Petone. Twenty dollars' worth of 91 unleaded, and he wanted a paper as well. It was a cold Sunday morning in August, and the light rain shoaled in with the wind from the sea.

Afterwards Patrick wanted a piss, and he went past the two aisles and into the lavatory that had a small black cut-out of a man on the door. That's where the killer was, although Patrick didn't know his identity at the time. The killer wore a black beanie, black jeans, leather boots and a grubby, blue windbreaker. He was smoking and looking reflectively at the roof as he pissed onto the stainless steel back of the urinal. Patrick took up his stance at the far end of the grating. Sometimes he'd noticed that men preferred to go into a cubicle if there was even one other person at the urinal, and that seemed oddly prudish to him.

The killer washed his hands briefly, and balled a paper towel. 'It's a real shit day out there, mate, isn't it? Bloody wind and bloody rain and bloody Sunday.' He was a thin, undersized man with a face like a chisel and a small goatee beard. He worked the zipper of his jacket up and down, and then left it in the same position as before.

'Nasty day all right,' said Patrick. He took his turn at the basin as the killer stepped aside to check his teeth in the mirror.

'I suppose a joker just has to keep on keeping on, eh, mate.'

'That's about the size of it, I'd say,' said Patrick.

So they came out of the lavatory together, and Patrick was only a step or two behind as they went past the aisles towards the counter and the door. Afterwards, Patrick would say that he noticed there was no one behind the counter, and had an uneasy feeling, but it wasn't true. What he did notice were the three policemen standing around the killer's car by the pumps, and he had a glimpse of others going around the back of the shop. 'Ah, fuck it, no,' said the killer, in a tone of both weariness and anger, and he reached to the back of his jeans and pulled out a knife with a straight blade. He waited until Patrick drew level, then he took him by the shoulder. 'What we do, see, is walk right on by so everyone's okay,' he said.

'What?' said Patrick.

'A hostage like, mate. And you and I walk right by the cops so you don't get hurt.'

'It won't work,' said Patrick. 'It's like stuff on video, and that never works in real life. Only cocks up things worse.' He didn't believe that on such a drab day anything of moment could happen.

For just an instant the killer looked highly brassed off, and Patrick half expected a blow, but then his companion said, 'You're right — course you are. Bugger,' and he dropped the knife and sprinted for the door. He was pretty speedy, even in boots, and he made the doorway before the police could intercept him, and hared away across the forecourt, leading with his narrow chin and goatee. A car of police reinforcements was coming out from the city, though, and they spilled out eagerly and brought him down. Whatever he'd done, Patrick still felt a certain sympathy to see the poorly dressed, skinny guy borne down by so many. There was something of an augury in it, perhaps.

The police showed some special interest in Patrick at first, but after the counter and forecourt men said he'd arrived separately from the killer they eased up, even letting him walk up close enough to the captive still on the ground to see the small grey stones caught in the matrix of the wet soles of his boots, and his thin, hairy wrists in the handcuffs. The killer lay passively, with one cheek pressed on the glistening road and his eyes half closed. It reminded Patrick of the way chooks are when you hang them by the legs. A sergeant said the killer's name was Geoffrey Madden Wenn.

A journalist arrived when Patrick and the two garage men were still giving information to the police, and he said he wanted to talk about what had happened. Then a TV crew came and were disappointed that the killer had been taken away. Patrick spoke briefly to them as well. It was the security camera footage, however, shown on the news the next day, that created the surge of interest. It caught Geoffrey Wenn gripping Patrick by the shoulder and holding up the knife, and although Patrick's words to the killer couldn't be heard, the trick of the camera was to make it seem that Patrick was full of composure rather than bafflement, and that his insouciant advice had put Wenn to flight.

So both the print and television journalists sensed the possibility of one of those passing, but profitable, instant celebrity creations so much a part of their trade. The security camera film was replayed in many contexts, and the revelation that Patrick and Geoffrey Wenn had talked together in the lavatory before the latter's arrest provided further ramifications. 'In Lieu of Danger' was the punning headline in one Sunday paper; 'Killer's Philosophy in WC' was the banner of another.

It wasn't that Patrick set out to tell any lies, or even to take advantage of fortuitous circumstance: he was just an ordinary guy unaccustomed to being sought out, unaccustomed to flattery, or being the centre of attraction. The attention of women journalists in particular he found strangely gratifying, and he was drawn into specious elaboration, exaggeration and conjecture by their open interest and familiarity. The brief conversation between Patrick and the killer in the men's room was spun out into an exchange of some depth and significance. 'I think he was oppressed by the dismal day and the sort of life he had,' said Patrick. 'He wanted to talk, and he said that Sundays were always a bummer for him. He was determined not to give in to despair, however. He told me that you needed to be resilient: to keep on keeping on. I got the impression, too, that he was a lonely, troubled guy. I don't know all the things he's done, of course, and there was definitely threat and anger in him, but he was reaching out as well, I reckon.'

What Geoffrey Wenn had done was run over a man who had discovered his cannabis plot in the bush behind the Butterfly Track: come down on him in his yellow Holden ute, the prosecution said, and run over him full tilt. The defence lawyer said the dead man was a known drug dealer who had threatened to take over Wenn's plot. The prosecution said the victim was a reformed man, innocently taking exercise on his doctor's orders.

It was a high-profile case, partly because the defence lawyer hinted that they could name some well-known Wellington personalities with links to the growing of marijuana. The publicity kept Patrick's name in the news also, and there were benefits in that. Globus Aluminium Mouldings had its head office in Wellington, and after his heroism were keen to have Patrick back on the staff. The CEO himself called Patrick in, and said that the regional manager who had sacked him had shown a regrettable lack of judgement. Patrick was offered the situation of deputy to the national sales manager, who was due for retirement within a year or so, and the position carried with it a new six-cylinder car and mortgage perks. The CEO also said that they hoped to structure a new advertising campaign around Patrick, which would stress the reliability and value of GAM products.

Patrick took the job. He was a reasonable salesman and understood he'd got a lucky break that could be the making of him if he worked hard. As the CEO realised, the publicity of the Wenn case was a definite advantage in attracting business. People liked the association with him, which gave them a talking point with their fellows and families. 'You know that guy who talked down the murderer in the Petone service station?' they might say. 'I had him in giving a quote for the new conservatory range frames today. He's GAM's chief salesman here. Seemed a decent bloke and we had quite a chat. No way was he going to back down at all even if the bastard did have a knife, he told me. Said he'd twigged right from the start there was something odd about him.'

Sonia Tonkisse was the accountant at GAM. She was a year older than Patrick, better qualified and with an equable temperament, which is very attractive in a woman. She was good-looking, too, in that way that emphasises grooming rather than obvious points of appeal. Patrick liked her and, rather to his surprise, Sonia favoured him too. They began going out together and getting to know each other in the rather measured sort of way that suited both of them. Patrick was still regaining confidence after his GAM dismissal, and Sonia was as scrupulous with life's decisions as she was with GAM's accounts.

Patrick bought a house in Seatoun: a double-storeyed roughcast-over-brick home with a glimpse of the sea. The price was a good deal more than he'd planned to spend, but he went along with Sonia's advice. Best to take advantage of the firm's low mortgage rates, she said, and the place was bound to appreciate considerably in that area and with that construction. She had contacts in the real estate business, and also there was the tacit understanding that she and Patrick might in time live there together.

Two women's magazines ran features on the couple. The cover photograph of the first showed Patrick standing at the bottom of the front steps and Sonia two steps up, leaning informally on his shoulder. The shot was nicely framed by the arched entrance, and the article stressed both Patrick's record of heroism and the romance he'd found since. The second cover showed the two of them framed by the lounge window and with the sea just visible. 'Killer confrontation forgotten' was the caption, by which the magazine hoped to keep the incident alive in the public mind.

Neither prosecution nor defence called Patrick at the trial, and Geoffrey Wenn received a sentence of fifteen years' imprisonment. The trial stirred up public interest once more, but it subsided more rapidly the second time: new trepidations and monsters soon filled the media and the national consciousness. Patrick, however, found the incident hard to put out of his mind. The image of the killer face down on the wet road: the sordidness and loneliness of that slight man borne down by the righteous supremacy of the police. Patrick had benefited from a random meeting with him, and felt obscurely under some obligation because of it. It occurred to him that maybe he should visit Wenn in prison. The idea came back more strongly on the day the GAM CEO called him into the office to congratulate him on orders, and confirm the expectation of Patrick's promotion after the retirement of the national sales manager. 'Susan and I would like you to be our guest on a yachting trip next weekend. Time we all got to know each other better. We're asking Sonia, of course, and a few friends we'd like you both to meet. I like to think of our management team as a family. We'll probably sail across to the Sounds and do a bit of blue cod fishing. Sheer heaven.' The CEO came from behind his desk and lingered at the door with Patrick a while to show the possibility of a new relationship. 'All work and no play, you know,' he said. The CEO's personal assistant in the outer office looked up and smiled at them both warmly.

Even the weather mirrored Patrick's fortune: calm and bright. He resolved to visit the killer in prison, aware of how their lives had diverged so sharply since that rainy day at the petrol station in Petone. He found, however, that this wasn't a simple matter. Geoffrey Wenn had been sent to Paremoremo in Auckland, and prison visits were initiated by the prisoners themselves, not visitors, and as well there was a whole sequence of applications, approvals, booking times and identifications required. Also Sonia wasn't in favour of his renewing contact. 'Nothing that he did was intended to favour you,' she said. 'He killed somebody, right, and he wouldn't have hesitated to kill you. Best to keep away from someone like that, and you don't want people thinking you've any sympathy for a murderer.'

'I suppose his life's hell,' said Patrick.

'And so it should be,' she said.

Patrick didn't mention his intention to Sonia again, but when the GAM CEO asked him to attend a sales conference at Titirangi, he wrote to the killer, who put the bureaucracy in motion. Patrick described his visit as being based on non-religious, yet compassionate, grounds.

Visits were allowed only in the weekends, so on the Saturday following his conference, Patrick drove to Albany and Paremoremo. He expected to be sitting before one of those glassed-in booths he saw on TV crime shows, but the visiting room was open and reminded him of his home-town polytechnic where he'd done his trade exams. Small, cheap tables beyond squinting distance of each other, and tubular chairs. There was one warder seated by the door, and two others wandered listlessly among the groups, or stood intent before the one window.

Patrick didn't recognise Wenn at first. He no longer had any sort of beard, and, although still scrawny, he'd lost the hard edge of freedom, had already slackened with apathy. He didn't regard Patrick with any apparent anticipation. He sat well back in the hard chair, with his knees apart, and, after a glance at Patrick, seemed more interested in people at other tables in the visiting room. He caught the eye of a fellow prisoner talking to a hard-faced woman in jeans, and gave the thumbs-up sign. Wenn made no attempt to start a conversation with Patrick, neither did he show any eagerness for his visitor to begin one. What need of hurry, what possibility of good news, could there be for a killer serving a long term? No doubt he'd had the odd Bible-basher call on him before.

'I brought you some cigarettes and biscuits,' said Patrick, 'but the staff took them to check, and said you'd get them later. Do you remember I was in the petrol station when the cops came to get you?' said Patrick.

'Yeah.'

'We came out of the lavatory together, and then you made a break for it when you saw the police.'

'That's right. Yeah, I remember.' But the recollection didn't cause him any excitement, or surprise. He remained well settled on the chair, and with his hands on his splayed knees. He sucked his teeth.

'You were in the paper and that,' he said. Patrick realised that their meeting that day meant nothing to the killer: nothing had come from it to benefit him, nothing to make it noteworthy in a day he wished to forget. For Patrick it had been a lucky strike with a string of consequences to his advantage, but for Geoffrey Wenn, Patrick was just a guy he had pissed next to before being arrested.

'Anyway,' said Patrick, 'I just thought maybe a visitor would be something of a break for you, and they tell me cigarettes are always useful in here.'

'Yeah,' said Wenn. He seemed to be waiting for Patrick to come to the point of the visit, to start talking about the capacity Jesus had for forgiveness, or reveal a programme of reading skills supported by the local Association of University Women. Yet Patrick had no further explanation for being there than he'd already given, and felt awkward.

'Can't be much of a life,' he said fatuously, and the killer didn't bother to reply, just let the bottom of his thin face twist a little.

The conversations at most other tables were equally desultory, and prisoners and visitors glanced around often as words failed them. In a way it reminded Patrick of visiting his father in hospital, where he'd been given an even more severe sentence. Only the woman in jeans seemed to be talking against the clock, on and on about her money troubles. Patrick heard snatches to do with back rent, hire purchase goods, Sally Army parcels, repossession of a free-standing hotpot, and the inability to afford a school camp for one of the kids. 'It's the kids, though, isn't it?' she said, not lowering her voice at all, oblivious to listeners in the intensity of her focus. 'I mean, okay, we've fucked up, but I can hardly stand what it does to the kids. You know?' The man had no hair, and his skull bones made uneasy conjunction. He nodded affirmatively, as if she had suggested a treat. 'You know how Shane is,' she said, and he nodded again. 'Sometimes at night I stand outside the little bugger's door, and I hear him crying in his sleep.'

Patrick tried to focus on the killer's face so that something to say would come to him, and the woman's life would recede. He felt that he was in some bog of existence and would be sucked under if he stayed longer. He wanted out. 'Am I allowed to give you money?' he asked Wenn. 'Just a few bucks I've got on me?'

'Stuff it up your arse maybe,' said the killer. He leant back a little more, and grinned at his bald-domed mate.

Patrick didn't know how to respond to such animosity. 'I suppose I'd better be going,' he said. The killer showed no interest. He remained seated as Patrick stood up and began to leave. When Patrick glanced back from the door, Geoffrey Wenn was still seated, his arms folded, and his attention on the bald man and his woman visitor.

In the car park a large woman struggled to get out of her Suzuki beside Patrick's. She seemed winded by the effort, and stood puffing for a while, her small mouth with dolly pink lipstick open wide. 'They don't think of us, do they?' she said. 'Oh no, no, they don't think what it does to the family, do they? Punish one, punish all: that's what they reckon, don't they? What show have we got, eh? *No* show at bloody all, that's what, isn't it?' It was another chorus to that of the hard-faced woman in the visiting room. She swayed off towards the prison buildings.

Patrick decided there was no need to mention the visit to Sonia: that there was no one to thank for what had happened to him over recent months. It was just the play of indifferent circumstances, sometimes supporting you above your fellows, sometimes pulling you down. As he drove he concentrated on a projected new range of aluminium struts for caravan and campervan awnings, and occupied himself by going over the specifications in his head. He'd always had a knack with figures, and found it reassuring to let them form and disassemble in those predictable patterns quite free of emotion, or any augury.

ANACAPRI

Professor Huchro gave the keynote address at the conference in Grenoble. It's an odd place perhaps for academics to gather to talk about Imperial Rome, but the university there offers excellent facilities, and the venue is popular because of the skifields close by.

The content of most such gatherings is predictable, even repetitious, and often location becomes the point of attraction. I'm not into winter playgrounds myself, but was interested when I read that Paula Huchro was to give a paper on the importance of sea power during the time of the Flavian emperors.

We'd met in our mid-twenties as assistants at a minor archaeological dig in Italy, had been colleagues there for six weeks. Before Grenoble I'd seen her only once again, fleetingly, at a symposium in Genoa. Paula is married, but keeps her maiden name, perhaps as a nod to feminism, perhaps more to pay tribute to her Polish origins.

I sat in the third-floor room of a modern wing of the university at Grenoble, next to Andrew Neiderer, reader in classics from the University of London, and listened to Paula's address. A window cleaner worked from an enclosed seat that travelled on a bar attached to the outside of the building. No noise intruded. He was youthfully agile, did his job well and I could see snow on the mountains not far away. Paula was poised, authoritative, deserving of the respect she was accorded in her field. She was short, still inclined to plumpness, but her hair was much darker than it had been when she and I were young in Italy. It appeared quite natural, although it must have been dyed.

Anacapri was the first archaeological dig of which I was ever part. I was one of two PhD students funded to gain experience. The widening of a walled street had revealed the remains of a first century BC domestic shrine, and a midden, the use of which went back at least a century earlier. The site was close to Axel Münthe's Villa San Michele, and the tourists going there would sometimes be attracted by our chatter and the signs of excavation, and walk up the cobbled slope to watch for a moment in the accosting sun. A canvas awning was stretched between poles to keep the glare from us as we crouched on the little terraces of stony soil amid the sectioning tape and pegs. The tourists soon tired of the meticulous sifting and scraping, the constant delay for recording, the lack of arresting discovery, and drifted back to the street that led to San Michele, where they could stand under cool arches and see the rich pickings of Münthe's classical collection displayed to advantage on the very spot where once Tiberius had a villa.

The archaeologist in charge was only a few years older than me. Colum taught at the University of California, and his industrious talent almost matched his overweening ambition. A lanky, ginger-haired and freckled guy who refused to cover up, and whose body refused to tan: burn and peel, burn and peel, so that always there were overlapping lines of sloughing skin like pale tide marks on his reddened body. His acumen in scholarly matters was indisputable, however, and he bested me with condescending ease in any professional disagreements. 'Good try, man,' he'd say, 'but you got a way to go yet. Keep taking the tablets.' He did some digging at the excavation, but most of his time was spent site mapping and cataloguing.

I disliked Colum most of all because he was having sex with Paula, who was the other graduate student funded for practical experience. Her tuition was more personal and intensive than mine, and at night I was kept awake for a time by her head butting the thin wall between our cramped rooms in Capri harbour, down the winding, narrow road from Anacapri. 'Come on, come on,' Colum would exhort, as if impatient for her to follow suit in a card game.

She was then a short, fair girl who, because of Colum's attentions, seemed to inflate during our stay, until dimples appeared on her cheeks and knees. Even her nose became a more dominant feature. Whether Paula's weight gain was the consequence of satisfaction, or guilt, I was unsure. She said little during her work both night and day during the first weeks on site. Faustus and Alessandro, the two permanent team members, were puzzled, I think, at her reserve, given her almost immediate openness with Colum.

Paula and I usually worked together, and at first there was constraint between us because of her relationship with Colum, although that was never mentioned. I admired her knowledge, her industrious enthusiasm and persistence. Fieldwork has never been the aspect of classical studies most attractive to me, and some hot afternoons, cramped from sitting and crouching, and also a little bored with the precise discipline required in a dig, I would wander off and take a long break: have a beer at the café cum bar with a view of the chairlift. Well, we weren't even getting paid. Paula didn't accompany me: Colum would lift his sandy eyebrows as if to say, boys will be boys.

It was the discovery of the coin that brought us closer. We were sitting on wooden slats on the shallow terrace of the site's level three, when her narrow trowel flipped out a denarius we later found had been minted by Sextus Pompey during his war with Octavian. An interesting coin to be there on the island of Capri. The day was unusual also: high cloud and a strong sea wind that puffed dust from Paula's trowel into our faces.

I lifted my head in excitement, and was about to call out to others of the team, when Paula put a hand on my arm. 'Shut up,' she said. 'Keep quiet about it.' The excavation was a shallow one as sites go, and my neck was above the level of the cobbles nearby. Because of the thrill I felt, I expected Colum and Faustus, working not far away, to be caught up in awareness of it, but their faces remained down. 'Just keep working,' said Paula. She rubbed the coin a couple of times in her fingers, then slipped it into her pocket. She began the scrupulous, small-scale excavation again in the dry soil, and the wind ruffled the orange site tapes and blew grit as before. Just the passage of a little time made me an accomplice, and without conscious decision.

We finished early because of the wind, and Paula and I went to the nearby café and had small glasses of yellow Limoncello liquor. Most of the tourists had already gone down the steep road to the harbour and the boats waiting to take them back to Sorrento, or Naples. Paula's lover was our superior and someone I disliked. That situation created wariness between us, but by saying nothing of the find, she created new ambiguity.

From the café patio we could see the chairlift that took visitors low over the last gardens and up to the mountain lookout. I went up several times during my stay, and enjoyed the quiet, skimming ride as much as the view from the island's top.

'You won't say anything about it, will you?' Paula said.

'Okay,' I said. 'What do you reckon it is?'

'A denarius of course.'

'Yeah, what period, though?'

'I'm not going to take it out now. Let's not even talk about it. You know what people are like round here. I'll clean it up a bit when I get a chance and you can have a look at it.'

'What about Colum?' I said.

'What about him?' Paula showed no embarrassment.

'Aren't you going to tell him?'

'He doesn't own me,' she said.

You could have fooled me. For the first time, sitting there in the cooling wind, I had a sense of her resolve and independence. Because she was short, quiet and plain, because she was pleasuring Colum at night, I'd assumed she was submissive, and reliant on others. How difficult we find it to avoid such superficial assessments. We didn't talk any more of the coin that day, but it marked special knowledge between us, and a basis for friendship of a kind. Later, in the darkness, I heard her head, or knee, tapping on the wall again, and Colum's exhortations, and knew their relationship more complex than he realised.

In my free time I went often to Villa San Michele to enjoy its spacious beauty, and examine the treasures Münthe had gathered there: Greek and Egyptian artefacts as well as Roman. Such views, too, and I could stand there and think of Tiberius looking out from that same place, feel thankful not to live in a despotic age. Torre was guide and custodian of the villa. He was as much interested in the dig as I was in San Michele, and we spent time together in both places, and time together in night restaurants drinking imported beer and Limoncello. Torre was middle-aged and had the darker skin and stockiness of a southern Italian. Arabs, I later heard a professor from Milan call them. Torre had a central bald spot around which small curls lapped, and a fine voice, but he sang vacuous American pop songs instead of arias, perhaps to display his command of English. Often he spoke of going to the USA, where he imagined wealth awaited everyone. His cousin in Dayton, Ohio, had two cars and was a member of a country club. The cousin said he wouldn't come back to Italy. It had too much of a past, he said, and not enough of a future.

I never went to Torre's house, never met his wife, saw only one of his large family — a barely adolescent son. On the few occasions that he and I stayed drinking late, the boy would track us down, and Torre would get up without demur, put an arm around his son and they would begin the walk home. I don't remember the son ever saying one word. 'Buona notte, amico mio,' Torre would say, and extend his free arm towards me as if about to make a declaration.

I told Torre that I had difficulty getting to sleep in the cramped room in Capri, though not of the noises that were the cause. I complained of the heat, the lack of space and privacy, the fag of having to go up and down the hill each day. It was a relief when he allowed me, in the last few weeks of my stay, to creep into the villa's kitchen, spread my rug on the pale tiles and sleep there. He gave me a key and his trust. His strict instruction was that I kip in no other room, touch nothing. I would wake in the morning with bright light glinting on the large, copper cooking pots, with the shelf of blue pottery, and a soft breeze through the open rooms. When Torre arrived to prepare for the day's visitors, and we passed with a smile at the door, there would be no evidence of my stay.

Colum went to Naples during the third weekend to give a progress report to the museum director there, and it was then that Paula showed me the coin. On Sunday we went down to the harbour and had lunch in the Sarzano family restaurant, well away from the tourists and the promenade cafés that served the insalata Caprese applauded in the travel guides. The cramped Sarzano room lacked ambience and faced a modern concrete wall with no niches for lizards, no quaint gates, only graffiti and casually parked scooters that leaked oil onto the pavement. The oil lay drably until rain came, then awoke, spread glistening, rainbow wings. The wine was bad, but the seafood made all worthwhile, and the prices were reasonable. The waiter was young, thin, with full lips, but an insufficient moustache. He'd taken a dislike to me because I didn't tip well. Waiters there assume all foreigners are rich.

Afterwards, Paula and I walked up to the little cemetery. So tidy, so obviously a place lovingly visited, with sealed photographs on many of the graves and plaques, and none of the vandalism so common at home. We sat on the stone step of the Vergotti family tomb and she showed me the denarius, no larger than my thumbnail, with the fine, raised head of Sextus Pompey on the obverse. We agreed it must have been minted about 40 BC. I have always felt a frisson of delight to hold history in the hand, and returned it with reluctance. 'Highly bloody unprofessional, you know,' I said. It was more envy than malice.

'Oh, bullshit,' she said. 'I love it. You love it. You know it's almost impossible to get anything out of the country legitimately now. And it would only end up in a drawer in the museum in Naples with scores of others, even more likely flogged off by some curator there.'

'You're right. Will you tell Colum before you go?'

'You don't like him, do you?'

'Not much, but then you do.' The well-kept graveyard had little exposed earth, or grass, but walls of polished stone inset with photographs and inscriptions like large filing cabinets of the dead. But Paula's enjoyment was to touch the silver coin, hold it openly for close inspection.

'I like you just as much,' she said.

'Come off it. You're sleeping with the guy. I was in the next room remember.'

'Colum's okay. The sex is okay too. The important thing's the commendation I'll get at the end of the stint, and maybe that'll influence the examiners when I hand in my dissertation, and the universities I apply to afterwards.'

I was taken aback, not so much by the calculation in her behaviour, as by her honesty in admitting it. We all act in our own interest, but usually disguise it, even to ourselves. I was flattered that she confided in me, although she was sleeping with Colum. I felt male regret too, that ours was a confidence of colleagues, that it was Colum who came to her room in the dark, exposed the pale, fullness of her thighs, took habitual and firm possession. I told her righteously that she was bright enough not to need that sort of help.

'My parents were immigrants from Poland: they're poor. I'm not exactly a beauty queen, no friends in high places. Nah, I have to make it happen, or it doesn't happen,' she said. 'I don't mean shagging every lecturer I've had. I haven't had the hard word put on me much actually, which shows the competition perhaps. But it hasn't been easy. Even a doctorate doesn't guarantee a decent position any more. I don't want to end up for life in a polytech, or a teachers' college, some provincial museum.'

Here was a realism foreign to me, and an unvarnished expression of it equally unusual. I had a sense of a background and struggle that made my own experience almost genteel. If she'd been confiding in me late at night after a good many drinks, I wouldn't have been so surprised, but it was mid-afternoon in a quiet graveyard. We sat in the patch of shade at the entrance to the Vergotti tomb, and between buildings was a glimpse of the yachts and fishing boats of the harbour. And she was absolutely right. You did what you could to give yourself the best possible shot at the career you wanted.

'But you're a bloody good student, aren't you,' I said. 'You wouldn't be here otherwise. You deserve the best opportunity.' On several occasions she'd shown understanding and knowledge superior to my own, but I was too proud to admit that. Perhaps I wasn't God's gift to academia after all. I had a quick, unbidden sense of how we looked together there, talking on a stone step in the cemetery. Myself tall, gawky, the lucky one of the family, my grandmother said: the spoilt one, Pops said. Paula, dumpy, with a face like a beachball under her large hat, and dangling a water bottle between her knees. Just for moment I saw us from the outside, as you see a photograph of exact replication, yet with the knowledge it has fallen into the past.

'You don't always get what you deserve, though,' she said. 'It's a different world for a woman.'

'Right.' But I wondered if men enjoyed as many advantages as she supposed.

During those last few weeks we achieved an easy comradeship at the dig. Colum was content to command her nights, and paid no special attention to her during the day. I don't think the reason was subterfuge. I found it preferable to be sleeping in the villa, and so not reminded of their amours by the noises through the wall. At night in the Villa San Michele there was just the sliding scuttle of lizards, occasional scooters far off, or soothing whispers of the wind from the sea.

Paula and I didn't discuss the coin any more. She never again quite approached the honesty expressed in the chapel cemetery, but we would talk often of our dissertations, our academic ambitions, our love of antiquity and the local food. She continued to put on a bit of weight, but I made no mention of that.

At the beginning of our final week together there was a night cloudburst that caused water to run into the excavation, and Colum asked Paula and me to spend the next day in the office cataloguing material from the midden. The office consisted of two rooms and a primitive lavatory washroom he had rented in a private home close to the site. The owner was old Signora Deluca, who spoke no English, but was always watching from the doorway when any of us were there. Despite her inability to understand what was said, she seemed to enjoy the company, and would laugh when we laughed, click her tongue admiringly when some shard of pottery, or a bone from a long-forgotten banquet, was lifted to the light.

Paula and I talked more than we worked, and all three of us ate Neapolitan sugar biscuits, Signora Deluca taking mere presence as a right to be included. Perhaps because it was a day so out of normal routine, perhaps because our time in Anacapri was coming to an end, Paula opened up more about her family. The room had green, wooden shutters, and as she talked the bright sunlight shimmered through them, and the sounds of other people's lives drifted in from the street. Her father had been a surveyor in Poland, but made political enemies, and emigrated. His qualifications weren't recognised in Australia, and he had to work as assistant to a carpet layer. Neither of her parents understood English well. I asked her if she spoke Polish, and she did so as a reply. 'I won't tell you what it means though,' she said. And when we laughed so did the old lady, putting gnarled fingers to her mouth as if she recognised some indiscretion in the words.

'I bet you've never felt different like that,' Paula said. 'Going to school, or other kids' homes, and knowing all the while that you're not the same. Spending so much time copying what the others do, picking up on what they think and do, and yet always you're different.'

'I've never thought much about it.'

'You don't have to, that's the thing. My parents were defeated by it, by the need to remake themselves, but I sure as hell wasn't going to let that happen to me. I had a shitty time at school too. I think that's why I loved history: the escape from where I was.'

'Ehi, aspettami,' wait for me, called someone from beyond the green shutters.

'Varsity was a lot better,' said Paula. 'Conformity isn't a doctrine there. It's everyone for themselves, and I prefer that. I stopped trying to be like other people.'

'It gets very competitive at uni, though, don't you think. A sort of ugly intensity to do well, especially at post-grad level.'

'I don't mind competition,' Paula said. Her appearance was so little a reflection of her character — an unlined, almost cherubic face and soft body. She was so much shorter than me that when we stood together I looked down on the stack of her short, blonde hair, or the stitching of her floppy hat. 'History's chock full of competition, isn't it, and the price of failure was a bloody sight more serious then.'

'The Romans were a violent people,' I said. Paula smiled, and Signora Deluca rattled like an autumn tree, and gurned at each of us in turn.

Paula left one day before me to travel to Rome, and from there fly home to Sydney. Colum drove her down to the harbour after a farewell lunch in our usual café. Faustus, Alessandro, and the three of us. Colum said the lunch would mark the end of stay for me as well as Paula, though naturally his comments in respect of her contribution were warmer and of greater length. Colum gave us both a photograph taken on site — he seated on level one with the Italians, and Paula and I below on level three — and an envelope containing a testimonial. Mine was temperate, but not vindictive. Colum saw me as neither rival, nor equal. As he spoke of us, he rubbed his sunburnt arms, and pale shreds of skin wafted away. Less than ten years later he died of a stroke while in Arles to advise on the preservation of the Roman amphitheatre there.

I could see people ascending the mountain in the quiet chairlift, one by one borne up over gardens and low walls towards the lookout. Once I'd seen a naked doll in the grass below, spreadeagled like a murder victim and with discarded clothes nearby. Once a man with hairy shoulders washing his upper body from a blue basin at his doorway.

So the parting between Paula and myself was quite public and routine. A quick hug at the car door, my cheerful contribution to the waving, and the shouted good wishes, as she was driven away. I remember wondering where she was carrying Sextus Pompey, and which of her scholarly attributes Colum had chosen to praise in his report. Her sun-bleached hair and round face were visible at the window for a moment and one hand held up in acknowledgement. 'An American girl comes next week,' said Faustus, and he caught my eye, gave a quick smile.

That last evening Torre came to the villa, and I gave him a bottle of good Umbrian wine for his kindness during my stay. He insisted we drink it together, although he wasn't able to stay long. We stood at the end of the open walkway and looked down on the harbour where the sharp outlines of the day were being replaced by the soft feathers of dusk, and the yellow lights were gaining strength. The breeze from the fading expanse of ocean was insistent and pleasant; sea birds were noisy on the mountain. Torre said one of his daughters was ill and getting worse, and although he made an effort to show interest in our farewell, his concern was with his family. 'Come and see me when you come back to Capri,' he said, but his free hand was opening and closing in a small agitation. He told me he'd miss our evenings together, but when I said I'd better pack for the next day, he left quickly. It was as it should be — family first. Our passing acquaintance would soon be forgotten on his side, but I've remembered his goodwill and desire to better himself in America. He left his glass on the wall with wine still in it, and I finished it, standing alone in gathering darkness.

I slept well that last night in the kitchen of the Villa San Michele, and in the morning made my own way down to the harbour and caught the small ferry to Naples. The six weeks at the Anacapri site had been a busy passage, gone almost before it could be fully grasped, yet the experience unpacks itself often in recollection. Years later I visited Münthe's grave in the Protestant Cemetery in Rome, and read his book which had been a phenomenal success in its day. 'I want my house open to sun and wind and the voice of the sea, like a Greek temple, and light, light, light everywhere,' he said. The sad irony was he became blind at the end.

Munthe wrote of spring at San Michele: myrtle and honeysuckle, hyacinths and crocuses, tortoises and Minerva owls. I saw none of those, but I did see skylarks coming back to the mountain above the villa, morning light on mottled marble pedestals which held the classical busts he had so lovingly collected, and I looked down from his rotunda to the startling blue of Capri harbour. I had been alone at night in that much-loved house, woken in the spacious kitchen of pale tiles, blue pottery and burnished copper, lightly touched and wonderingly observed artefacts whose beauty was given lustre by antiquity.

Some of all that came back to me as I listened to Paula Huchro, and the window cleaner worked himself soundlessly out of sight so that the mountains behind Grenoble were unobscured, the dark pines a uniform cover until the snow at higher altitude. Later I would sit with Paula and three other colleagues with glasses of pinot gris, and discuss points arising from her address, before the conversation moved on to Cicero, that eloquent old braggart, yet how loving to his daughter. There would be passing mention of our time together at Anacapri, and our even shorter meeting at the symposium in Genoa. 'Oh indeed,' she'd say, 'Dr Malcolm and I go way back.' She would smile and meet my eye, but nothing would be said of Sextus Pompey, nothing said of burning Colum and the thinly partitioned rooms in the harbour of Capri, nothing of the Vergotti family tomb above the harbour, nothing essential of our former selves.